I0577421

DECODED

PHISHING FOR LOVE
BOOK 1

DECODED

PHISHING FOR LOVE

BOOK 1

Meribeth Richards

Contents

Copyright © 2025 by Meribeth Richards

All rights reserved.

No part of this publication may be reproduced, distributed, or transmitted in any form or by any means, including photocopying, recording, or other electronic or mechanical methods, without the prior written permission of the publisher, except as permitted by U.S. copyright law. For permission requests, contact author@meribethrichards.com

The story, all names, characters, and incidents portrayed in this production are fictitious. No identification with actual persons (living or deceased), places, buildings, and products is intended or should be inferred.

AI was not used in the creation of this book.

Original Cover Design created in Canva

Cover Artwork created by Alyssa's Illustrations

First Edition: October 2025

Paperback ISBN: 979-8-9997692-1-3

This book is dedicated to anyone who hasn't ever felt like enough.
You are more than.

Keaton and Anna's Playlist

Glitch
Taylor Swift

Let's Go to Vegas
Faith Hill

What Makes You Beautiful
One Direction

...Baby One More Time
Britney Spears

Painted You Pretty
Hudson Westbrook

Can't Help Falling in Love
Elvis Presley

Keeper
Trevor Martin

Pour Some Sugar On Me
Def Leppard

T-Shirt
Thomas Rhett

Glad You Exist
Dan + Shay

Always
Bon Jovi

But Daddy I Love Him
Taylor Swift

Forever and For Always
Shania Twain

Content Warnings

This book is intended for an adult audience. There are scenes , including those with sexual content, that are not suitable for children.

Unfortunately life isn't always pretty, and when I try to make my characters relatable, that carries over into their lives. I feel it is important to note that the MMC and FMC neither one are performing the acts listed below. Please review this list for any possible triggers:

Fat Shaming

Sexual Harassment

Sexual Assault

Death of a Parent

Depression

Drug Overdose (not resulting in death/suicide)

Your mental health matters. If you feel additional content warnings need to be considered, please reach out at author@meribethrichards.com

Chapter One
Anna

Anna

> At the airport and waiting on my plane to board. I cannot wait to see all of you tomorrow!

Pressing send, I lean back in the hard, plastic seat positioned in front of large windows showcasing the planes as they fly in and out of the small airport. I take in my surroundings of the slow, sleepy terminal and send a silent prayer of thanks out to the universe for the upcoming respite. Working at Brenner & Associates this year has been taxing, to say the least. As an executive assistant to the CEO, I've had to schedule and coordinate all of the things for my boss, but mostly I'm exhausted from dodging his creepy advances.

After I graduated college with two degrees, one in business management and the other in photography, I had taken a job as an administrative assistant at the center for the arts. Sadly, it had to close its doors almost two years ago leaving me jobless and with way too little in my savings account for comfort. I had to find a job fast before I was forced to move back in with my parents. When my dad's best friend offered to make me his executive assistant at his accounting firm, I couldn't exactly turn it down. My dad wouldn't have *let* me turn it down, for that matter.

Daniel Brenner and my father had been college roommates, so he's been around my entire life, attending every celebration and most family dinners. He had always been kind, but when his wife left him for another man a few years ago, I noticed his demeanor had changed, particularly toward women. He openly makes lewd comments about their appearances, and when my dad chastised me at his Christmas party this past year for going back for seconds, Daniel assured him that many men like a woman with some meat on their bones.

What my father didn't know as he laughed and agreed with his friend was that Daniel was talking about himself. For almost the entire duration of me working for his company, Daniel has been sending me suggestive messages about what he wanted to do to me and my body, as well as what he had hoped I would do to him in return. At the office he would find ways to touch me. They were innocent enough that I couldn't pin him with anything, but they were still unwanted. I shivered knowing those advances were only getting worse and more frequent.

That is why this annual girls' trip could not have come at a better time. I fully plan to immerse myself in sunshine, booze, and my besties for the next three days. Looking back down at my phone, I smile at the girls who have become my lifeline in this crazy walk we call life.

Jasmine

I hate that you're going to be there all alone tonight.

Penny

Where are you staying? Have you booked a room yet?

Anna

Oh, I think I can find somewhere in Las Vegas with a vacancy tonight. Maybe I'll treat myself and stay somewhere fancy, like the place in that movie George Clooney and Julia Roberts were in.

Skyla

You should stay at The Venetian! It seems so romantic!

Anna

Well, considering there's a snowball's chance in hell of me having a romantic escapade tonight, I guess I'll be steering clear of that one.

Skyla

Girl, stop! You're a hottie. There's gonna be plenty of singles amidst the thousands of bachelor parties that will be taking place tonight and at least one is gonna be looking for a front row ticket to your incredible rack.

I laugh at my ridiculous dreamer of a friend. Skyla always believes love is just around the corner for everyone.

Jasmine

Just be safe. Check reviews and make sure you don't end up in some cheap motel that reeks of cigarettes and has stains on the bedspread.

Anna

I'm a big girl. Don't worry about me.

Skyla

But we do worry about you! We love you!

Penny

Have fun, but not too much fun without us. Maybe don't go drinking until we get there?

Anna

You just want me to sit in a hotel room by myself when I am single and free in Las Vegas? Girls, where is your sense of adventure?

Jasmine

Girl, where is your sense of safety?

I snort as they continue texting back and forth about what I should do tonight in their absence. It isn't ideal that the small airport I fly out of only has certain days it flies from Kentucky to Nevada, but it's a nonstop flight for a ticket I can afford. The idea of being a single woman all alone in Las Vegas should probably terrify me to some degree, but I need this trip so desperately that the only thing I feel is excitement. Besides, anything is better than spending another day in the office with Daniel Brenner.

My phone buzzes again and I look at the screen expecting another group text from my Boozy Besties, but my smile quickly fades, my soft stomach tightens, and disgust runs through my body.

Daniel

> The office sure isn't as beautiful without you here.

The acid from the bile traveling up my throat burns as I swallow it back down and another message comes through.

Daniel

> I'm sitting here in my office, growing hard while thinking of you. I know you're probably dripping thinking of me, too.

Daniel

> I'll be sure to send you a little something later tonight so you don't feel so alone.

His words disgust me, and I thank my lucky stars that the man is all talk, or at least he has been so far. The last thing I want is a dick pic from my skeevy boss who is thirty years my senior. I quickly close out the text and take a deep breath, repressing the panic attack that is trying to break through. Humiliating myself in the middle of this airport isn't the way I want to kick off this getaway.

My phone buzzes again and I can't bring myself to look at it right now, fearing what, or *who*, might be on the other side of the screen.

Instead, I pocket my phone and press the little button on my pods that are safely tucked into my ears. I'll just listen to a few chapters of my smutty book before boarding so I can forget about my boss and focus on the adventures that await me in Sin City.

When I reach the part where the heroine realizes the guy she's been hooking up with in the secret sex club where everyone is forced to wear masks is actually her ex-boyfriend's dad, I hear an announcement from my gate:

"Ladies and gentlemen, we are now boarding all remaining passengers for flight 756 to Las Vegas, Nevada at this time."

Pulling out my phone so I can let my friends know I'm about to board, I breathe a sigh of relief to see no more disturbing messages from my boss.

Jasmine

Whatever you decide to do, just be careful. We don't need anyone else falling into a cactus on vacation.

Skyla

That was one time!

Jasmine

Once is one time too many.

Penny

Turn on your app so we know where you are in case some creep tries to steal you away from us.

Anna

Everything is going to be great. I'm getting ready to board. Love you all. See you tomorrow!

My phone begins chiming with what I'm sure are messages of affection from the best girls I've ever met. I smile to myself as I pull up my boarding pass on my phone. This weekend is going to be everything I've needed.

Chapter Two
Keaton

"It should be a pretty straightforward trip. I've gone over everything with them and they just have to sign the contracts. Odd that they refuse to digitally sign with a cybersecurity company, but I guess their company is a bit old school in that regard."

"Whatever it takes to get them to sign and move forward," I say to my younger brother, Camden. He's both a partner in the business we own together with our other sibling, Lincoln, as well as a damn good attorney.

The crackling of an intercom system garners my attention. "Ladies and gentlemen, we are now boarding all remaining passengers for flight 756 to Las Vegas, Nevada at this time."

"I've gotta go, Cam. I'm about to board the plane."

"Stay calm, the last place you want to be having a complete freak out is on an airplane. Just remember that more people die each year from car accidents than they do plane crashes," he assures me.

"Gee thanks, I feel so much better now that you've said the words plane and crash together. It definitely made me forget the fact I'm about to ascend into the air while trapped in a giant, steel tube of doom."

I disconnect the call and make my way into the long line for boarding, not eager in the least to take this flight. I try to swallow down the nausea that always comes with flying, but it's no use.

Fortunately, the career I started with my brothers has given us an incredible opportunity to travel all over the country. Unfortunately, this is really the only way to get where we need in an efficient amount of time. You would think frequently flying would help ease my fears, but it has yet to happen.

In desperate need of a distraction, my eyes track over the smaller domestic airport trying to find anything to focus on and get my mind off the fact that I will be thousands of feet in the air and no matter how many birthday wishes I made in my youth, my Superman ability of flight has never quite kicked in.

They manage to come across a voluptuous blonde leaning over her carry-on, seemingly checking to have everything intact. As she makes herself aware of all the contents in her luggage, she fails to notice that leaning over in her low-cut, pale purple top has the mouthwatering soft globes of her full chest spilling out. This woman was blessed with a chest and a half, and my hands twitch at the desire to find out how much of them I could cup in my palms. I'm a boob man. And I'm not ashamed.

My tongue darts out to wet my lips as my eyes reluctantly leave her swelling chest to track the rest of her luscious curves. I can feel my pants tightening as my gaze lingers over her soft stomach, even if her flowy top covers it and those wide hips I'd love to grip while thrusting inside her. Thick thighs lack a gap between them, and I become embarrassingly hard in the middle of the airport as I think of what a fucking victory it will be when I pull them apart to sink myself into the mound that lies between them.

Shit, I run a hand down my face as I realize I'm being a fucking creep. This beautiful woman does not deserve to be objectified, no matter how badly I need to get laid. I start to count the months in my head and realize it's been a while since I took a woman home with me. With my time being limited between my business and family, I really only have time for the occasional hookup, which isn't easy to come by when you live in a small town where everybody knows your business. Driving the two hours to the city to find someone isn't nearly as easy as it was in my twenties and thirties. Hitting forty this year has taught me that many things aren't as easy as they used to be.

Deciding I'll immediately hit up a bar when I touchdown in Vegas and find myself some much needed relief for the night, I rid myself of the incredibly inappropriate thoughts of this complete stranger. I will the pretty impressive semi I'm currently sporting to go down, and move forward in the line as we begin to board the plane.

With the dirty thoughts of a stranger no longer filling my head, the fear has settled back in. My stomach is churning, my palms are sweating, and I'm pretty sure my face is whiter than the unexpected seven inches of snow that blanketed my hometown this past January. I nod at the attendant as she scans the QR code on my phone, then slowly make my way through the creaky tunnel leading me to the plane.

After storing my carry-on in the bins above, I settle down into seat 10C, noting the two empty seats to my left. Being as how I have absolutely no desire to look out the window and see just how far my feet are above the earth when I know damn well how gravity works, I always opt for the aisle seat. I will gladly take the chance of my elbows being hit with the drink cart if it gives me a little peace of mind about plummeting to my death.

I place my earbuds in and start my audiobook up, shielding my screen and turning the volume down slightly. I'm not ashamed of the romance novels I read. They're entertaining and good for research purposes when it comes to those wild nights I do manage to have a few times a year. Still, it's best not to make anyone around me uncomfortable by overhearing the dirty words they like to say. The dirty words I like to record in my notes to use for later. I take a deep breath in and remind myself I can handle the four hour flight ahead of me. Releasing it, I close my eyes and settle in.

"Are you comfortable, sir?" I abruptly pause my book right where the girl calls her ex-boyfriend's father Daddy as he smacks her ass with a flogger. My eyes open and take in the flight attendant with the light brown hair pulled up tight in one of those fancy bun things women at country clubs wear. She seductively bites her lip that's painted in a shockingly bright shade of red. The plane hasn't finished boarding yet, so there's only one reason she's talking to me now instead of helping the other passengers find their seats.

Not to sound like a cocky piece of shit, but having a healthy past of hookups has made me privy to when a woman is coming onto me, and there's no doubt that's why she's here. While becoming a member of the Mile High Club may be on many a man's bucket list, it holds no appeal to me. I'd much rather stay safely buckled in my seat while aboard Fear Force One.

Not to mention, while there's no doubt the woman next to me is attractive, she doesn't so much as make my cock twitch compared to the curvy goddess I couldn't take my eyes off of earlier.

"I'm good, thanks." I answer politely and go to return my earbuds, but she reaches out and grazes my hand before I can go back to ignoring her.

"Well, if you need anything, anything at all," she says breathily, "I'm Sheila. You just let me know and I'll be sure to take care of whatever it is you need."

Attempting to end this one-sided attraction and conversation, I nod and settle back into my seat, but apparently Sheila isn't used to men turning down her advances. "I'll be around with the drink cart and a snack shortly after takeoff, but don't hesitate to push that button if you need me to come back for any reason, no matter how big." She not-so-subtly glances down at my crotch before meeting my eyes again.

"Or small?" I ask, trying to complete the phrase.

"What's that, handsome?" she asks, fluttering her eyelashes at me.

"You were saying no matter how big, but the phrase is, no matter how big or small. Just completing it for you." I'm not trying to be a smartass, but I'm also not *not* trying to be one either.

"Right," she says with a giggle that makes me fight a grimace trying to cross my face, "you just let me know if you need anything from me at all." Her flirting is thankfully interrupted from a heavily annoyed man barking her name.

Thanking the Lord above for giving me enough height to see around Sheila and over the seats, I notice another flight attendant a few rows up ahead. He looks annoyed as hell with his hands on his hips and a disapproving scowl on his face. Seated directly in front of him is the beautiful woman I was drooling over earlier. What did my curvy vixen do to piss him off?

Chapter Three

Anna

0   1 0   1 0   0
1 1   0 0   1
0   0 0   1 1   0   0 0   0   0
1   0 0   0 0   0   1   1
0   1   0 0   0   1   1
0   1   0   1   0

"**M**a'am, you're not allowed to use that." The flight attendant snapped at me.

I glance down at the seat belt extender in my hands, puzzled. "Oh, sorry, I didn't know. It's just that I have used them before."

I speak in a hushed tone, a silent signal for him to quiet down. Spoiler alert. He doesn't. Instead, Flight Attendant Dickhead rolls his eyes and huffs like the big bad wolf and I'm the stupid, fat pig trying to shove my butt into a seat clearly made for those without hips.

"Not on this airline you haven't. Hey Sheila," he hollers over the rows behind me, trying to gain the attention of the pretty flight attendant I've seen walking up and down the aisle. I feel my jaw drop and I wipe my face for any drool that's leaked out as I notice she's standing beside the most gorgeous man I've ever seen in my life.

This gorgeous specimen must be the spawn of a burly lumberjack and a Greek goddess. There's an effortless, rugged charm to him. His hair is mostly dark but is beginning to gray right above his ears and silver flecks seem to dance throughout it. It's perfectly styled and slightly spiked on top, making it appear as though his hair defies gravity and grows towards the sun. His salt and pepper beard is trimmed neatly, close enough to his face that he probably doesn't have to worry about food getting caught in it, but long enough to leave a delicious amount of beard burn between your thighs. I shift uncomfortably in my seat, both at the lack of room, the angry flight attendant, and now the moisture that has started to collect between my legs from dirty thoughts of the slightly silver stranger.

"Grab me a seat belt extender, will you? We need one up here in 8F." Sheila walks towards the back and the silvering fox looks at me, the look of disgust in his eyes. I bury myself in my seat, embarrassed that the flight attendant is drawing attention to my predicament and slightly pissed off by the reaction of the handsome stranger.

This is not my first flight. I have had to use seat belt extenders before because heaven forbid them to make a standard sized seat belt that is built to protect those with curves. Typically, the flight attendants are discreet and kind. I don't know if the purchase I made after checking out plus size travel tips is what set this one off, but clearly he's not happy about the fact that he's having to deal with me at all.

"Here you go," Sheila dumps the seat belt extender in my hand and walks off. She wasn't exactly kind, but at least she didn't make a scene like Flight Attendant Dickhead.

As I buckle up with my airline approved extender this time, a man who appears to be in his late forties or maybe early fifties stops at my row. The man in the aisle seat nods at him and stands so the new, slender man can come take his seat between us.

"Just great, they sat me by a fatty," he mutters under his breath, but still loud enough for me to hear. He makes a bit of a show as he settles down, throwing elbows and ramming one into my side. Pretty sure that wasn't an accident, but I keep my wince and comments to myself. That old bullshit nursery rhyme about sticks and stones pops into my brain. It's completely wrong because words do fucking hurt, but I've learned it's best to just try and keep quiet when dealing with assholes.

"Can you scoot over into your spot?" he huffs out at me.

"I...I am in my spot." I stammer. He's even louder than Flight Attendant Dickhead was being and I can feel my face flush in embarrassment.

Huffing loudly, the man hits the call button. "We'll fix this," he says glaring at me. I look down at my lap, willing my body to close in on itself and become smaller. Why couldn't I have been born a damn turtle?

Flight Attendant Dickhead returns to our row and while my anxiety could be making things up in my head, I'm fairly certain he's glaring at me for causing even more trouble. I swear I'm just trying to go see my friends and enjoy my weekend.

"How can I help you, sir?" He smiles at the man, a gracious act he certainly never bestowed upon me.

"This woman is obviously too large for her seat. She should have purchased two tickets. Now I'm stuck on this multi-hour flight having to be crammed and uncomfortable because her fat ass is spilling into my spot. Can she please be moved?"

My eyes blink rapidly so tears don't fall at the man's harsh words. I overhear the not-so-hushed whispers of the women sitting in the aisle behind me, and the unshed tears continue to build at their pity. "That poor girl. They just need to move her and get it over with. I'm sure she'd be much more comfortable sitting somewhere else."

As much as I love my friends and look forward to this girls trip every year, I am beginning to regret this entire ordeal. Maybe it's not too late to just head home.

I have been a big girl my entire life, and I've embraced my larger body. Sure, I have days where I don't like who I see in the mirror, but as I get older those days are fewer and farther between. I am usually very confident in who I am, regardless of what society may have to say about that, but no amount of self-worth is keeping me from feeling the utter humiliation this entire fiasco has brought on.

"Sir, the flight is full, but we will do the best we can." Flight Attendant Dickhead turns to me, "Ma'am, as soon as we close the doors, we can move you to a different seat, preferably one in an empty row if one is available. That way you won't bother anyone else. You will have to take that extender with you." He eyes the additional buckle at my waist with cold disapproval.

I'm so ready to just say fuck it and leap over the man beside me, hopefully smashing my fat ass right into his stupid face, then sprint for the door of the plane and head back home. Unfortunately, they just sealed the door, so instead I sink down in my too-small seat, completely mortified and miserable. Maybe we will crash before we make it to Vegas, and nobody will ever remember about the fat girl who was publicly humiliated on the plane.

I'm looking out the window watching the little vehicles zoom around the plane with suitcases when my daydreaming is interrupted. "Ma'am, there's a seat available for you at 10A. You need to go ahead and move as quickly as possible so we can take off. Nobody wants to be delayed." Flight Attendant Dickhead snips at me before briskly walking towards the back to join Sheila, no doubt gossiping about what a pain in their asses I've been.

As if moving seats on a full aircraft after everyone has been seated isn't humiliating enough, I have to ask the two men to my left to get up so I can get out of the aisle, making the mad man huff and puff all over again. I may or may not have not-so-accidentally stepped on his foot. It may be petty, but just because I'm fat doesn't mean I have to be the bigger person.

Slowly I complete the walk of shame to aisle 10 and when I want to do nothing but cry, I find myself biting my cheek to hold back a laugh when I realize I'm standing next to the gorgeous man whose face couldn't hide his disgust earlier. This day really is after me, it seems.

His head is tilted back against the seat, and I can't help but notice how beautifully peaceful he looks with his eyes closed and his earbuds in. I tap his shoulder and he quickly pauses his phone, looking annoyed, but when he catches my gaze, a soft smile graces his face.

"Hi there. Can I help you?" His voice is as rich as that chocolate cake the poor kid in Matilda had to eat in front of the entire school.

"Umm, I've been moved to sit in 10A. Do you mind stepping out so I can get through?"

He smiles fully at me now and damn, I'm pretty sure my panties just disintegrated. A dimple pops out on his left cheek and I kind of wanna lick it. Maybe I was imagining things and he wasn't disgusted with me at all.

As the real-life dream man stands, I realize he's the perfect headrest height. You know, where your head can perfectly tilt and land on his shoulder? I can also smell his cologne of tobacco and vanilla, not too strong. Just fucking perfect. It's an incredible blend and makes me want to curl up next to a fire. When I get home, I'm immediately going to the store and sniffing every damn candle at every single home goods store until I can find one that matches the delicious fragrance.

He steps out into the aisle and I shuffle my way into the seat next to the window. I quickly try to secretly latch the seat belt extender before he sits back down and look out the window so I can't see his reaction just in case he did manage to catch a glimpse of the embarrassing action.

His smooth voice washes over me, "I'm sorry they made a scene like that earlier. You don't deserve to be treated that way. It's ridiculous and I truly hope this airline doesn't condone that behavior. They shouldn't have forced you to move seats. You should reach out to them, but I don't mind speaking on your behalf and tell them what I witnessed."

My legs squeeze together on their own accord, knowing that we do love a handsome, kind man with a touch of activist in him. I shake my head to get rid of the fantasy that a man this gorgeous could be interested in a girl like me. Especially a girl he pities.

"Oh, it was nothing, really. Besides, the man beside me smelled like ass." I try to downplay the encounter with my horrible former seatmate.

"Farm animal or body part?"

I grin at him. "I'd say a mixture of both."

"Well lucky for you I opted for Tom Ford instead of Eau de Jackass this morning."

I huff out a laugh at his silly joke as we both settle into our seats. I go to resume my audiobook, and the man who made me smile again goes back to listening to whatever it was he was so concentrated on before I messed up his prior seating arrangement.

A few minutes later the flight attendants are in the middle of the aisle going over the safety procedures. I glance over at the distinguished gentleman beside me who has removed his earbuds and is now staring at Sheila intently. Go figure a man who looks that damn fine is transfixed by the tall, thin, and perky flight attendant who was fawning over him earlier. They were probably scheduling a rendezvous for later when she got interrupted to fetch me the extender. "Oh, you've got to be kidding me," I mutter.

"Do you not take airplane safety seriously?" He asks, his tone sharper than it was with me earlier.

"Oh, no, I do. I definitely do." I assure him. He nods at me and goes back to watching Sheila, his brows furrowed and a determined look of concentration on his face. I keep my mouth closed and roll my eyes internally this time knowing this is the way the world works.

As the flight attendants finish their spiel, he speaks again. "I'm sorry I snipped at you. I just didn't want to miss anything they said." Mr. Sexy sucks in a large breath and exhales slowly. His hands are gripping his armrests so tight his knuckles are whitening. Could this big, strong man be afraid of flying?

"Umm, is this your first flight?" I ask.

He laughs and I can't help but notice how lovely it sounds. It's like a deep melody that could soothe you to sleep. "No, I actually have to fly fairly often. I just hate every minute of it."

"I take it you travel for work?" I'm genuinely curious, finding myself wanting to learn as much as I possibly can about this attractive man with aerophobia.

"Mostly, yes. My brothers and I also fly out to a place we share down in the Caribbean every year. Deep sea fishing and mischief, mostly. But, the majority of my destinations are work related. Are you also flying for work?"

"Oh, no, I don't get to travel much for my position. I would totally love that, though. I'm actually headed to Vegas for a girls' trip. Every year some of my friends from college and I choose a destination. It's my one trip a year and it's seriously one of the things I look forward to the most."

While his grip doesn't loosen, he does smile at me, the sexy little dimple popping out on his left cheek. "That sounds like a lot of fun. My name is," he interrupts himself with a gasp as the plane finally begins to ascend. We've been talking enough that I was able to distract him on our drive around the airstrip, but the lift off has his whole body tensing up. I don't know where the boldness comes from, but I reach over and swipe my thumb across his knuckles, trying to give him some comfort. I brush back and forth a few times, and as I go to take my hand away, he flips his over and grasps mine. The embrace feels so damn good and tiny flutters fill my chest. There's an odd satisfaction in how perfect it feels for this complete stranger to be holding my hand.

Facing forward with his back aligned perfectly straight, he repeats his deep breathing exercise. Then he looks down at our hands wrapped together and quickly drops mine. "Sorry about that. I was trying to say that my name is Keaton."

Though I miss the warmth and feel of his hand, I pop a smile on my face. "I'm Anna. And you have nothing to be sorry for Keaton."

The precious dimple pops out again and it's a good thing I'm sitting down, because my knees go weak. "So, where are you from?" He asks.

"Oh, born and raised in the city. Go Cats!" I pump my hands in the air, making him chuckle. "How about you?"

He runs his hand over his brown hair with the silver speckles, and I bite my lip to stifle my laugh. I wonder if the little spikes on his head poke his fingers. "I'm from a small town a couple hours south of you. But also, Go Cats." He winks and my body heats, falling a little harder for the kind stranger with Daddy vibes.

Chapter Four
Keaton

Anna is animated as she tells a story about her and her college friends on their trip to Cancun last year. "She was so drunk, and we tried the best we could to rein her in, but she started dancing, flailing her entire body about, and fell right into a cactus. We had to haul the poor thing to the infirmary, where they pulled twelve of those dang needles out of her. Twelve!"

Her infectious laugh makes me do the same and I realize how easy it is to do that with her. We've been talking and laughing these past few hours of the flight and it's really helped ease my fears. I've appreciated her sitting here with me to get my mind off things. Having the opportunity to look at her has been incredibly nice, too, especially when she laughs making those luscious tits of hers jiggle. "So, Cancun last year and Las Vegas this year. Y'all choose a different place every time?"

She nods. "Yeah, on the last day of each trip we have brunch and that's when we decide where we are going next. We all put a destination on a slip of paper and put it in a glass. Then we pull the slips out one by one. Each one we pull out is where we will *not* be traveling to, so when we reach the last strip, that's our destination."

"That sounds like a fun tradition. Where all have you been?"

"This is only the third year we've done it. We all agreed on New York City for our first trip, then Cancun last year, and Vegas this year."

"What destination do you plan to enter into the drawing this year?" I ask.

Anna's eyes light up and I can tell how much this woman loves to travel. Something inside me wants to help her discover the world, but I push that odd feeling down as I take in her answer.

"I know it's super basic, but I really want to go to Paris. I've dreamed of going there ever since I was a little girl. I want to visit The Louvre and see the Mona Lisa, of course, and take in the views of the city from the Eiffel Tower. And I want to go to a little café to drink coffee and enjoy the croissants." She says the last word in a fake French accent that is too adorable to not make me chuckle.

"Well then, I hope Paris is the last one pulled this year." Her smile widens and she beams at me. I have to dig my thumbnail into my palm to stop myself from reaching out and cupping her cheek. I so badly want to kiss this woman, but trying to do that on a plane when she has no way of escaping me is not the way to go about that. So instead, I distract my dick by asking her more questions about her and her friends.

"Penny is an elementary school teacher. She's taught third grade the past several years, but they just transferred her to first grade this year and I just know she's going to be great. Her heart is so big and she's gonna love those babies so much." Her beautiful face lights up as she talks about the people she loves.

"Then Jasmine is an attorney. She's such a badass and I want to be her when I grow up. She refuses to take shit from anyone, but she's secretly a lot softer than her rough exterior lets on.

"Finally, we have Skyla." The soft smile on her face lets me know she cares deeply about her friend. "She's our dreamer. I don't know if there's a place in this world that could hold on to that girl for too long. It's not unlike her to call us up and say something crazy like, 'I wanted to see a live Toucan, so I'm in Costa Rica.'" She lets out a laugh and it warms my chest. "She's so silly, but I love her so much."

"It's obvious y'all have a great bond. So, there's the dreamer, the attorney, and the teacher. What about you, Anna?" I notice she deflates slightly with my question.

"Oh, I'm nothing quite as impressive. Right now I'm an executive assistant for an accounting firm, but can I tell you a secret? I haven't shared this with anybody, so I'm trusting you to keep quiet." She whispers and I lean in closer, breathing in her scent and knowing I need more. I can't help but smile as I give her a nod, urging her to go on.

"I've been trying to find work somewhere else. I actually just applied for a position at this one company where I've heard nothing but incredible things about the owners, even though I can't seem to find anything online about them at all. I would be an executive assistant again, so I have hope that since I've got some experience in that area, I'll be chosen for the position. The only downside is I've never lived outside of the city and it's in a small town just a couple of hours from home. If I manage to get the job, I know it will upset my parents, and I really hate letting them down."

"I take it you're close with your family?"

She shrugs her shoulders in a noncommittal gesture. "We are, but, well my dad can be pretty hard on me. He has some high expectations, and I seem to fall short of those more often than not. He loves me, but well, it's complicated."

"I get complicated. My family is very close," I tell her. "Sometimes too close. My brothers and I work together. Well, my brother Lincoln and I work in the same office. My brother Camden is an attorney, and while he works with us, his office is downtown. It's a lot of togetherness, sometimes too much if I'm being honest. We work together all week, typically get together to get into something on Saturday, and then we have family dinners every Sunday."

"Oh, we do that, too!" Anna gushes. "But I'm an only child, so it's just me and my folks usually. Occasionally my boss will come over."

"Your boss attends your family dinners?"

She nods before answering. "Yeah, he and my dad are best friends. Have been since college. It's how I got the job, actually. The company I had been working for previously just closed and I needed a paycheck. My dad practically demanded that I work for his friend and I didn't want to disappoint him. I also didn't want to move back home, so here we are."

Her incredible smile has dimmed and I immediately miss the light it brings. "I take it that being an executive assistant isn't exactly your dream career?" I ask, hoping she will share all her hopes and dreams with me.

"I graduated with a degree in photography. But apparently that was a waste of an education and to make my dad happy, I double majored in business administration. Photography is definitely my passion, though. There's just something about capturing that special moment. That special place. That special feeling. Oh, I love it so much."

The sparkle in her eyes takes my breath away as she shares her passion with me.

"Do you still get to practice photography, then?" I ask, truly hoping this woman gets to pursue her passion, but sadly she shakes her head.

"There's not really time for it. My boss is," she trails off, shuddering slightly. "Well, my boss really wants me to be at the office when he's there, which is a lot. Every now and then friends from school will contact me to take some family photos for them. Occasionally I try to travel to nearby locations and take some pictures, but that's just for fun. I went to Mammoth Cave a few weeks ago. Have you been? So beautiful."

I look at Anna's round cheeks, full lips and emerald eyes. *So beautiful.* I find myself leaning in her direction, my hand reaching out and brushing a stray blonde hair from her cheek. *Am I about to give in and kiss this woman?*

Suddenly, the plane dips and I find myself pressed back against my seat. Short, quick breaths escape between my lips and I think I'm about to hyperventilate. Are we about to crash? If so, why is the only thought running through my mind that I will die before I ever get to kiss the incredible woman beside me? The woman who has scooted into the middle seat so she can cup my cheek and swipe her thumb over it. Back and forth, back and forth. Her calming movements feel so good, and I find my body relaxing.

"That's it, Keaton. You're doing great. Take a breath with me." She breathes in through her nose and I find myself mimicking her actions. When she releases through her pouty lips, I do the same. "So good, Keaton. You're doing so good."

I listen to her soothing voice with just the slightest touch of twang to it and my body relaxes. We repeat the breathing exercise, and this time after I've exhaled, I can't help but lean closer and brush my lips ever so lightly against hers. Her soft, full lips are perfect as they match my pressure. My hand comes up to the back of her head, brushing the golden waves of her hair. I've never had a reaction to a woman as quickly as I have to Anna, and now I'm kissing her on a fucking airplane. I'm not sure what has come over me, but I'm not ready to release her from my hold just yet.

All good things must come to an end, though, because all too soon the crackling sound of the plane's intercom system has us separating far too quickly. As we straighten in our seats, I look to my left and see the sweetest shade of pink tinging her cheeks. She looks over at me, a sheepish grin on her face, and I can't help but smile like a fucking opossum eating persimmons. Knowing she was just as into that kiss as I was has me wanting to pull her back over here and take her lips again. Hell, I want to pull her on top of me and take her right here on this fucking plane and let everyone know this incredible woman is mine now.

"Sorry about that, folks," the pilot says, "we've run into a bit of turbulence. We ask that you please remain seated with your seatbelts fastened as we navigate these bumps over the next few minutes."

"See, just some turbulence. He has it under control. Feel better?" Anna asks, her voice genuine, but breathy from the tender moment we just shared.

"I do, thanks to you." I rub my thumb across her hand. "Would you stay here beside me?"

The pink on her cheek returns as a blush blooms across her beautiful face. "Oh, do you think you'll be comfortable?"

I know she's thinking back to the cruelty of the man who sat beside her earlier and damn if I let her think for one second I wouldn't want her beautiful body on me. "I imagine being closer to you would make me very comfortable."

Capturing her plump bottom lip between her teeth she nods, and even though I see her unclasp the extra length of seat belt from her previous spot and click it into her new seat, I look away so she doesn't get embarrassed again.

"Maybe you should have been the one to switch seats. Don't you want to look out the window?" she asks.

My body tenses and the fear has officially crept back in at the thought of what I might see. "Absolutely not."

Anna laughs lightly, "Okay, no worries. Umm, Keaton. I know we just met, but apparently you're really good at keeping secrets. Mind if I tell you one more?"

I want to tell her that I'm dying to uncover every single one of her secrets, but I don't want to frighten her off. "You can tell me anything, Anna."

"That was my first kiss on a plane," she admits, pink smattering her cheeks. "And it was pretty fucking incredible."

I smile at her as my heart does a full-on touchdown dance inside my chest. "That was my first one too, and I'd say you're fucking right."

She catches her bottom lip with her teeth and I want to release it and give us both the chance for a second in-flight kiss, but the crackling of the intercom interrupts.

"Ladies and gentlemen, we will be descending into Las Vegas in approximately ten minutes. At this time we ask that you throw away all trash, return your seats to an upright position, and fold up those tray tables. We thank you for flying with us."

"So, are you meeting up with your friends this evening?" I ask, secretly hoping she has no plans.

"Not tonight. Since I rely on a smaller airport than the rest of them, my flight came in a day early. I'll meet up with everyone else tomorrow. Tonight I plan to drink until I forget about this god-awful plane ride."

"I hope it hasn't been totally awful," I smirk at her.

"Oh, no. I didn't mean that. You're great. I mean, you've been great. I mean, I've loved talking with you." Her flushed face is adorable as she stammers over her words. "Anyway, I also have to find a room for the night. We don't technically have reservations until tomorrow, so I should probably be a responsible adult first."

It takes me just a moment to process what she just admitted. When in Vegas, I suppose one should take a gamble.

"Well, if you're needing a room, I just so happen to have one you could stay in."

Anna's entire body flushes and I can't help but light up inside at her reaction. Then, those gorgeous green eyes lock on mine. "I think I'd like that."

1 1 1 1 1 0 1 0 1 0 1 0 0 0 0 0 0 1 1 0
1 1 0 0 1 1 0 0 0 1 0 1 0 1 1 1 1 0 0 1 0
0 0 0 0 0 0 0 1 1 0 0 1 1 0 0 0 0 0 1 0 1
1 0 1 0 1 0 1 0 0 0 1 1 0 0 0 1 1 0 0 1 0
0 0 0 0 1 1 1 1 0 0 1 0 0 0 1 0 0 1
0 1 0 1 1 1 0 0 1 0 0 1 1 1 0 1 0

Chapter Five

Anna

1 0 1 0
1 1 0 0 1
0 0 1 1 0 0 0 0 0
0 0 1 1 0 0 0 1 1
1 0 0 0 0 1 1
0 1 0 1
0 1 0 1

"**I** can pull up the ride share app and get us a car." I offer to Keaton as we make our way through the airport.

"No need. I have a rental car ready. Walk down with me to get it?" He extends his hand out and I tentatively grab it, even though butterflies bloom inside my belly. It's in my nature to fall fast and hard, but things with Keaton seem to be moving at warp speed. If I had a notebook right now. I'd be doodling our names together inside of a heart.

He strolls up to the rental kiosk, with no hesitation like he's done this a million times. I'm constantly fumbling over myself, and new situations always make me incredibly awkward, but there is none of that in him. Keaton looks every bit the professional. While we learned a lot about each other on the plane, I'm not exactly sure what he does other than he owns a business with his brothers, but I have no doubt that he's highly respected. He just has this air about him that makes you know he's one of the good ones - a good boss, a good man, a good lover.

While my mind begins to dream up deliciously dirty desires at the thought of Keaton taking me back to his room and having me in every way he sees fit, warning bells simultaneously tell me to beware. Am I seriously going to spend the night with a man I just met? I mean, I'm no stranger to a one night stand, but it's always been on my terms and on my own turf. Plus, one of my girls always knows where I am.

My stomach flips as Keaton signs off on some paperwork and I decide I should probably text my friends about what's going down, just in case. But before I can reach for my phone, he takes the keys from the attendant and is walking back my way.

I should heed my friend's words and get a room of my own. I should tell him I can't do this and thank him for the one kiss I got. The one kiss that had me feeling things I haven't felt before. But when Keaton grabs my hand as we walk to the black luxury vehicle he has rented for the weekend, I look down at the way our fingers entwine. I could totally get used to that.

Opening the door, Keaton helps me into the vehicle before walking around to the driver's side. "So, these drinks we're getting," he asks, "are you thinking about the minibar at the hotel or do you want to go out on the town?"

Did this man just offer to take me straight to the room? I mean, I know it was implied that I would be in his room tonight, but he's seriously considering no stops along the way? No time for me to change my mind? No bites to nibble on before the big feast?

The nerves in my belly begin to stir again, but when I look over and see his handsome, patient face, I realize he isn't just looking for a trip to pound town. He wants whatever I want. And he's giving me the time I need to decide.

Do I want this man to take me straight to the room? Boy, do I ever. I want him to kiss me like he did on the plane again. Then I want him to release my lips and repeat his actions, but this time with a ferocity that tells me he wants nobody but me with him tonight. I want him to kiss every inch of my body. And then I want him to give me a night I know can result in nothing but endless pleasure.

Jasmine's cautious voice pops into my head and reminds me that I need to get to know the guy a little more, and I realize I want to get to know him. I want to learn his drink order when we go out to the bar. I want to know if the stops I hope to make at all the tourist attractions make him grin or groan. I want to test how many times I can make that adorable dimple of his pop out.

"How about we go to the hotel to check-in and drop our bags off? Then we can hit the strip and get those drinks. Maybe get to know each other a little more." I offer, and Keaton replies with a smile, that sweet dimple making its appearance. I make a mental tally mark. There's one.

"That sounds like a perfect plan, Anna." My name rolls off his tongue, drenching my panties that are practically ruined from the way this man has been staring at me all night. Maybe when we get to the hotel, I can sneak away and change into a new pair before we head out. Or take them off completely. Easy access and all that.

Keaton connects his phone to the Bluetooth of the vehicle, but instead of the monotonous sound of the navigation system, we're blasted with the seductive sounds of narration.

"Oh, Daddy. Yes, Daddy fuck me hard." Her screams echo around us and it just makes me that much harder.

"That's right, Baby Girl. You want to come on Daddy's hard cock don't you?"

My eyes go wide, and I stare at Keaton who is completely panicking as the graphic scene is described to us. He turns the car off, but the story continues. I assume he has to open the door in order for the fancy dash system to stop, but I'm frozen in my seat and unable to suggest the idea to him. The narrators continue.

She whimpers as I continue thrusting into her pussy. "Bet my son never fucked you like this, did he?"

"Oh my gosh," I cry out, "turn it off, turn it off!"

"I'm trying!" Keaton hollers, then grabs his phone. He manages to stop the book from playing any longer and we both just sit in silence, too stunned to say anything and too awkward to make eye contact. Awkward laughter begins to bubble up out of me.

"So, I can explain." Keaton refuses to look at me, instead staring at the dash with a look of betrayal. It's clear to see he's mortified by the unexpected confession of his reading tastes. "It's embarrassing to admit, but I do listen to the occasional romance novel."

"No, no, don't be embarrassed. I promise I'm not judging." He glances over at me with a look of total disbelief on his face. Even though we've arrived in the city past sunset, I can see the faintest flush running through his cheeks and traveling up his neck. He opens and closes his mouth a few times like he can't decide what he wants to say, so I finally calm myself down to explain.

"Keaton, I'm not judging you, I promise. I just asked you to turn it off because I'm pretty sure I'm reading the same book, but I'm not at that part yet. I just didn't want any spoilers."

His gorgeous icy blue eyes feel like they're staring into my soul and then I see his shoulders begin to shake, and a sound of amusement bursts from his lips. We sit there laughing together in the cab of the vehicle at the total ridiculousness of it all until finally I'm wiping away tears and the beautiful sounds spilling from his lips fade.

Keaton gives me that megawatt smile of his and reaches out to brush the tears of laughter from my cheeks. I'm overcome by his thoughtfulness and my heart and pussy both urge me to be bold. I pull at his shirt until he's within reach, and then my lips slam against his. There's no hesitation from him as he pokes his tongue against me, asking for silent permission to further explore.

And I don't hesitate either because this man is delicious. I can taste the subtle flavor of the ginger ale he had on the plane, but there's also the taste of just him. His lips are soft, but he's kissing me with a vigor that cannot be described as the same. I need more of this man and I need it now. Reaching towards his belt, I try to free what I know must be the most incredible dick. This man is the epitome of big dick energy, and I would like to confirm that I'm right about it.

"Wait, wait," Keaton breaks his lips away from mine and grips my hands, stopping me from my destination.

Humiliated, I yank my hands back like they're on fire and cover my face. "Oh my god. Keaton, I'm so sorry. I shouldn't have assumed it was okay to do that. I'm sure you are just trying to be nice to me after everything that happened. It was way too bold for me to assume you were interested in that. It was nice of you to offer me a ride, but I'll just get a rideshare. Again, I'm so sorry."

I go to grab the door handle, but hear the click of the locks before I can open it. Great, I fully embarrassed myself in front of this man and now he's probably going to kidnap or kill me. The girls were right. Don't leave Anna Laura Keith unattended, she will humiliate herself and then get in cars with total strangers.

"Are you finished rambling?" I don't know if I want to slap or kiss that sinful smirk on his lips right now, but I somehow manage to keep myself from doing either and simply nod.

"First of all, you were right to assume. You may not have noticed me, but I first laid eyes on your gorgeous face in the airport, and those fucking fantastic tits of yours were spilling out of that top. Do you have any idea what it's like to be standing in a sea of strangers sporting a hard-on?" I shake my head. His confession is hard for me to believe, but I'm dying to hear more.

"I tried to shake it off, but then divine intervention had you sitting down next to me on the plane, and I got worked up all over again. Your body is fucking perfect, Anna. Your lips, your curves, and I don't know what you did to deserve the set of breasts you've been blessed with, but you must have been a good fucking girl."

We may be in the desert, but there is no chance of a drought from how wet things have managed to get between my thighs. I squeeze them together as he continues.

"Then I had the privilege of learning that not only are you the most beautiful woman I've ever seen, but that you're the most caring one, as well. When I was freaking out about the flight, you helped me work through it. So you won't call a rideshare. You're gonna sit your fine ass in that seat and I'm going to take you to the hotel, and then we're going to have some fucking fun. And if I'm lucky baby," his thumb strokes down my cheekbone and I can't help but lean into it, "I'll be giving you another ride later tonight."

There is a pulsing need that has my entire body on fire and the desire to completely devour this man is insane, but his words don't explain why he stopped me from trying to move forward.

"But you pushed me away," I say softly, looking for some clarity.

"Hardest fucking thing I think I've ever done," he admits. "The only reason I did is because your touch had me only a couple seconds away from coming completely undone. I promise you can touch me anywhere, any way, but I would rather wait just a little longer so I can calm down enough to not embarrass myself tonight."

I offer him what is probably the dopiest grin in the history of smiles, but his words have brought me such satisfaction and have given me a much needed jolt of confidence after tonight's events. "Then let's go get those drinks."

"Seriously?" I squeal and can't help but gush, taking in the sights of the beautiful casino and resort. The fountains are going off and it's beyond stunning. I've never been somewhere quite this fancy. "I've always wanted to visit here after watching a movie I once saw! In fact, I was just joking with my friends about it. Are we seriously staying here?!"

Keaton gives me a satisfied smile before leaning over and brushing his lips against mine. "I'm happy this makes you happy. You go ahead and explore while I take our bags and get us checked in."

I let out another squeal before rushing out the car door and through the walkway to see the fountains. Taking in the beauty and wonder of it all, I can't believe I'm standing in this place right now, with an incredible man offering me what is no doubt going to be the most amazing night of my life. Warm hands wrap around my waist and pull me in. "You feel so good in my arms, Baby," Keaton whispers in my ear before pressing his lips to my neck.

I melt into him, and we stand there and watch the fountains shoot up into the air. When the water starts to die down, he takes my hand and together we walk the Las Vegas strip, taking in the sights and each other.

I smile at myself knowing I was right. This weekend is going to be everything I needed.

Chapter Six
Anna

If Las Vegas is considered the City of Sin, then the man sitting beside me is the devil incarnate. He has brought out every dangerous desire inside of me and the more I look at him, the wetter I get. Drinking with him is the weirdest foreplay I've ever experienced.

Our first stop is at one of the bars inside our fancy hotel. It is all creams and golds, and we sit here talking while munching on popcorn and chips. My third lavender lemon drop sits in front of me and Keaton is on his second or third old fashioned for the night. We talk about our family, reminding each other about his brothers and my lack of siblings. A sad moment passes by when I learn that he lost his dad several years ago and he speaks of his mom ever so gently, mentioning that she's still a beautiful and incredible woman, but one with a broken heart.

Finishing up our drinks, we decide to go to Caesar's Palace. We pose with several obscene statues, snapping pictures to commemorate our time together, laughing the entire time. "Wow, you really are a photographer. These are so good and all you're using is your phone." Keaton praises and I can't help but blush.

"Well, I didn't exactly plan on an impromptu photoshoot, so I don't have my fancy equipment with me. But it helps to have a marvelous model to work with." I lean up on my toes and press a kiss to his lips. "Come on, let's go to the casino and see how lucky we can get."

As I try to pull away, Keaton tugs me to him and kisses me again so passionately I think we may end up needing to book a room here. "You're going to get so fucking lucky tonight, Baby, but there's no doubt that I'm the luckiest motherfucker in this town."

My breath catches at his words, but before I can react, he's walking to the casino, and I dutifully follow like the lovesick puppy I am.

Neither the blackjack tables nor slot machines were doing anything for us, but the drinks were plentiful and there's a beautiful buzz in my head. We head outside for some fresh air, thankful that the temperatures have cooled a bit. Glancing up and down the strip, I spot the hotel Skyla mentioned earlier, but then my eyes light up at the sight across the street. "Let's go!"

Tugging Keaton's hand, he follows me as we cross the road and step in front of the beautiful pink display. As gorgeous as it is, I take us in a different direction, laughing as he tells me to slow down and asks where we're going.

"Look, Keat!" Shortening his name like I've known him all our lives feels right and the nickname falls off my lips easily. "I'm in Paris!" I twirl around in front of the resort, giggling with excitement and am full of joy I don't think I've ever experienced with anyone else. "Can we go see the Eiffel Tower?"

"I'll take you anywhere you want to go." The way he looks at me has me thinking he truly means it.

The views from the observation deck are incredible, but the view I've had all night is even better. Keaton is so fucking hot from the silver flecks that glisten in his hair to his strong hands with these lickable veins that run through it. Who knew veins could be a turn-on, but here I am wanting to run my tongue down every single one that lines his body. I never knew forty could look so good, but he pulls it off flawlessly. I don't know why I've never considered dating an older man before, but I certainly see the appeal now.

On top of the fact that drool drips from my mouth and down my thighs when I see him, he's just a great guy. We've talked and laughed, and I can see how much he loves his family. His face lights up when he mentions his niece and it makes me wonder what this incredible man would be like as a dad. No doubt better than my own. There's no way Keaton would force his child to work for a slimy man.

I take a drink from the martini we ordered before heading up here, expunging all thoughts of Daniel from my head. When I pull the drink away from my lips, I notice Keaton smiling at me. Every smile he gives me makes my heart flutter. I should probably see my doctor as soon as I get back and make sure there's no chance of a murmur or something more serious. It's probably not normal to have all this activity over someone I've known for less than twelve hours.

"How's your first night in Paris, Baby?" I flush at the pet name he's been calling me all night. The endearment squeezes my chest every time he says it.

"Perfect. This is absolutely incredible. You really should stop spoiling me, though." Keaton had insisted on paying for everything tonight, from our drinks to our tickets here at the tower. Even when I wanted to just experience the slot machines for the first time, he insisted it's more fun to gamble with someone else's money.

"I've enjoyed spoiling you," he wraps his arms around me and brushes his lips against mine. "And I plan on spoiling you a lot more later."

My thighs tighten as the mound between them begins to pulse in need. I try to hide my arousal by looking back at the busy goings on beneath us. There's nothing near this busy back home in Kentucky, even in the bigger cities.

So many gorgeous and infamous hotels and casinos line the street, including the one I am so excited about staying at tonight. Future brides and their friends wear sashes as they stumble along the pavement. A little wedding chapel advertises that your wedding there will be fast, fun, and legal. A giant sphere glows like a prism behind a terrifyingly large Ferris Wheel.

"I don't get it, Anna," Keaton says quietly, bringing my wandering attention back to him.

"What's that?"

"I've never wanted anyone the way I want you. I don't want to fuck you."

The alcohol in my stomach turns sour at his confusing confession. I'm officially at the limit where it's a fine line between a good time and a breakdown and even drunk I'm not sure I can handle a breakdown in front of this man. Apparently, my face doesn't hide the pain I'm feeling from his comment.

"Shit," he quickly follows up, "I didn't mean that. I mean I don't *just* want to fuck you. I want to talk to you and hold you and sleep with you. Not the sex kind. I mean, yeah, the sex kind. But the other kind, too. I want to know your favorite color and what songs you sing in the shower. I want to know everything there is to know about you."

The tears that were forming dry up as fast as they came on as I realize Keaton is trying to say that he likes me and not just for a hookup. I swallow down the lump that had formed in my throat before I speak.

"Green," I say. "My favorite color is green."

His lips tilt up as he hums, "Hmm, like your gorgeous eyes."

"And in the shower, I'm definitely belting out 'Hit Me Baby One More Time'. Or 'Oops I Did It Again'. Really, anything by Britney Spears."

"I'm more of a silent showerer myself, but I'm man enough to admit that Tay Tay comes up in my shower karaoke rotation every now and then." Picturing this man singing in the shower has a smile spreading across my face, but I force myself to be serious for the next thing I'm going to say.

"And I don't want to just fuck you either," I admit and my heart pounds in my chest. This is the part where he runs. In the past, I've been told that I'm more of a "behind closed doors" type of girl. I'm not the one that hangs on a man's arm as he proudly introduces his partner. But I should have known Keaton isn't like the boys I've been with. Tonight I'm with a man. A man who looks at me as though I've just bestowed upon him the greatest gift in the world and that makes me feel pretty damn special.

"I really fucking like you, Anna." Before I can return my sentiment, his lips descend upon mine causing an inferno to build inside me. I can't seem to get enough of him, grabbing his shirt and pulling him into me. My hands find their way under the shirt he has on that matches the shade of his eyes. The rest of the world has faded away and it's only the two of us here in this tower, devouring one another knowing it's likely this is our one and only night together. It's not until Keaton pulls my leg to wrap around his thigh, and we hear a gruff voice rudely telling us to get a room, that we crash back into reality and become aware of our very public surroundings.

"I need you," he growls out, "are you ready to go back to the hotel now?" I must admit that falling into bed with him sounds so fucking good. Just as I'm about to say yes, I look back out at the view and my eyes land on a place they scanned over moments earlier.

There's probably enough alcohol in my system to tranquilize an elephant, but I know when I want something, and by golly, I want Keaton. The desire I have for him, along with the fact I'm three sheets to the wind right now, are a lethal combination and I quickly realize that I'm a goner. More than anyone else in my life, he has made me feel seen, beautiful, and desired. Maybe that knowledge paired with the liquid courage coursing through me is why I risk saying the next words that come out of my mouth.

"Would you mind going to one more stop with me?"

Chapter Seven
Keaton

Typically on business trips I arrive, grab dinner somewhere, and then stay in my room and work until it's time for my meeting. Instead, Anna has dragged me all over the Vegas strip tonight and I can't lie and say I hate it.

If I were a stronger man, I would be in my room right now, hunched over, reviewing logistics, and preparing for my meeting tomorrow. Caruso Enterprises is the fastest growing casino and resort empire in the country, and currently our newest and largest client. Such a high-ticket client demands extra support and care which our smaller clients have no current interest in. Thank goodness, because what this company is asking for is a lot.

On top of the layered encryption protocols, custom-built firewalls, and twenty-four hour monitoring most of our bigger clients ask for, they're demanding "invisible redundancies," shadow networks that even their own staff can't access. They want contingency systems without explanation, private channels locked down tighter than military grade grids.

All the additional expectations have me wondering if they are looking to simply keep hackers out, or hiding something they don't want uncovered. Throw in the fact that the men we worked out negotiations with wore sleek and expensive all-black suits and looked more like the people who throw the drunks and cheats out of casinos than the type of people who want to invite the lucky and the losers into them, and it had my mind recreating scenes from some of the old gangster movies I used to watch with my dad.

This company would probably have me 'sleeping with the fishes' if I mess up our meeting tomorrow to sign the contract, or any meeting after that. Which is exactly why I should be back in that hotel room like the controlled, responsible company CEO I am.

But Anna's laughter pulls me from any hesitating thoughts about being with her and inviting her to stay with me tonight. I'm completely intoxicated, not from the alcohol I've consumed, (okay, maybe a little from the alcohol I've consumed) but mostly from how this woman I was lucky enough to meet teases me with her curves and pulls a smile from my lips faster than anyone I've ever come in contact with before.

She's the type of addiction that has me taking pictures with indecent statues, drinking far too much to know how I'm even standing upright at the moment, and falling head over heels for her.

Tomorrow I will be the man Caruso Enterprises needs. But tonight? Tonight I will be anything Anna allows me to be.

"Would you mind going to one more stop with me?" Anna asks, sweetly. Her golden hair and beautiful face look ethereal as we stand here on the observation deck looking over the illuminated city.

If this girl knew just how far gone I was for her, she wouldn't even have to ask. There is no doubt in my mind that I'd go anywhere with this woman. But I can't let her in on that, just yet.

I wrap my hands around her waist, pulling her into me and kissing the skin on her neck. It's smooth, though slightly warm from the heat of the desert evening. "Hmm, it depends. Are you naked at this next stop?"

"Keaton!" She pushes at me to get away, but I just bring her in closer, this time capturing her delicious lips. They press back against mine, soft, but needy. When I dip my tongue inside her mouth, a delightfully gentle moan escapes her, an invitation for more. My hands twirl the strands of hair brushing her shoulders and when I tug at it, a gasp of excitement sounds from her.

"I need you so bad," I say between kisses, never wanting to let this woman go.

"One more stop," she answers breathily, "and then I'm yours."

Chapter Eight

Anna

G iggling and somehow managing to keep our hands on one another, we stumble our way into the hotel room. No, this isn't a room, it's a suite. A very expensive suite. Keaton is fancy as fuck and has to be loaded, too. I want to explore this amazing space in my dream hotel, but his lips on my neck are as distracting as his big hands that roam over my body.

"I want you so fucking bad, Anna, but I don't want to take advantage of you," he admits in between kisses that make a path down to my shoulder. I know he's referring to the both of us having drunk our weight in alcohol, but the need for him is so strong.

"I appreciate you being so honorable, but if you keep your cock away from me any longer, my entire body might combust." I brush my hands down his strong chest and sculpted torso until I reach the crotch of his pants and press against his impressive bulge, making him release a groan and creating a flood in my panties.

Keaton grabs my hips and hoists me onto the biggest king size bed I've ever seen, like I weigh nothing at all. Never has a man handled me in that way and I want more of it so badly. I love that he's so strong and my curves don't deter him, but instead he seems to genuinely love those parts of me. Lying in the humongous bed on my back, I prop up on my elbows to see the little show he's giving me at the end of the bed. Slowly he pulls off his shirt and swings it around the air like some sort of cowboy before he tosses it to the side. The man on the plane memorizing the safety pamphlet and watching how to administer the oxygen masks with rapt attention is long gone. I have a feeling I am seeing a side of this man he doesn't typically let out very often. And I'm loving every second of it.

"You gonna strip for me, Keaton?"

He gives me that sinful smirk of his where that damn dimple pops out and nods. Giving me a little wiggle of his hips, his hands move to his jeans.

"Let me." I push myself up and crawl over to him on the bed. Looking into his crystal blue eyes, I have to ask, "If I try to unbuckle your pants, are you going to push me away again?"

"Baby, I will never push you away again. Now undo my pants before my dick gets a fucking imprint from my zipper." Eagerly, I get the man unbuckled, unbuttoned, and unzipped. My hand reaches into his gray boxer briefs and gently grazes the tip of his hard, thick, and extraordinary cock.

"Fuck, that feels good," he moans, but his eyes never leave mine.

My hand wraps around his shaft fully and I pull out the most beautiful cock I've ever seen. Dicks aren't pretty. It's just a fact. But Keaton's deserves a shrine. My hand pumps up and down, trying to show my appreciation, but as I go to move off the bed so I can have a taste, Keaton stops me.

"You first."

His hands reach around and tug at the zipper on the cute dress we bought at our last stop for the night. As he moves it down, my nipples harden in anticipation. The dress gets caught at my full hips, but Keaton just presses me back against the bed so he can shimmy it off the rest of the way. As he does, his hands massage my hips and thighs, making noises of satisfaction that have my heart racing. God, he feels so good, and he's barely touched me.

Once my dress is tossed to the floor, he repositions me so he can wrap around and unsnap my bra. I love the way this man just moves me around as though I'm weightless. With the final clasp undone, my breasts spring free of the barbaric contraption. Keaton lets out a deep moan that sends a jolt straight to my pussy. Large hands begin massaging my breast and then his mouth is descending upon them, first one nipple, then the next. "God, Anna, you're so fucking perfect. I've wanted these gorgeous tits in my mouth from the second I saw you."

I'm usually a girl who needs some help for things to come to fruition and so I have an arsenal of toys in my bedside table. Tonight, however, I think I could come from Keaton's words alone.

After a generous amount of time appreciating my breast assets, he reaches down to the band of the simple white, cotton panties I'm wearing. I'm a little insecure that I don't have something a bit sexier on, but the last thing I was thinking about when I got dressed this morning was that I'd be in a hotel suite with an absolute Adonis of a man treating me like a queen. He looks at me with a question in his eyes and just above a whisper I give him the confirmation he needs.

Keaton leans in and places a kiss on the inside of both thighs before peeling the fabric down my legs.

"You smell so good, Baby. I bet you taste even better."

With no hesitation at all, he brings his tongue to my core and licks through my seam before placing a kiss at my clit. He repeats the process again before he begins lapping me up like he's dying of thirst. I've always been self-conscious about oral in the past, but between the alcohol and passion coursing through my veins, not to mention the fervor in which he's tonguing my pussy, there is no room for my insecurities.

"Oh Keaton, that feels so good. Don't stop, please don't stop."

His hands grip behind my thighs and then I'm yanked down until my ass is hanging off the bed. A whole new ravenous side of him comes out. Keaton's tongue is relentless as it runs up my slit, circles my clit and then sucks my swollen bud into his mouth.

"Yes, Keaton! That feels so good. You're so good at this," I cry out.

His tongue continues its exploration, darting inside of me, then languidly licking my lips. I try to remain in position so he can continue but before I know it, my back is arching off the bed. My legs wrap around his back, pressing my thighs into his cheeks. He lets out an appreciative moan but doesn't lose focus. Then I'm screaming through the most intense orgasm of my life.

I come down from the shattering moment with Keaton pulling me into his arms. "You're fucking delicious, Baby." Then he presses his lips to mine so I can taste it for myself. I've never experienced my own flavor before, but it mixed with the taste of Keaton is giving me a head rush of euphoria. When our lips are finally swollen and sore, we pull apart.

"Mmm, I like when you call me Baby. But what should I call you? Want me to reenact the book we're both listening to?"

"You want me to be your Daddy, Baby?"

I bite my lip and decide to try it out. "You fuck me so good, Daddy."

Keaton's eyes widen and lock onto mine. I feel my lips tilting up in amusement. Then both of us are barking out laughs.

"No," I huff out, "no I really don't. Damn, it's hot to read about, but I just can't in real life. Ugh, I was really hoping to give you a name."

"I have a name, Baby," Keaton smiles at me, lifting my hand and placing a gentle kiss on the fourth finger of my left hand. "You can call me Husband."

Chapter Nine
Keaton

My phone rings relentlessly the next morning, waking me up with a piercing pain in my head. Somehow I'm able to locate it under my pillow and answer just before the call is sent to voicemail.

"Hello?" I manage to croak out.

"Why the fuck do you sound hungover?" Oh great, I get to start my morning with the grumpiest asshole I've ever met.

"Because I am," I admit to my younger brother, Lincoln.

"Keaton Fisher, are you telling me that the one time in your life you decide to be reckless is the night before one of the biggest acquisitions we've landed since starting this company? Did you forget you have a meeting today?"

Shit.

I look at the clock on my phone. My meeting with Caruso Enterprises is in forty-five minutes and according to the maps app I pull up, it takes at least twenty minutes to get there.

"I didn't forget." *I totally forgot.* "I'll make it," I assure him.

"What the hell is this? You turn forty this year and have a midlife crisis? You're the fucking CEO. People come to our company because of your professionalism and dedication. One trip to Vegas and you've gone and fucked things up."

His condescending tone is the last thing my headache needs, but I bite my tongue and refuse to get into a pissing match with him so as not to wake the gorgeous woman who is still asleep next to me. Anna. My wife. Did I really fuck things up?

It's been years since I've let my guard down and drank like I did last night. Definitely before I started our company. As the oldest brother, I had to step up when my dad passed away. I was eighteen, Lincoln just a couple years behind me, and Camden was ten. Mom was an absolute fucking mess. She couldn't get out of bed for about a month after the funeral. I know the saying is that it's better to have loved and lost than to never have loved at all, but in the case of my mom, I'm not sure that's true.

She stopped taking care of us. Hell, she stopped taking care of anything. I was about to graduate high school and was set to go to the University of Kentucky just a couple of hours away, but there was no way I could leave my brothers to try and fend for themselves. Especially Cam. Damn he was so young, way too young to lose a parent, let alone two, and then a brother on top of it.

So, I ended up enrolling in the community college, creating a schedule of classes that were built around taking my brothers to school and their extracurriculars. I enrolled in mostly business and technology courses, with no clear direction of what I wanted to do, but I enjoyed it, and when it came time to make something of myself, I put the knowledge I gained from those classes to good use.

Once Lincoln had his driver's license, it helped a lot. Mom was still a mess and became a recluse, only going out for her monthly hair appointment and a ladies luncheon. She'd put on a brave face and act like everything was perfect, then come home and wallow in sorrow until the next month came around. Ten years ago, she stopped going out at all. Things got incredibly dark during those days, and we didn't feel like it was safe to leave her, so Lincoln moved in. Now that his daughter, Charlie, is living there too, we see more smiles out of Mom, but she's not the same as she used to be and I'm not sure she ever will be again.

A therapist would probably tell me that's why I was content with nothing more than just the occasional hook up with a woman. Relationships can completely redefine who we are, and we can lose ourselves in our partners if the feelings are strong enough. Feelings create messes and between the business and making sure our family is okay, I don't have time for messes. Looking back down at Anna, I feel a tug in my heart, and I know things are about to get a whole lot messier in my world.

I reassure my brother that I will get the job done before hanging up as he grumbles something about how he should have been the one to come out here, but we both know Lincoln's growly tone doesn't always do the best in business acquisitions.

As quietly as possible, so I don't wake Anna, I slip out of bed and rush to the bathroom to prepare for my meeting. As I cross the bedroom to change into my suit for the day, I pick up the white dress we purchased at the chapel before we got married.

Anna took my breath away the moment I saw her in that airport but seeing her in that white piece of polyester that hugged her curves in all the right ways, knowing she was about to promise herself to me, I'd swear there's nothing more beautiful than that.

I'm not an idiot, I know what we did was fucking crazy. When she asked me to stop at one more spot with her, I expected her to be hungry or want one of those impressively tall margaritas. The last thing I expected was for her to drag me into a wedding chapel, the gleam in those emerald eyes looking at me like I hung the damn moon.

When you're the CEO of a company, you have to be calculated. Structured. Intentional. Making huge decisions based on a whim can lead to some pretty dire situations that could put your business on a path you want to go down. Impulsive was not something I had a luxury of being.

But how was I supposed to say no to her? And why would I fucking want to?

I look down at my woman lying in the bed where we joined as husband and wife last night. I note how she looks so beautiful and peaceful while she sleeps. I'm not sure how I managed to be the lucky bastard she ended up next to on the plane, but I will forever be grateful for it. Her blonde hair is tucked behind her ears. Her lips are still swollen from all our activity last night and they're gently parted so that the slightest, softest, sweetest snore can escape them.

The temptation to lean down and kiss her awake is strong, but I fight the urge to wake her so she can sleep, and I can get to my meeting. Waking her up will just lead to me not wanting to leave this fucking hotel room, and that will without a doubt piss my brother, and our new clients, off even more.

Not wanting to leave her without so much as a goodbye, I search both the desk and the nightstands in the room but can't find a single thing to write a note out on. Running out of time to get out the door, I pick up her phone and hold it up to her face to unlock, then I add my contact information, hoping she will see it and reach out in case she wakes up.

The meeting shouldn't last too long. I'm just needing them to sign the contract. I hate to leave without saying goodbye, but hopefully I'll make it back before she wakes up. I'm eager to spend the rest of the day with Anna, then follow today up with the rest of my life.

Chapter Ten
Anna

I wake with a smile on my face as the hazy memories from last night fill my head. The night may have started off horribly, but the soreness between my legs is a reminder that it ended in the most unbelievable of ways with the most handsome man showing me tons of affection. I roll over to snuggle next to Keaton, but all I find is a cold sheet.

"Keaton?" I call out, hoping he's just retreated to the living space or bathroom to keep things quiet as I sleep. There's no response, though, so I decided he must have run out to grab breakfast or coffee. I smile at how thoughtful he was all last night, knowing that's probably carried over to this morning and I have nothing to worry about.

Leaving the amazingly comfortable bed with a sigh, I get up and walk my naked self to the bathroom. Getting into the shower brought back the dirty words he said to me last night.

So fucking beautiful, Anna. Look at the way you take me, like you were meant just for me. Do you feel that, Baby? Do you feel how we were meant to be together?

Oh, how I felt it. That man made me feel things I have never felt before, in both my pussy and my heart.

I grab some of his body wash and pour it onto a washcloth, loving how the smell fills the shower stall with his scent. Wanting to keep the smell of him and the memories of last night lingering all day, I lather myself in the tobacco and vanilla fragrance.

Stepping out, I catch my image in the mirror and automatically wrinkle my nose. My body is larger than average and mirrors are always willing to show me the truth of that fact. I smooth my hand over my rolls and think about how Keaton touched them with such passion last night. They didn't keep him from touching and tasting every inch of me, so instead of shaming my body like I typically do when I have a standoff with my reflection, I smile and thank my body for where it's gotten me.

I smile at the thought of seeing him again this morning, my heart full for the first time in a long time. There was just something about the way he made me so comfortable last night. He listened and wanted to get to know me, asking questions and telling me about himself. Unlike my last boyfriend, Keaton didn't shy away from touching me, kissing me often and running his hand over my hips. Everything about last night just seemed perfect.

After drying my hair and putting on a cute flowy dress, perfect for meeting up with the girls, I stepped out into the living area and noticed it was still empty. "Keaton?" I called out again but received no answer in return.

I was trying to keep the positive vibes flowing, even though a heavy weight formed in my gut. It had been about half an hour since I woke up. If he had left just before, walked to get breakfast, stood in line, and then walked back, that could easily take longer than that. I just needed to be patient.

But what if he woke up and saw me, instantly regretting the decisions we made last night? What if this was his way of letting me down easily?

Memories from college rushed back. I was at a frat party and this guy started flirting with me. His compliments seemed sincere, the tugs on my hair were playful, and so after a fairly public makeout session, he asked me to go to his room and I said yes. When we entered his room, he turned me face down over his bed and pulled my dress up. He grabbed a condom, thank god, but then plunged in without any foreplay and started rocking back and forth into me, not touching me anywhere else. As soon as he got off, he pulled out, thanked me for the easy hundred bucks, and walked away. I felt disgusted but mostly confused. When I walked back out into the party, I learned it was some stupid bet to prove that he would, in fact, fuck the fat chick.

I shook my head dismissing those concerns. Everything about Keaton was different. The way it didn't feel like just sex, but an emotional act when he took me in bed, and then in the shower, and then in bed again. But if it was so different, then why am I sitting here on the sofa with tears down my face instead of lying in bed in his arms?

I'm jolted when I hear buzzing from the bedroom. Wiping the tears away, I walk in to see my phone lighting up with messages.

Skyla

Anna! We're in Vegas, my bestie bitch!

Penny

Want to meet us for brunch?

Jasmine

Anna, where are you? Where did you stay last night?

Jasmine

Why aren't you answering us? I swear if you stayed at some shady spot and now you're in a dumpster chopped up into tiny pieces, I will find every last one of them and glue you back together just so I can chop you back up myself.

Penny

Whoa, Jaz! That got dark.

Skyla

Jeez, Jaz. You've got to calm down. You're fine, aren't you Anna? She's probably just sleeping in after a solid dicking.

Anna

I'm fine. And all my body parts are still intact, Jaz.

Except maybe my heart.

Penny

There's our girl! What did you end up getting into last night?

Anna

> Way too much to text. Just tell me where to meet you.

Texting makes me wonder if Keaton input his number in my phone at some point. I scroll down to the K's, but there's no Keaton listed. Defeated, I'm about to toss my phone on the bed, but vibrates in my hand.

Daniel

> Couldn't stop thinking about your fat ass and huge tits last night, sweet girl. Look what you do to me. [Video]

I know I shouldn't, but curiosity gets the better of me as I press play. I knew nothing Daniel sent could be good, but a video of him stroking himself while moaning and saying my name is not what I had expected. Why the fuck would he send me something so vulgar? I have done absolutely nothing to show any sort of interest in my father's best friend.

Disgusted, I note that it's now been an hour since I've been awake and Keaton hasn't returned. He isn't coming back. And he just left. With no word. He could have woken me up to say he had to leave, or hell, that I had to leave. Something. Anything. But nothing at all?

Tears begin to flow down my face again and my body shakes, but instead of being from sadness, these tears morphed into anger. Fucking men. Fucking ex-boyfriends who always acted like they were doing me a service by dating me. Fucking college frat boys and their fucking bets. Fucking Daniel thinking he has any right to talk to me the way he does and touch me without my permission. Fucking Keaton for playing with my heart and then leaving me without so much as a word.

I'm done with all of them.

Chapter Eleven

Anna

"Anna Banana!" Skyla shouts as I step into the fifties style diner they messaged me the details about. Her auburn curls bounce as she rushes up to envelop me in one of her signature hugs. I didn't realize I needed it so badly, but I wrap my arms around my sweet friend and let the ribbons of red tickle my skin.

"I cannot wait to hear about all the fun I just know you had last night." She pulls me through the place to meet up with our other best friends who are seated in a booth near the back of the restaurant.

The diner they chose to meet up at is super cute with teal and pink vinyl booths situated around large glass windows. Tables with chairs padded in the same colors are strewn throughout the middle. Black and white tiles adorn the floor in a diamond pattern, and the walls are covered in Elvis memorabilia, but also the cutest cat clock where the tail swings back and forth.

As I pass the jukebox, Jasmine and Penny stand up to greet us. Giggles and shrieks make us a spectacle as my friends engulf me in unconditional love I didn't realize I needed so terribly in this moment. These girls are seriously the best friends I could ever ask for and I hate that I don't see them more often than a few times a year.

Skyla and I met in college where we were roommates. We immediately became besties. She is so full of life and can always put a positive spin on even the worst of situations. She's from the same hometown as Jasmine and Penny, who were rooming together. When she introduced them to me, Penny was incredibly kind, but I had the strangest feeling that Jasmine absolutely hated me. Turns out, that's just Jaz. Her exterior comes across pretty rough, but she's truly one of the sweetest people I know. Penny is a good blend of Jaz and Sky. She struggles badly with anxiety, but she knows how to have a good time and let loose.

Our unexpected, but immediate friendship means the world to a girl who grew up without any true best friends. I mean, I hung out with people and was nice to everyone, but I never had someone I always knew would be in my corner. Thinking about the love my friends have for me brings the tears back and I begin shaking in their arms. Penny seems to be the first to notice.

"Anna, what's wrong?"

"I'm okay," I sob, "it's just been a really shitty morning."

They pull me into the booth and Skyla hands me some napkins from the dispenser so I can blot at my face.

"Who do I need to kill?" Jasmine demands. Her dark hair is tied up in a severe ponytail, showcasing her high cheekbones and looking entirely like the badass I know she is. Like the rest of our friend group, she's bigger than the average woman, but Jasmine is solid muscle. There is not a single doubt in my mind she can take down anyone whether it's in a courtroom or otherwise.

"Before anyone goes on a murder spree, do you mind me taking your order?" An older woman who looks to be in her sixties appears at our table. Her abundant bleach blonde curls are stacked on top of her head in a messy bun and she gazes at us with big brown eyes that tell me she's lived a life full of stories.

After we place our orders, myself ordering a slice of chocolate pie for breakfast, because why the fuck not, Jasmine looks over at me. "Spill."

"I hate men," I start out.

"Naturally. But explain. Be specific," Jasmine continues.

Not wanting to exploit my naivete just yet, I opt to keep my story about Keaton under wraps for now and begin with the issues I'm having with my boss, Daniel. I've shared other things he's said and done with them before, so at least this is familiar territory. "That's so fucking gross!" Penny shouts after I tell them about the messages yesterday and then the video I received this morning.

"Anna, I know you've told me no in the past, but we need to file a sexual harassment lawsuit. Hell, we could even pin him with sexual assault after that time in the workroom." Jasmine has been relentless about me pressing charges, especially when I told them about the time in the workroom when I was pulling a granola bar out of the cabinet and he pressed his body up against mine, poking his small, hardened dick into my backside as he reached over me, seemingly for the same thing.

"Do you feel this, pretty girl?" His hot breath made me want to gag as he pressed his body further into me and whispered in my ear. "You come into this office dressed like a little slut and this is what it does to me. Do you want me to bend you over my desk? Is that why you wore this tiny little skirt? I'd love to hike it up and make you feel so damn good. Come to my office and let me take care of you."

Thankfully we heard people making their way towards us and he stepped back and walked away before his hands could travel anywhere else. My coworkers had come in before I could adjust my face and when they asked about me, I just said I thought I was coming down with something. It wasn't a complete lie, because when my body came out of shock, I rushed to the bathroom where I immediately got sick. I sank to the tiles of the floor and hugged the toilet, choking out sobs.

I had been so excited about wearing the outfit I had chosen that day. Penny and I had gone shopping and found this adorable pleated black skirt. I don't typically like showing off my larger legs, but the way it hit just above my knees made me confident instead of self-conscious, so I decided to purchase it. I had paired it with a soft pink v-neck sweater because I'm always a bit chilled in the office and threw on a pair of black kitten heels to finish the look.

As soon as I got home, that skirt I loved so much was thrown into the trash.

"I know, Jaz, I really do. And I want to, but I can't afford to lose this job right now. Plus, he's my dad's best friend. It's just going to cause more issues. I can keep ignoring him."

Skyla leans over on my shoulder, "I love you, Anna, but it isn't healthy to ignore this. These are serious acts he's committing."

"We just want you safe and happy," Penny continues. "You are the best person ever and don't deserve to be harassed. Do you think if you told your dad what was going on, he'd put a stop to it?"

I snort. My relationship with my father is complicated, at best. He's never been downright mean to me, though he does like to make little digs about my weight more often than not. I do believe he loves me, but I've never come first, and there's no way he would choose me over his best friend.

"Absolutely not," I say with a shake of my head. "He and Daniel Brenner have been friends for years. There's no way he would believe me over him."

"But you have proof," Penny suggests, gesturing to my phone.

"I know my dad, guys. He could watch it happen and he'd blame me for it. I think I'm just going to start looking for other jobs. It seems like that's the easiest solution at this point." I don't confess to my friends that I've already applied for one. Something in me is scared to put it out in the world and risk losing it, even though it's something I easily told Keaton.

Thinking of him makes a place inside my chest pinch. I was really hoping to spend a little more time with him before seeing my friends. My heart ran away and started dreaming up scenarios of this the older-than-me man with the sweetest smile wanting more than one night from me. But as always, my heart was wrong. So very wrong.

"That's not a bad idea," Penny says, snapping me back to reality. "Maybe you can even look at doing something in photography. You're so good at it and I know you love it so much."

"Not sure I can afford that right now, but maybe." It would be incredible to do something I'm actually passionate about, but I'm barely capable of paying my bills as it is, so photography will just remain a hobby for now.

Thankfully the conversation shifts to what our plans are for our time here in Vegas. No surprise it's going to consist of a lot of pool time, casino time, and drinking. We finish up our breakfast, my delicious slice of pie long gone. As I stand to walk out, Jasmine grabs my left wrist.

"Anna, can you explain why there's a fucking wedding ring on your finger?"

Chapter Twelve

Keaton

Driving back to the hotel, I can't help but be furious about having to waste my money, time, and resources. The trip out here was just a power play for Caruso Enterprises. We're a fucking cybersecurity company, so digital signatures should always suffice, but some people we work with demand in-person meetings, usually to ask any additional questions or attempt more negotiations. Today there were no questions or negotiations. I simply got the signatures we needed to make this happen and then was expected to sit and chat while sipping on overpriced scotch.

Dealing with this company, though, is what led me to meeting the woman I haven't been able to get out of my mind all morning. After seeing what my dad's death did to my mom, I had absolutely no desire to let someone wreck me in the same regard. Relationships just weren't a thing for me and that was that. Now this beautiful, curvy goddess has entered my world, and I will do anything in my power to make sure she never leaves it.

The thought should scare me, especially how suddenly it happened. I should be skeptical of how easily we got along. Don't get me wrong, I generally get along with people, but usually there's some flaw that you notice in others. With Anna, there's literally not a damn thing about her I would change.

I toss my keys at the valet and jog through the lobby to the elevators, eager to get to my woman. It's been hours since I had to leave her this morning and my cock aches to be buried back inside of her. If I'm lucky, she will let me feast on that delicious pussy of hers first. I doubt she's still sleeping, but if I'm lucky, her friends aren't in town yet and she stuck around.

Swiping my key, I rush to the bedroom, only to find it empty.

"Anna," I call out, glancing around the room and noticing her things are missing.

Shit.

"No, no, no," I mutter under my breath, my chest tightening in panic. I look everywhere for any trace of the woman who captivated my mind, body, and soul, but the only piece of her I find are the white cotton panties I tore from her body last night. Pocketing them, I sit at the end of the bed.

Rocking back and forth, my hands buried in my head, my brain searches for some possible way to find my girl. We talked about how she and her friends were going to go all out this weekend, but she didn't mention a single specific event. Hell, she didn't even tell me where they were staying.

Stewing in turmoil, my phone begins to ring with a conference call from both my brothers. "What?" I bark.

"Whoa, big bro. What's wrong?" Camden asks, concern clear in his voice. He's a gentle giant, taller than both me and Lincoln, but a helluva lot kinder than either of us, too.

Lincoln, ever the pessimist, says, "Did you not get the contract signed? Were you late to the meeting, motherfucker?"

"I made it to the meeting. Got the contracts signed, then did the whole schmooze routine like a good little puppet."

"Thank fuck," Linc says. "So was your asshole greeting just because of the hangover you're still nursing?"

"Hangover? You got drunk? Mr. Responsible? Mr. All Work and No Play?" Cam teases.

"I don't have time for either of your shit right now, I need help with something."

The line goes quiet for several moments. It's not like me to ask for help. As the oldest, I tend to take on the problems and try to fix them without disrupting my family in the process. When Mom couldn't take care of my brothers anymore, I stepped in. When my brothers and I needed an opportunity in our small town, I got our business started.

Cam's teasing was officially over. "Shit. What's wrong? What can we do?"

I take a second to consider how deep into detail I want to go regarding my situation with Anna. "I met this girl last night on the flight. Her name is Anna, and we spent the night together here in my room. This morning I had to leave for the meeting, but she was still sleeping and I didn't get a chance to say goodbye or get her number. I need to find her."

"Why do you need to find this girl, Keat? Did she steal from you?" Lincoln asks,

"What? No of course not," I realize I'm immediately defensive of her, but also not entirely sure she didn't steal from me. I didn't even think of considering that as an option because there's no way the Anna I met last night would do anything like that.

Camden's voice takes on a different pitch, "Lincoln, has Keaton ever asked us to find information on any of his past hookups?"

"You know baby bro, I can't recall him ever giving enough of a shit about them to so much as get their number. I wonder what's different about this one."

"I have a few of their numbers, asshole," I mutter. Though, he kind of has a point.

"So tell us, Keaton, what's different about this girl? What makes her special enough to seek out?" Lincoln presses, sounding ever the smug asshole he truly is.

"I can't really get into it right now," I dodge, "I just need help finding her."

"Does Anna have a last name?" Camden asks.

Yeah, mine.

"I don't know it," I admit. "But like I said, we were on the same flight. Think we can somehow pull the logs to get her information?"

"Brother, we are a cybersecurity company. Our whole mission is to stop the kind of shit you just asked us to do," Lincoln chastises.

"You don't think I fucking know that?" I'm off the bed and pacing my room at this point. "I wouldn't ask for this if it wasn't important."

"So, it's imperative that you find this girl, to the point you're asking us to do some illegal shit, but you can't tell us why she's so important to you?" Camden asks calmly, the mediator of our bunch.

My stomach is in knots. I feel like I'm trapped in one of those hourglasses where the sand is pouring down on me. Every second that passes without her is another grain drowning me in my grief. That grief turns into anger at my brothers for slowing this process down.

"Would the two of you stop dicking around and help me find my wife?"

Shit. I definitely didn't mean to let that detail slip through, but here we fucking are, I guess.

"Your fucking what?" Lincoln shouts through the phone. "What the fuck do you mean by that?"

Camden once again tried to diffuse the conversation, "Umm, Keat, can you say that again?" He laughs, "Kinda sounded like you said your 'wife' there for a second."

I groan and damn myself for losing my temper and confessing the secret I meant to keep until she was officially with me. Living in my house. Sleeping in my bed. Under me every night.

"I did. We kinda sorta got married last night." I go over the details from the night before with my siblings. I smile through the pain when I think of the way her face lit up in that little chapel.

"Do you think Elvis is gonna marry us?" Anna giggles and it's the cutest damn thing I've ever heard in my life.

"The king might be a bit busy, Baby, but if you want Elvis to marry us, I can see what we can do."

She shakes her head, that gorgeous smile lighting up her face. "As long as I get to be with you and keep feeling this way, I don't care who it is that marries us, but maybe we can at least have him sing at our wedding. We are getting married in Vegas, after all."

Anna walked down the aisle to Can't Help Falling in Love while wearing a little white dress she had picked out in the chapel's store. She was the most beautiful woman I'd ever seen. And she was mine.

"Keaton? Did I lose you?" Camden's voice crashes me back in the present and the memories of my beautiful bride fade.

"Sorry, what was that?" I ask, obviously having missed something.

"How do you 'kinda, sorta' marry someone?" Lincoln asks.

"I guess you don't. Legally, Anna and I are married." I stand from the bed to find the paperwork from the chapel last night. Surely her name is on there somewhere and with a full name, we are more likely to locate her.

"You married her after what, just a few hours? How much do you know about this girl? I'm going to assume you didn't have a prenuptial agreement signed, with this being a drunken wedding. We need to move forward with an annulment to protect your assets."

"Protect his assets?" Lincoln fumes. "You mean our assets? His dumbass decision has put the fucking company in jeopardy? What if we fucking lose everything? You want Charlie out on the fucking streets, Keat? Way to fuck everything up." There's a click on the phone and I see that he's hung up.

There's no way Anna would be cruel like that, not the Anna I married. She is the sweetest, most caring, and wonderful person I have ever encountered in this life. Hell, this is probably just one giant misunderstanding and she'll be running back into my arms as soon as we meet up again.

"Keaton, I hate to say this, but Lincoln wasn't wrong when he said she could come after the company. A drunken wedding could easily be granted an annulment, but we have to move fast."

I take in Camden's words. I was a bit reckless when it came to marrying Anna last night. I mean, who marries someone they've known for only a few hours? But the thought of losing her for good? The thought of acting like last night never happened? My stomach churns and I know I can't let that happen.

Locating the papers I was searching for, I find her full name beside my own.

"Keith, Cam. Anna Keith. And no annulment. Just help me fucking find her."

1 1 0 0 1 1 0 0 0 1 0 1 0 1 1 1 1 0 0 1 0
0 0 0 0 0 0 0 1 1 0 0 1 1 0 0 0 0 0 1 0 1
1 0 1 0 1 0 1 0 0 0 1 1 0 0 0 1 1 0 0 1 0
0 0 0 0 1 1 1 1 0 0 1 0 0 0 1 0 0 1
0 1 0 1 1 1 0 0 1 0 0 1 1 1 0 1 0
0 1 0
1 0 0
0 0 0 1 1 0 0 0 0
0 1 0 0 0 0 1 1
0 1 0 0 0 1
0 1 0 1

Chapter Thirteen

Anna

"Okay, there are options. We can look at an annulment, but those are only granted under certain situations. Neither of you are underage, right?" Jasmine asks.

"Gross! Of course not. In fact, Keaton's older, in that sexy silver fox way."

"Ooo, a daddy!" Skyla exclaims and I bark out a laugh, shaking my head.

"No, definitely not, a daddy."

She pouts a little but moves on quickly. "Still, older men are so sexy. I bet he's super experienced, too."

"Speaking of," Jasmine moves on, "the other option would be that you didn't consummate the marriage. You didn't sleep with him, did you?" I bite my bottom lip and she winces at my reaction. "Of course you fucking did."

"If you saw him your legs would have fallen right open, too," I protest.

"I definitely need more details about this man and the night the two of you had," Skyla says with a wink, making me smile.

"It was honestly the most incredible night of my life, Sky."

"Yeah, until he ended up being a complete asshole leaving you after a one night stand with nothing but a broken heart." Penny gives me a knowing look. She's been the product of giving someone her heart, only for them to leave town and her behind without so much as a reason. Her sweet face softens again. "Sorry, Anna. I didn't mean..."

"No, you're right," I admit, even though it pains me to do so. "We had an incredible night together and then he just left. He was an asshole. I'm sick of being disposable." For what feels like the millionth time in less than twenty-four hours, tears begin to well in my eyes.

"Sweetie, you are not disposable," Skyla rubs my back reassuringly. "You deserve the world and one day you will find the right man who is prepared to give it to you."

The sad thing is, I thought I had found him. Yes, the relationship between me and Keaton was rushed, but it was so real. The tears begin to pour, and I can't seem to get them under control. Our server comes over and places a second slice of chocolate pie in front of me with a wink, letting me know this one is on the house. I'm so pathetic that strangers are giving me pity pie. Still gonna eat it though. It's fucking great pie.

My tears begin to dry, and a slightly maniacal laugh escapes my lips. The girls just stare at me in concern, but the laughter continues bubbling out of me. "I'm sitting here with pity pie because of this man. I'm so done. Obviously, he's the world's most impressive player because I was blindsided by him just leaving like that, but it's over. I'm over him. Now let's go enjoy our weekend."

Maybe if I lie to myself that I'm over Keaton, I'll finally believe it. But one thing for sure is that it feels a lot better to be angry with him than sad over him.

"That's the spirit," Penny insists, "Your first night may not have started off great, but that's just because your girls weren't here. The four of us are going to have a great time and put all this behind us. Fuck men. We don't need them."

The rest of my friends agree with her, and we pile out of the diner for our day in the city. Determined to have fun and savor these memories with my besties, I put a smile on my face and force out all thoughts of the man I married.

"Thanks so much," I shout at my driver as I slam the door, running as fast as my chubby legs will allow towards the security line at the airport. I cannot believe I overslept and almost missed my flight. The line is long, so I hold my breath, cross my fingers and wish for the air traffic control gods to speed this process along so I don't miss the only flight back home today.

Finally through security, I make a mad dash for my gate right as I see the airport employee about to close the doors. "No!" I shout at her. "I'm here."

Bracing myself for another encounter like I had with Flight Attendant Dickhead, I'm shocked when she smiles at me and wishes me a good flight.

Shuffling down the aisle, which is not at all generously spaced, I make my way to my seat, noting there's only two in a row instead of the three we had on the way here. At least I'll only have to climb over one person this time.

"Excuse me, but I have the window seat," I say with a smile to my seatmate. But when the handsome face with the neatly trimmed salt and pepper beard flashes a gorgeous grin and blue eyes so pale they look like they belong in the high sky, my smile quickly drops.

"Keaton," I whisper, acknowledging the man who has haunted my dreams the past couple of nights.

"Hi, Anna."

This can't be happening.

Shaking my head in a panic I say probably much louder than I should, "No. No, I'm not doing this. Fuck no and fuck you." I scan the aisle searching for anyone who can get me both home and the hell away from him. Landing on a graying woman with a kind face, I quickly flag her down.

"Miss!" I hiss and wave to the flight attendant standing a couple of rows back. "Miss, I am so sorry to be a bother, but is there another seat I could take?"

She walks my way and looks at the empty seat before turning back to me. "Ma'am, I am so sorry, but the flight is completely full. Is there something prohibiting you from sitting there?"

Just my husband who is looking way too good for me to sit here and act like I'm not bothered by him the whole way home.

Not wanting to get into that huge debacle with the patient woman waiting for my response, I try again. "Are you sure there aren't any other seats available?" I try to show her the desperation in my eyes, but sadly it doesn't seem to help my case.

"There's really nothing we can do. Everyone has already taken their seats and, as I said, it's a full flight."

Defeated, my shoulders slump as I realize I will be sitting directly beside my husband for the next few hours. "I understand. Thank you."

"Is there anything else I can help you with? Perhaps a drink?" She takes a quick glance at Keaton then turns back to me with a lifted eyebrow. A drink is the last thing I need since it landed me in my current predicament, but I do appreciate the solidarity. I turn my back fully to Keaton when I whisper, " No thank you, but could I have an extender, please?" She gives me a kind smile and discreetly places one in my hand.

"Just let me know if you need anything else, Sweetie." As she turns and walks towards the back of the plane, I face my husband and huff.

"Move," I demand, crossing my arms and positioning myself so Keaton won't touch me as he steps into the aisle so I can take my place next to him. Once seated and buckled, I turn away from him and look out the window, pointedly ignoring the hulking hunk beside me. But he refuses to provide me my peace.

"Anna Baby," I roll my eyes but refuse to look at him, so he presses on. "Please don't shut me out. Just let me explain why I wasn't there the other morning."

I can't help but scoff and even though I really don't want to speak to this man, there is no way I am going to sit here and listen to him drone on about his feelings when he doesn't give two shits about mine. "Don't shut you out? What? Like you did to me?"

"Baby, I never," I throw my hands up, cutting him off.

"Stop," I hiss at him. "Stop it with the whole 'Baby' shit, it just gives me the creeps."

It definitely doesn't, but I'm not about to tell him that.

"I don't want to hear a word you have to say. I went from having one of the best nights of my life and experiencing so many things I had only dreamed of and on top of that, you had made it seem as though you cared about me, too. Like you really liked me. I mean, hell, you fucking married me."

"Anna, I do care. I do really like you. And I want to stay," I cut him off again before he can finish that statement.

"You want to stay? Because you sure didn't stay. Do you have any idea how humiliating it was to wake up the next morning stranded in the hotel room without so much as a clue of where you took off? The longer I sat there waiting for you to return, the more humiliated and heartbroken I became. Until finally it dawned on me that you were never coming back for me."

"I was coming back, Anna. I promise."

"Well excuse me for not believing you. Actions speak louder than words, Keaton. There is nothing you can say to take away the way I felt when I woke up and you weren't there. I don't want to speak to you. I don't want you to speak to me. We are going to fly home and go our separate ways. Do you understand?"

He looks at me with sad eyes, his mouth opening like he's prepared for rebuttal, but eventually he nods and leans back against his seat and I do the same. The flight attendants go through their safety procedures and we head to the runway. Noticing the man beside me is white knuckling his armrests as we go to take off, against my better judgment, I reach out to hold his hand through it, providing him with a comfort he doesn't deserve.

His body instantly relaxes at my touch and my heart pulls in his direction. It's really hard to hate this man, but the pain I felt the morning after we said those vows is coursing through my veins and powering my fury. It takes everything in me to fight the desire to keep my hand on his even when we're in the air and above the clouds. But the memories of me sitting in that incredible hotel suite alone remind me why I have to do it. I remove my hand and place it on my lap, then turn to look back out the window.

Letting go of his hand allowed me to release so many things that were keeping a firm grip on my heart. I let go of the desire that filled me with his touch. I let go of the sweet memories we created with one another. I let go of the hope and dreams of a future with this man. I let go of my husband.

Chapter Fourteen
Keaton

The mild panic attack I'm currently breathing through has nothing to do with my fear of flying and everything to do with the fact I've lost the woman who means so much to me. I sure as hell didn't expect to come across a beautiful woman on an airplane that I would eventually want so badly I decided to dedicate my life to her, but it happened all the same.

And then I went and fucking blew it.

I knew it was naive, but a part of me thought maybe she would simply listen to what happened and realize that I didn't mean to leave her the way I did. That it was just all a big misunderstanding. But the other part knew if I hadn't heard from her yet, there was a good chance she was livid with how I left things.

But I wasn't prepared for the devastating blow when her first reaction to seeing me was trying to get the hell away. Seeing rage instead of lust or care in her eyes when she saw me in the seat beside hers sent an eerie chill through my body. I never wanted Anna to look at me in that way. And I would do anything to make sure she never looked at me like that again. Though, if she had it her way right now, she would never look at me period.

When my brothers discovered Anna Laura Keith would be on this flight coming home from Vegas, we managed to do some light hacking and make it where I would be seated beside her. There was only one seat remaining on this flight, but there was no way I was letting a man named Phil from Arkansas sit next to my wife, so he just luckily managed to score an upgrade. I'm sure he is much happier now sitting up in first class.

Now if only Anna was happy to be sitting next to me.

As the plane begins to ascend, I grip the armrests. I hate flying with a passion, but I'd fly hundreds of times if it meant she would give me another chance. I suck in deep breaths through my nose and release them out my mouth, trying to practice the exercises I've learned through the years. They don't really help. Nothing helps. But then the softest hand caresses my skin and rests on top of my own. I look beside me, hoping to stare into Anna's gorgeous greens, but she's staring out the window. She may refuse to look at me right now, or to even speak to me, but I smile all the same. The simple touch by my kind wife has given me something even more than comfort. It's given me hope.

The flight home is painfully silent and as much as I want to say something to her, it's not fair for me to try and force her into a conversation when she has no opportunity to leave. So I sit there, stealing glances at my beautiful woman who exchanged vows with me only two nights ago, whenever I know she isn't looking. The only contact we have is when she reaches over once more while we descend. How I managed to find an angel on my way to the city of sin, I have no idea, but I remember to thank God that I did.

As everyone files off the plane, I notice how she manages to push herself forward so there's distance between us. Once we're back in the airport, she moves in a hurry. I have no doubt she's trying to rush out of my life, but I can't let her go just yet.

"Anna, wait, please." We're in the terminal as I call to her and I'm thankful since it's a small airport and late at night, there's not many people around to witness me groveling and begging my wife to stay.

I don't expect it, but Anna offers me the tiniest bit of grace. She stops. She keeps her back to me, but that's okay. As long as she can hear my words, maybe I still have a chance. "Baby," I watch her back tighten and quickly correct myself.

"Anna. I know you're upset with me, and I know that you have every right to be. What I did was wrong and it was not the way I wanted to leave things between us. If I'm being honest, I didn't want to leave you at all, and I still don't." Her shoulders begin to soften, and I want nothing more than to cradle her into my body, but I respect her too damn much to invade her space like that and go against her wishes.

"I know you probably want nothing to do with me right now. And I know that right now could be for a really long time. But I want you to know I'll wait for you. I will wait as long as it takes for you to forgive me. Do you know why?"

She doesn't react.

"I will wait, because you are my wife. Because you are worth it. Because I want nothing more than to know what it's like to wake up next to you every day for the rest of my life. To know what it's like to kiss your lips good morning, goodbye, and goodnight. I will wait because you're it for me, Anna. So, when you decide to stop making me wait, give me a call. I'll answer so damn fast and meet you wherever you are."

I want to see her walls crumble down. I want to see her turn to me, with the desire I know she once felt. But I don't get that. Instead, Anna lets out a huff, fisting her hands onto those wide hips of hers I want so badly to grasp.

"Give you a call? A call, Keaton? And how the hell do you think I can manage that? I searched everywhere for a note or something from you, so of course, like a lovesick puppy, I checked my phone. There's not a Keaton listed anywhere in it."

Her angry eyes pool with tears. My heart twists in that moment, mimicking the pain I know she had to feel thinking I had lost all desire for her the morning I left. Anna hating me isn't at all what I want, but I understand now just how much I deserve it.

"It's under your name for me, Baby. It's under Husband."

I watch Anna's jaw drop ever so slightly as she processes my words. I can't determine if the red in her cheeks is there from the anger over me calling her the pet name I love to say so often, or a flush of heat at remembering how incredible we are together and the promise we made in a little chapel that one night. I want to cup that smooth crimson skin of hers and pull it to me so I can kiss the pain and shock away. But I don't. As much as it hurts to see Anna standing there in front of me, just an arm's reach away, I know what I have to do for a second time. I leave my wife.

"So, how was the flight?" Camden asks. We're sitting at our favorite booth in Kalli's Corral, our one and only local bar here in Cheatham. A tumbler with two fingers of bourbon sits on the table in front of me and with the shape I'm in, I know I'll be drinking down a few more.

"She wouldn't even look at me," I confess. When I got home after the best and worst long weekend of my life, I allowed myself to wallow in the grief over losing Anna. I'm constantly looking at my phone, hoping she calls or texts. Anything to offer me some sort of hope that she hasn't completely let me go.

"It's for the best, brother," Lincoln tips his beer in my direction like we're celebrating my broken heart. I know his ex, Nicole, left him, their baby, and this town behind, but the way he's been looking for someone to replace her ever since has me surprised at his defeatist attitude. I shake my head at him and try to focus on something other than the woman I fell so quickly for and lost even faster.

"Tell me about work. Have they posted for my assistant position yet?"

"Yeah, it got posted before you left for Vegas, pretty sure," Camden confirms. "You gonna handle your own hiring?"

"Nah, I'll let Janine take care of it," I say, referring to the head of our HR department. She's kind of scary, but she's damn good at her job and that makes everyone else we employ damn good at theirs, too.

"Think Janine would hire a nanny for me?" Lincoln asks, catching us off guard. He's incredibly protective of both Mama and his daughter Charlie, so the fact he's considering someone coming in is a huge deal.

"Is Mama okay?" I ask and he shakes his head with a grim look on his face.

"The other day she was watching Charlie when I went out on a date. When I came home, Mama was sitting on the couch with a dazed look and Charlie was still awake even though it was past ten. When I tucked her into bed, she confessed she had to make herself one of those microwavable mac and cheese cups. Apparently, Mama had been like that most of the night."

He lets out a defeated sigh. "I don't know guys, some days I feel like she's doing better, and then it's like she takes ten steps backwards the next. Think we should schedule her to see somebody?"

"Yeah, because that went over so well last time," I remind him. When Mama became fully reclusive about ten years ago, we had no idea what to do. I asked a buddy of mine who's a doctor if he had any suggestions and he recommended therapy. We made an appointment, but when we told her about it, she flipped like we've never seen before. She started tearing the house apart, throwing picture frames off the wall, breaking the dishes in the kitchen and then she went to the pantry, grabbed a bag of marshmallows off the shelf, and started pelting the three of us with them. We were both terrified and genuinely impressed with her aim.

"We've got to do something. She's getting worse and it's becoming dangerous for Charlie." Lincoln looks as defeated as I feel right now. He has a lot on his shoulders with raising his daughter and taking care of the woman who raised us.

"Talk to Janine," I encourage. "I bet she can find someone who would be a great fit for all three of you. Maybe having someone else around will help Mama, too."

Camden nods, then adds, "I can draw up a contract and send some expectations to Janine. It'd be awesome if we could find someone who has a degree in psychology or something. They may be a little more empathetic about the situation."

Lincoln sighs. "Yeah, I like that idea. If you can get that started for me, I'd appreciate it."

Mentally checking items off the list I keep in my head, I mark off hiring an assistant. Now if I can just check off the item that reads "get over my wife."

Chapter Fifteen

Anna

"I can't believe you're really leaving us," Kristy says to me as I take a bite of my salad. It's been almost a month since I put in my application to Phisherman's Cybersecurity and I will be officially starting my new position there on Monday as executive assistant to the CEO. "We're going to miss you so much."

I smile at her but internally roll my eyes. Kristy is nice enough to me at work, and we enjoy lunch together on occasion, but we aren't exactly friends. She has never once reached out to me about doing anything outside work and the few times I've asked her to hang out, she's always had something better to do than hang out with me.

"I'm really excited about it," I tell her honestly. "The woman who interviewed me said nothing but incredible things about the owners and I've already seen a sight of that. When I explained that I couldn't accept the job until I had housing lined up, she let me know about the guest house the CEO has and offered it for me to stay in for no charge until I can find my own place."

"Are you shitting me? That's awesome! Of course, any boss would be better than Mr. Brenner. He's always been a jerk, but he's been on a real tirade the last couple of weeks," Kristy says while chewing on her sandwich.

She isn't wrong. Once I put in my two weeks' notice, Daniel has been a complete asshole to everyone at work. His messages to me have become more frequent and while they're typically just vile and downright gross, they've become slightly threatening.

Kristy lifts her water bottle up and says, "To new beginnings." I tap my bottle to hers. I can definitely drink to that.

Packing up the last of my things from my desk, I feel his presence before he speaks.

"Anna, I need to see you in my office," Daniel's raspy voice has a bit of a bite to it today.

I look up at him, his dark brown eyes as muddy as the river my dad likes to take his boat on. His hair is greased back, and I know for a fact it's filled with hair dye to try and hide the fact he'll be sixty at the end of the year. It's not fooling anybody.

Following him to his office, he allows me to enter and then shuts the door behind him. Immediately my shoulders tense and my mouth goes dry. Daniel has shut the door with me in his office before and I've never left afterward with a feeling other than pure repulsion.

"Why are you doing this to me, Anna?" he asks, coming over to stand behind me. I scrunch my nose up in confusion because I'm not doing a damn thing to this man. His hand grabs my hip, and I flinch at his touch, only causing him to squeeze tighter. "Why are you leaving me when you know I've been so good to you?"

I want to yell about how he definitely has not been good to me. When looking for other opportunities I found that my pay is abysmal in comparison. He often keeps me past my workday and I never receive compensation for it. Oh, and then there's the fact that he has been sexually harassing me for a year. I want to say all that but instead calm myself before I find my voice. "While I've appreciated the opportunity to work here, Mr. Brenner, I need to explore my options." I'm hoping that if I keep things professional, he will too, but I should have known better.

"Your options?" He huffs out a laugh and his grip tightens to the point of pain. "Sweet, stupid Anna. What other fucking options do you think you have?"

His hand slides from my hip and he cups my ass over the gray pencil skirt I chose to wear today. I try to pull away, but his other hand is on my stomach, and he grips that pesky roll of fat that won't seem to leave there no matter what I try. "You think any other man wants this? You think any other boss is going to be sweet to you like I am when you look like this? You're lucky I like a girl with meat on her bones, sweet girl." His hand manages to find its way underneath my blouse and again I try to pull away, but he clamps down on my breast so hard there's no doubt I'll have a bruise tomorrow. "Though these fucking tits could easily bring any man to his knees."

There have been a few instances where Daniel has pressed himself into me, or touched me, but never like this. Sure, those were inappropriate, but this is something else entirely and I have to fight it.

"Daniel, stop," I demand as he pulls the cup of my bra down to fully expose me to him. "Daniel this is too far, let go of me. Now."

"You think you can fucking leave me, Anna?" He doesn't yell, but his menacing tone has me cowering all the same. "You're mine," he claims, pinching my nipple so hard tears spring to my eyes.

"Stop! Now! Let me go and I'll walk away. I won't tell anyone what happened, I promise."

He laughs, channeling every evil villain in movie history. "You think anyone is going to believe you? Poor, pitiful, Anna. I will ruin you. I'll make sure that the only one that will get sympathy is the boss who eventually had to let you go after your advances became too strong and you wouldn't take no for an answer. My, my, Anna. Your father is going to be so disappointed in you."

Daniel hits where he knows it hurts. My whole life I've tried proving myself to my dad, and every time I disappoint him is like an ice pick to my heart. Unfortunately, it's been pretty often in my life. If it's Daniel's word versus mine, I have no doubt my father will side with his best friend.

"Please let me go. I don't want this, please."

"Stop lying to yourself, sweet girl. I bet your pussy is drenched thinking about all the things I could do to it. Let me check."

I buck against him, trying like hell to push him off me, but his hand on my ass pulls up my skirt, and his fingers manage to skim underneath my panties. I'm screaming and shouting for someone, anyone to help, but it's too late. He dips his finger inside me, completely violating a piece of me I would never willingly give to him. Tears fall down my cheeks, shuttering my cries for help, as he continues pressing into my back and probing me.

A knock at the door stalls his actions, and I have never been so grateful to hear Kristy's sweet voice behind that door. "Anna? Mr. Brenner? Is everything okay? I thought I heard screaming."

Daniel leans into my ear, tugging my hair so that my scalp screams in pain. "You don't say a fucking word." He pulls his fingers out of me and makes an obscene spectacle of tasting them, then pulls my skirt back down over my ass. I adjust my shirt as he walks away from me but continue facing his desk, so my back is to the door that he cracks open.

"Hi, Kristy. Thanks for checking, but we're all good. Miss Keith just tripped over the chair and was shouting for help, but thankfully for her I was there, and she fell right into my arms. We're all good here."

I can't see Kristy's reaction and I'm too scared to turn around. She must be satisfied with his answer because I hear footsteps retreating. My body shivers as I stand there knowing my saving grace has walked away.

"That will be all Miss Keith. I hope your new place of employment brings you as much satisfaction as I know this one has." I slowly walk past him, but he grabs my wrist and yanks me to his chest before I cross the threshold. "And sweet girl, I will never let you go."

Something about Daniel's words sound ominous, but I keep my mouth shut and shoulders back as I walk out of his office and pick up the box with my things from my desk. I hold my head high as I walk to the elevator bank and then get the hell out of Brenner & Associates.

Chapter Sixteen

Keaton

It's the end of another long week without hearing from Anna. My new assistant is set to move in this weekend, so I've bribed my brothers with beer and pizza to come help me finish up the guest house so that it's to Janine's standards. Apparently plain drywall is unacceptable, and gray is "very in," whatever that means. This new assistant better be fucking worth it.

"Why are we doing this?" Lincoln asks for about the fiftieth time this hour.

"I've told you that the new girl needed housing and Janine was so gracious to offer my place." I roll another layer of paint on top of the already gray walls.

"Yeah, but I mean why are *we* doing this? You couldn't hire someone to paint the place and fix things up?" He complains again.

"*We* are doing this because we aren't pretentious pricks who aren't capable of doing the damn job themselves. Why? Did you have another hot date planned that won't go anywhere because nobody is good enough for you and your baby girl?"

"Fuck you. You know, everyone thinks I'm the grumpy asshole, but this past month you've really stepped up like you're vying for first place," Lincoln grumbles.

I know it was a dirty dig at my brother. He has been looking for love for both him and Charlie after Nicole left them just days after Charlie was born. Either he is incredibly picky, or the dating pool is slim pickings because he's gone on dozens of first dates this past year, but I don't know if any have resulted in a second one. I get back to painting as Camden comes whistling into the room, his glasses sitting slightly askew on his face.

"The bed is put together. Whatcha need me to do now?" He asks, sitting on the new white sofa with a smile, his glasses slightly askew. He's always a ray of fucking sunshine and today I hate it. In fact, I've hated just about everything since my trip to Vegas.

"We're adding the last layer of paint and then we're done. I don't know why Janine thinks we needed to do all this. The guest house was fine before." I look over to find my brothers staring at me, eyebrows furrowed. "What?"

"It had walls, lawn chairs and a poker table. That's pretty much it. How did you expect someone to live here without any furniture?" Camden states.

"Anyone that has to be your assistant deserves this and a whole lot more." I've had enough of Lincoln's smart mouth.

"Then how about the both of you get the fuck out of here and I'll finish it my damn self. I don't need the two of you bitching at me all night."

"Fine with me," Lincoln puts down the paint roller and turns to leave, but Camden stops him.

"We're here to support you, brother. When does your new roommate move in?"

I roll on the last bit of paint before putting the roller down and taking a seat beside him. "Tomorrow night. Janine said she will move in and then start first thing on Monday. I told her she could have a couple of days to adjust if she needed it, but Janine said she insisted on starting right away."

"That sounds promising," Camden says while pulling a beer from the freshly stocked refrigerator. "She sounds like a go-getter, and with your schedule, you're gonna need that."

"You think she'll make it longer than a week?" Lincoln's smirk has me clenching my fists and fighting back, punching him in his pretty face.

"What the fuck is that supposed to mean?" I growl.

Camden interrupts before Lincoln can smart off again, "It's just that you've been a bit prickly these past few weeks. All the temps that Janine has found to fill in before your new assistant got here haven't made it very long."

I think back to the temporary assistants Janine has hired. Usually, the woman is spectacular at her job, but these past hires have been complete let downs. The first girl to replace my last assistant was supposed to be back from lunch at one, but she was ten minutes late, claiming traffic held her up. I don't care how bad the traffic is, punctuality is important and if she couldn't be on time her first fucking day on the job, then this wasn't the job for her. The next one was some guy who couldn't tie his necktie correctly. If he can't figure that out, how am I supposed to trust him to keep my schedule updated among the millions of other things my executive assistant has to do daily.

"They all deserved it. None of them were good enough."

"What about Linda?" Lincoln asks.

"Who?" The name doesn't ring a bell.

"Your last assistant. She didn't even make it to lunch before you had her crying and packing up her things. Heard it was because you told her, and I quote, 'You smell so bad I can't even be near you without wanting to gag.' Does that sound familiar?"

"She wore those fucking essential oils. You know I can't stand those. How am I supposed to work with someone all day, every day if I can't even get past the way they smell?"

I stare at my brothers and shake my head. "Fine, maybe I've been a bit of an ass. I just miss Anna so damn much."

"You knew her less than twenty-four hours," Lincoln deadpans.

A rumble from my chest moves up, spilling out of my lips in the direction of my brother. I feel my fists tightening again. It doesn't matter if I had known Anna less than twenty-four minutes, there was no doubt she's the woman I was meant to be with. Admittedly it sounds crazy, especially for a guy who has not been in a real relationship in over two decades. It doesn't negate the fact that Anna is it for me and I would do anything to get her back.

"How about that pizza you promised us?" Camden suggests before Lincoln and I break out into a brawl.

"Fine, but then we're going to Kalli's after. I need a beer."

"Yeah," Lincoln agrees, "because drinking led you to some pretty great choices a month ago."

I didn't plan on landing the blow that had my brother losing his breath and doubling over, but for the first time in a month, I felt a smile tug at the corners of my mouth as I headed out to my truck.

Chapter Seventeen
Anna

After today's events at the office, I'm kicking myself for asking my parents to have family dinner. It's my last night before I move to the small town of Cheatham, population of 1300 and while it doesn't have a supermarket, they do proudly boast two dollar stores.

I've never lived more than twenty minutes away from my parents, so I had asked them if we could get together, but I never expected to be assaulted only hours ago. The way Daniel touched me has me wanting to hide from the world, but I know I'll regret not spending time with the people who have given me so much in this life.

My mom pulls my favorite chicken casserole out of the oven as I finish up the salad when we hear the front door open. "Hey, Craig! Thanks for inviting me." I dropped the tongs to the counter at the sound of Daniel's voice.

"Everything okay, honey?" My mother asks.

"Dad invited Daniel?" She cocks her head at me and gives me a confused look. This isn't the first time he's been at family dinners, being as how he and my dad have been practically inseparable since college. "I just figured with it being my last night here, we would be having dinner as a family."

"Don't be rude, Anna Laura," my father chastises from behind me. "Daniel is family."

I turn to see the two men standing beside each other and Daniel puts a hand to my dad's shoulder. "Oh, she isn't being rude," he says with a grin, "she probably just thought we said our goodbyes at the office today. Told you I wouldn't just let you go, sweet girl." He winks at me, and it takes everything in me not to toss my cookies into the tossed salad ready to be served for dinner.

"Is supper ready?" He changes the subject. "It smells great in here, as usual, Kara."

My mom smiles at my attacker, ever the gracious host. "Sure is, why don't you two men go ahead and have a seat at the table. Anna and I will bring everything in."

I help my mother take everything into the dining room, where my dad is seated at his usual place at the head of the table. When Daniel is over for dinner, he usually takes the chair opposite him at the other end, but I notice that tonight he has chosen to sit in the chair directly beside my typical spot.

I drop the salad bowl to the table and go to sit in the space beside my mother, but Daniel speaks up. "I'm afraid I spilled my drink in that chair, Anna. But you're welcome to sit in your typical spot. So sorry for the spill, Kara."

"No need to be sorry," my dad says on my mom's behalf. "Anna Laura, why are you being weird? Go sit where you always do."

Reluctantly I walk around the table to my typical chair and sit down beside my former employer. Dad dishes out his serving of casserole then passes the dish to me. As I scoop a spoonful, he stops me. "Anna Laura, give it to Daniel first. You're likely to eat the whole damn thing. It would be rude to invite a man over for dinner and then not have anything left for him to eat." My dad and his best friend chuckle and my cheeks flame.

"Craig," my mom says, cutting her eyes at my dad, ceasing his laughter.

"Just a joke. Everyone's so damn sensitive," he grumbles and then digs into his dinner.

It's September in the Bluegrass, so there's talk about the first few football games and the fact that this could be the year the Wildcats bring home another national championship in basketball. When Daniel and my dad are together the talk is always sports, but something else must be weighing on my dad's mind.

"I just don't understand it, Anna Laura. Why would you leave such a good job? Daniel was kind enough to give you that position and now you're just leaving him high and dry."

The *kind* man my father is talking about slides his hand over to my thigh and squeezes. The tablecloth covers the actions so my dad is none the wiser about how unkind his friend can truly be.

"Oh, Craig. She's young and wants to spread her wings. Can't say I blame her," he speaks for me, rubbing his thumb back and forth across my soft skin.

My dad scoffs. "She's thirty. That's not young enough to be making dumb decisions with your life. Anna Laura, it's past time you grow up and start really living. Daniel is a good man who gave you a good job. You could have saved up and made quite the nice nest egg staying with his company. In fact, Daniel, would you mind teaching Anna Laura some of the ins and outs of accounting? She could go back to school and get her degree, then work for you in another capacity. I bet a few long nights and some hard work is all it would take for her to figure out what she would need to do to succeed."

"I would love nothing more than to keep Anna around at the office. If she's interested, I'd be willing to have as many long nights as necessary. Accounting can be long, hard work, but I have no doubt she would be amazing at it." As he talks, Daniel dips his hand into the gap between my thighs, causing a light gasp to escape me at his movement.

My mom's eyes flash over at mine with what I think is a knowing look, but then she quickly averts her gaze and goes back to her meal.

"Well then, it's settled. Now thank Daniel and we can put all this leaving business behind us." I look over at the man my father wants me to thank and see the biggest shit eating grin spreading across his face.

"Dad, there are a few problems with that scenario," I calmly explain and Daniel squeezes my thigh again, this time even tighter and with his nails digging into me to the point I think he may have drawn blood. "First of all, I've already accepted the position at the cybersecurity firm and they're expecting me to move in tomorrow and start on Monday."

My dad waves his hand in the air before taking another bite. "You're not set to sign that contract until Monday and people change jobs all the time. That's an easy fix."

"Well, there is the issue that I have no interest in being an accountant."

"Young lady, you don't seem to have an interest in being much of anything. Now accounting is a good job and will provide you with a good, steady income. You see how successful Daniel is and that could be you some day."

"Money isn't everything, Dad," I mumble.

He huffs, "You only think that because you grew up accustomed to a certain lifestyle. When you're struggling to get a mortgage, you'll see that money is a lot more important than you think."

"Well maybe the man she marries will take care of her," my mother steps in trying to resolve things, but just making me want to groan. She means well, but she also grew up with the belief that you married for provisions and not so much love.

My dad shakes his head. "I wouldn't count on that. Men with money don't marry women that look like her."

I should be fucking pissed, and a part of me is, but I can't help but think of the gorgeous husband of mine I haven't spoken to in over a month. The husband who is obviously financially loaded if he can book a suite at an upscale hotel in Las Vegas. Unable to hold it back, I let out a snort.

"Men aren't exactly attracted to that either," Daniel adds to the conversation.

I keep quiet for the remainder of dinner and Daniel keeps his hand on my thigh, every now and then bringing it up higher as a silent reminder to how he touched me earlier in the day. My favorite meal has been tainted with tonight's conversation, and I've never been so glad to see the last bite of it eaten and dinner officially over.

After dinner my dad and Daniel escaped to the living room to watch some documentary about the infamous Kentucky and Duke game from the nineties. They watch it just about every time they get together and every time, they get mad at the result as if it's the first time they've ever seen it.

My mom and I are in the kitchen washing dishes and cleaning up. "I really am excited for you, honey," my mom says to me as I take the dish from her to dry. "I know your dad and Daniel are close, but I also know it's important to harness your independence and see what you can do without relying on your parents. I'm proud of you."

I smile at her. "Thanks Mom, I really appreciate that. And I am really going to miss you so much." I look over to see my mom wringing her hands, a sour expression on her face. "What's wrong?"

"Has Daniel done something, honey?" Her tone is hushed, and she glances into the living room as the man in question sits with his best friend.

"What do you mean?"

"It's just that you looked so uncomfortable at dinner. I saw you tense up multiple times and I noticed he was eating with his left hand. Daniel's right-handed, Anna."

I stay quiet, drying the dinner plate in my hand with more focus than if I were facing off in an Olympic sport.

"Anna, was his hand on you during dinner?" I nod.

"Did you want it there?" I shake my head.

"Honey, please tell me what's going on."

I desperately want to tell her the truth. I want to confide in her about the messages and videos he's sent me over the past year. I want to have no doubts that she will stand up for me when I tell her how he touched me against my will this afternoon in his office. I want to tell her everything, but I don't, because the man she's asking about walks into the kitchen with us.

"Every time I watch it hoping somehow the ending will change. And every time we fucking lose." My mom lets out a nervous giggle, and Daniel takes another step in my direction. "I guess I'm headed home for the night. Thanks for dinner, Kara. Anna, you probably need to head home yourself. Let me walk you out."

"Oh, no, that's okay. I think I'm going to stick around here just a bit longer."

"The hell you are," my dad says coming into the kitchen. "I'm ready for bed and after making the dinner you requested, I'm sure your mother is tired, too. Stop making things difficult for everyone and let Daniel walk you out."

"Now Craig, we don't know how long it will be before we can see our only child again. She's going to be busy with her new job and all, so I think it's okay for her to stay a little longer." My mom gives me a weak smile, as she tries to save me from being alone with the man she now knows has been taunting me.

"That's her decision, Kara. Now I'm tired and it's time we all call it a night."

Tired of fighting with him and not wanting to make things worse for my mom, I give in to my dad and say my goodbyes. Daniel places his hand at the small of my back as he guides me through the house and out the front door. Once we're in the driveway, he grabs my wrist and spins me so that I fall into his chest. A hand wraps around my neck, and he tugs me to him, placing his lips over mine, refusing to stop even as I try like hell to pull away.

"You really are so fucking difficult," Daniel says, moving his hand from my neck to the back of my head and forcing me against his lips again. This time his tongue tries to find entrance and when it pushes past my lips, I bite down until I taste his blood in my mouth.

Daniel pulls back, but an evil chuckle rises out of him. "Oh, sweet girl, if you like it rough, you just had to say so." I manage to pull away from his hold and rush over to my car, slamming the door and locking it so he can't get to me. Daniel just stands outside my door and laughs. "Oh, Anna," his muffled voice comes through my window, "always playing hard to get. I left you a little care package so you can remember me." He jerks his head in the direction of my passenger seat where a neatly wrapped gift has been placed. "I'll see you soon, sweet girl."

My breath comes out in pants as I sit in my car and watch Daniel climb into his Jeep, then drive away. Once he's out of sight, I finally allow my body to relax, and I head for home. On the drive to my apartment, I can't help but think back to the man who kissed me so differently mere weeks ago. I may still be mad at him, but I can admit that I miss Keaton, and the comfort his arms gave me is exactly what I could use right now.

I park in the apartment garage for the last time and get ready to head inside, but my eye catches on the box in my passenger seat. I swear if there's a fucking head in there I'm going to be so pissed.

I hate to compliment anything about Daniel, but the box really is beautiful, trimmed in black with a gold bow around it. I lift off the lid to find a thick, veiny dildo inside, along with a note and a picture of me with Daniel Brenner from last year's holiday party. I open the note and read the scratched writing I recognize as belonging to my former boss.

I will never let you go.

Anna

I just made it here! Love you both!

My phone rings through my car's speakers and I roll my eyes knowing exactly who is on the other line.

"Anna, it's your mother."

"I know, Mom."

"We just got your message. I'm on speaker with your father here beside me." It should be annoying, but I can't help but smile at her full report.

"I just wanted to let you know I made it. I'm about to go into my new place."

I look out at the guesthouse at the end of the stone path. The white siding pops against the black roof and shutters and it looks so sparkly clean. The place is so cute, and more than enough space for me, but compared to the mansion beside it, it may as well be a shack.

"We love you so much, honey. Have a great first day of work and know that we are so proud of you. Tell her, Craig. Tell her how proud you are of her."

I don't expect my dad to say the words my mom is trying to force out of him, but I wait for him to come on the line anyway.

"Anna, it's really brave of you to pack up your life and start somewhere new. I think a fresh start is good for you."

"Thanks, Dad." He may not have said he was proud, but his words mean a lot just the same.

I hang up with my parents and look back at the guest house where my new life will begin.

Here's to fresh starts.

Chapter Eighteen
Keaton

I 've been on this call with Caruso Enterprises for over two hours and I'm ready to fire my newest client. The excitement of acquiring the huge resort and casino fades with every one of their lengthy follow-ups with some concern or another. "I understand," I say for the umpteenth time. "We will take a look into that right away and I will personally see that your concerns are addressed."

I hang up just in time for my brothers to saunter into my office because obviously I can't catch a break today. They both have huge smiles on their faces, and I wonder if I could stand them side-by-side and slap it off them at the same time.

"Have you met your new assistant yet?" Camden asks.

"Haven't had the time. I've been stuck on the call with Vegas for the past two hours. Next time I'm letting one of you fuckers deal with them." This weekend I did catch a glimpse of a blonde moving things into the guest house. I was probably a dick for not offering my help, but I didn't have it in me to care.

Honestly, I couldn't give two shits about the new woman moving in. There's only one woman I want living on my property and in my home.

"We just had the pleasure. Spoke with her for a little bit and I think you're *really* gonna like her," Cam continues.

Lincoln tags on, "She's your type, you know. Blonde. Beautiful. Curves for days. You may actually decide to keep this one around awhile."

Camden nods vehemently. "And if Janine hired her, she's gotta be smart. Though, I'm sure she's made *some* bad decisions in her life."

"Would you both shut the fuck up?" My voice is raised, which isn't something I do at work except in circumstances when I'm talking to the two dickheads standing in front of me. "I don't care what my goddamn assistant looks like. She could be fucking Miss America for all I care. I don't care if she's good at her job. I don't care if she's fucking married to the Pope. I just care..."

"Mr. Fisher." I'm cut off by the sound of my name followed by the clearing of a throat. Janine, the head of our HR department, is in my office with her signature retired school principal look. "I'm here to introduce you to your new assistant."

Taking a deep breath and cursing myself for letting these motherfuckers get to me, I look at the woman standing beside one of my most trusted employees. Her golden hair has the slightest curl through it so that it looks like waves drawn in the sand. Plump lips painted in a beautiful shade are slightly parted. My gaze travels down to her ample breasts that show just a tease of cleavage in her cream blouse that's tucked into a navy pair of pants that have a cute tie at her waist. A waist I remember holding in my grip all too well.

"This is Anna Keith," Janine introduces me to the woman I've been obsessing over for the past month.

I look Anna in her wide eyes as she takes me in. "Nice to meet you Mr. Fisher. I'm excited to be here, but I should inform you my husband isn't the Pope. He's actually a real asshole." Then she abruptly turns and storms out of my office, away from me.

My brothers are still in my office, Lincoln snickering and Camden masking his laughter behind his hand. "You knew?" I growl at the pair of idiots. "You knew my wife was hired as my fucking assistant? You knew that the woman I have been obsessing over was steps away from me, just on the other side of that door and neither one of you fucking told me?"

Camden holds his hands out like he's Chris Pratt and I'm a raptor. "Calm down, Keaton. We had no idea Anna was your assistant until this morning. We would have told you if we had known."

"Would we have?" Lincoln's smug smirk has an intense rage building up inside me. I take a step toward him, but then he throws his hands up, not wanting to deal with my fury this morning. "Well, are you gonna go get your girl?"

"Yes, Mr. Fisher, I think it would be best if you go see if you still have a freshly hired assistant who stood out among all the other applicants and would benefit both you and the company. Then maybe the other Mr. Fishers won't mind filling me in on what exactly is going on here."

Shit. I forgot Janine was still standing there and she not only saw me almost punch my chief financial officer but now she knows about my marriage to Anna. Not that I want to keep it a secret. If Anna would let me, I'd send an email out informing my entire staff about our wedding and even include the pictures the chapel emailed me thanks to the package we purchased. But I can't do that if I don't have a wife, and that's going to be the case if I keep fucking things up with her.

I leave my brothers, who have been smirking at one another like a couple of schoolboys who just pulled a prank on their teacher, to Janine. My human resources manager has her arms crossed, her hip popped, and a look that tells me she's about to knock them down a peg or two.

Couldn't happen to two better people. Those two dumbasses deserve to be incurring her wrath today. I have more important things to deal with. Like making sure my wife doesn't leave me. Again.

A few of my employees pointed out the direction they saw a small, blonde woman huff in and now I've been standing outside this bathroom door for about ten minutes. Usually, I'd be running through my neverending to-do list in my head, but the only thing I can think about right now is making sure Anna is okay. When I hear the click of the bathroom door, I straighten and smooth down my shirt. Do I smile? Where should I put my hands? Why is this awkward?

Anna steps out with her head down, bumping right into me. My arms raise to grip her shoulders and when she looks up at me, her eyes are rimmed in red and puffy. Even still she's the most beautiful woman I've ever seen. "Anna, Baby, I'm so sorry." She brushes my hands off, then taking a deep breath, she straightens up to her full height, fixing her eyes directly in front of her at my chest. "Mr. Fisher," she begins.

"It's Keaton, please. Please, Anna, call me Keaton." I'm begging to hear my name from her lips again. Her eyes flick up to mine briefly before she centers them so that she's staring at my chest. Her chin lifts and even though I know she's probably about to say something I don't want to hear, I'm so damn proud of her for being so strong in this situation. This shitty situation I've put her in.

"Mr. Fisher," she starts again, "I want to thank you so much for the opportunity to come and work for your company." A sniffle escapes her but she's able to compose herself quickly. "But I think it would be best if I go ahead and decline the position. This position just turned out to be something I wasn't expecting." Her voice turned squeaky towards the end as she tries to hide her pain from losing this job that I know she was excited to begin.

My head and heart both feel like they're splitting in two while yelling at me to pull my head out of my ass and figure something out fast that will keep this woman in our life.

"Anna, Baby, you can't quit. You were excited about this opportunity, and I won't let you leave on account of me. You just moved here."

"Stop calling me Baby," she grits out between her perfectly white teeth. "And yes, I did just move here. Into *your* guest house. I will have to see you every day at work and then when I can finally go home, there's still no break from it because you'll still be there."

Her voice comes out in sobs and those big, beautiful eyes stare up at me, shiny with the tears she's holding back.

"I can't do this," she whispers.

I need this woman to know that she can do anything she puts her mind to and that I will be the man standing beside her cheering her on. "You absolutely can do this. I have no doubt that you are capable of doing anything. This was my fuck up, Anna. What do I need to do to get you to stay?"

"Sell your company," she snorts. I know she doesn't mean it, but it doesn't stop me from taking a second to think. Am I seriously considering selling everything I created in order for this woman to take a chance on me? That's fucking terrifying and I guess my face doesn't do a good job of hiding the fear because the next thing she says is, "Oh my gosh, Keaton, I'm not serious. Calm down."

I shake the thought of turning over my company from my head. "Anna, we can make this work. I've been wanting to talk to you every day since we met. I need to explain. I had a meeting..." She throws her hand up and cuts me off.

"I'm not interested in hearing your explanation. You could have had a meeting with the Pope for all I care, there's no reason for you to have just left me there without a single word. I sat in that hotel room like a fool waiting, finally coming to the realization that everything from the night before meant nothing to you. That *I* meant nothing to you." She whispers her next words, "I'm so sick and tired of being the fool."

Her defeated tone has my already broken heart breaking down even more. It kills me that this woman sees herself in that way, and I know it's all my fucking fault.

"You are not a fool, Anna. You are a beautiful, intelligent, and talented woman. You are thoughtful, kind, and funny. If anyone's a fool here, it's me. And I'd be an even bigger one to let you walk away from this job."

To let you walk away from me.

Anna sniffles and appears to be contemplating my words. Her bottom teeth pull her plump lip into their grasp, and it takes everything in me not to pull it free and place a kiss on it. We stand there in silence for several moments before she finally looks up at me. My breath catches as I await her response.

"I need to go." I start to interject, but she shakes her head at me.

"Apparently my new boss has a thing against essential oils and being late and I happen to share those sentiments." A small smirk briefly crosses her face but disappears way too quickly. "I will be at my desk if there's anything you need, Mr. Fisher."

As she turns to the direction of my office, warmth spreads in my chest. Anna's here. And she's staying. Now to just let her know that the only thing I need is her.

"Let me get this straight," the woman whose job it is to make sure our people here are just as secure as our tech looks at me with a raised eyebrow, "you went on a work trip to Vegas. And while there you got excessively drunk and married your new executive assistant?"

"I don't know that I was excessively drunk," I mutter. Janine leans over and taps the ring on my left finger. The ring I haven't taken off since the night Anna put it there. "Fine, that's fair. But she wasn't my assistant at the time. In fact, I didn't even know she had applied. And even if I did, I didn't know her last name when I married her."

"I don't believe that's the flex you think it is," Janine quips. "Mr. Fisher, I am just trying to look out for you. While we don't have a non-fraternization policy in place, you are in a position of power over her. And while I'm not trying to pry, from an outsider's perspective, your relationship doesn't appear to be in good standing."

The words 'position of power' have me picturing myself straddling a very naked Anna while she's tied up to my headboard, and I'm plunging into the tight pussy I haven't been able to stop thinking about for weeks. I shake off the thoughts before things get super inappropriate in front of my personnel manager.

"There will be no issues between Ms. Keith and myself while she's employed here," I assure Janine. "I am sure Anna will find she loves working here at Phisherman's Cybersecurity."

She offers me a soft smile. With her no-nonsense attitude, they are few and far between, but that makes them even more genuine.

"I'm sure she will find many things she loves here, Mr. Fisher." Janine turns and walks out of my office.

I hope like hell she's right.

Chapter Nineteen

Anna

"So now he's my husband, my landlord, and my boss." I'm video chatting Jasmine, Penny, and Skyla while hanging up clothes after the most awkward first day on the job in history.

I spent most of the day at my desk learning the different programs I'd be using and sneaking glances at the most handsome man I've ever laid eyes on through his open door. He had no business looking that damn good in a black button up with his sleeves rolled up showing off the strong arms that wrapped around me so tightly just a month ago. And those dark khakis he had on hugged his ass so well my mouth was watering by the end of the day.

Keaton has made it clear that he wants to make this thing work between us. I don't know how I am going to resist him when he's in my space all day, every day. I wonder if there's a way I can be his assistant and work from home. But then I would miss the way his arms flex when he twirls his pen while thinking. Or the way his brows furrow when he tries to concentrate on whatever it is he's looking at on his computer screen. I'd even miss the petty spats between him and his brothers when they swing by his office.

One day in and he's already got me forgetting that I'm furious with him. If I'm being honest, I'm more sad than mad, but I'd rather him see my anger than my tears. I don't want him to know that I'm an insecure girl who sat in the hotel room wondering if his beer goggles had fallen off and he saw my curves and ran away. My feelings may have been intensified by alcohol, but they were still strong and present. Knowing that he's like the other men from my past would devastate me. So, I pretend I'm pissed, even when it would be so easy to believe he's truly sorry.

"Maybe it's the universe trying to bring the two of you back together," suggested Skyla. "I think it's kind of romantic that your paths crossed again."

Shaking my head at her, I finish hanging the rest of my clothes.

"Maybe it's the universe testing my strength. Y'all, he looked so damn good today and all I could think about was crawling under his desk and showing him how much I've missed him." My knees ache at the sexy office fantasy, while my heart flutters.

"Eww. None of that," Penny says. "That man swept you off your feet, married you, then broke your heart the next morning. We do not condone that behavior." there's one thing that woman knows how to do, it's hold a grudge against a man.

"Exactly. I can draw up the divorce papers and then he just becomes your boss and landlord, making him off limits." Jasmine's been hounding me to have her draft the documents I need to go ahead and divorce Keaton since before I even left Vegas. I know we were drunk when we got married and clearly, we didn't know much about each other when it happened, but a part of me hopes things will still work out between the two of us. I don't dare speak of it while Jasmine and Penny are on the call, but I could see where spending more time with the man I fell for is only going to bring back those initial feelings. This time maybe even stronger.

"And how exactly would that look? 'Here you go boss, you need to sign this contract, lunch will be delivered at noon, and if you could just sign these papers so we can file for divorce, I'd sure appreciate it.'" I shake my head after mimicking the impossible scene to my friends.

"I know you're there when I'm ready, Jaz, but please just let me have some time to adjust first." With my clothes and shoes unpacked, my closet is officially finished, so I walk over to tackle some of the other boxes as we continue our conversation. For someone who didn't think she had a lot to pack, it's like the amount to unpack has doubled.

"That would be awkward," Skyla admits with a heavy breath, "best to just get over it and get under him. Or maybe you like it better on top. Ooo, or do you prefer him behind you? Might as well try all three!"

"Not helpful, Sky." Laughing at my silly friend, I open a new box and freeze as I see the goodbye "gift" Daniel gave me. I didn't know what to do with it since all my stuff had already been loaded and so the next morning, I just shoved it in a box I found in my car. Now it's the same problem all over again. I want to burn it, toss it in the trash and forget everything about that creep, but Keaton would probably freak out if I started a fire my first night at the place, and if I throw it in the garbage, I risk him seeing it.

"Everything okay, Anna?" Penny asks.

I haven't told my friends about anything that went down between Daniel and myself on my last day of work at his office. I have no doubt they would swoop in and try to fix everything. Hell, Jasmine would probably actually kill the guy. Her loyalty can be scary at times, and I'm certain she knows some people who could help her get away with it. I hide the box out of sight from the camera before answering.

"Yeah, everything's great," I lie, "Just a little overwhelmed with everything I still have to unpack. I'm gonna let you guys go so I can finish up here. Love you!"

My friends say their goodbyes and end the call while I frantically search for a place to put this fucking box. Not finding anywhere better, I shove it in the closet and close the doors, hoping it keeps the memories of my former boss away.

After a long shower and a large glass of wine, I settle into my bed and press play on my phone to listen to my new audiobook. One that has no ties to the man who apparently shares my taste in books.

I realize the mistake in my new selection when I get to the part where the assistant and her boss are trying to hide their relationship from everyone in the office.

The fucking universe and its fucking signs.

As I listen to their moaning while he has her bent over his desk, I can't help but imagine Keaton putting me in a similar situation. I'm so confused about how I feel about him right now, but there's no denying he's insanely attractive with his silver streaked dark hair. And his muscular build. And that stupidly adorable dimple. I miss the feeling of his soft lips on mine. The way his big hands cover my body. His thick, swollen cock inside of me.

My hand slowly trails over my breasts and stomach, remembering the way Keaton's hands cherished my body. I begin to rub when they find my swollen bud that's been begging for attention since I saw the man I can't help but think about constantly. The man who is in the house just outside my doors. The man I will be working for. The man I will see every single day.

My fingertips caress up and down, running through the wetness that's gathered there from the thoughts of my husband. Reaching over to pull my favorite toy from the excellent selection in my bedside drawer, I position myself for my self-care session, using my fingers to massage my clit as I plunge the vibrator inside of me. I can't help but compare it to Keaton and realize it doesn't quite measure up to his impressive length and girth. Thoughts of his hands and mouth on me as he brought me to orgasm repeatedly that night invade my mind.

The phallic instrument does its job well as I repeat my motions. *Right there.* Visions of my boss in the office with his rolled-up sleeves flash through my mind. *That feels so good.* Images of my landlord taking me right here in this guesthouse on the kitchen counter have me shuddering. *Yes. God, yes.* And picturing my husband in a bed of our own that we share, our rings clinking together as our hands are joined, has me writhing and moaning. The overwhelming rush that comes over me has me crying out the only thing on my mind.

Keaton!

Chapter Twenty

Keaton

Anna has completely taken over all available space in my life. She looked fucking sexy as hell in the office today chewing on a damn pen cap while learning how to use the systems necessary to do her job. I had to stay hidden at my desk so I wouldn't scare my staff with the impressive hard-on I was sporting the majority of the day.

Now I'm home and she's just a few steps away. There's a stone path that leads from my back kitchen door to the front of the guest house. I pace back and forth in my kitchen hoping the movement is enough to keep me from racing down it to see her.

Seeing her again today lit me up inside in a way I can't describe. It's been decades since I gave a woman a second thought and now, I'm a smitten soul over this woman I married in a drunken stupor. It completely gutted me when she stepped out of the office bathroom, knowing the tears that fell were because of me. I thought I was doing the right thing not waking her before I left, but I can see where it had cut her.

My beautiful wife had some insecurities, and I was determined to eradicate every single one of them. I have no doubt that the cruel way she was spoken to on the plane isn't the only encounter she's had with fatphobic fucks who are so insecure in themselves they have to pick out flaws in everyone around them.

I had watched her on the plane, trying to make herself smaller. She kept her head down and tucked her limbs into her body like she was trying to hide. If she'd let me, I'd make sure she never felt ashamed of her body by worshipping it every second of every day.

Since the pacing is doing nothing for me, I yank open the door and follow the stone path over to the guest house. When I reach the small cottage-style building, I knock. There's no answer, but Anna's car is here and I'm so sure I can hear someone talking inside. I knock again, but still no answer. Debating whether I should let myself in or just give up and head back to the house, I decided to text my brothers.

Keaton

Hey Cam, what side of the law would I be on if I broke into a place I technically own?

Lincoln

Whatever the fuck you're thinking about doing, don't.

Keaton

I didn't fucking ask you.

Camden

I'm not offering legal advice without more context.

Lincoln

> In other words, don't fucking do whatever stupid think you're thinking about doing.

Keaton

> I hate you both.

Deciding that since I own the place it's not really breaking and entering, I move forward with my plan. Besides, Anna won't press charges against me. Probably.

Twisting the doorknob, I creep inside like I'm a damn spy in some movie. The voices are coming from the bedroom, so I walk across the living room to the smaller space. As my hand goes to knock, I hear Anna moan and my whole body goes still.

"Right there, that feels so good. Yes. God, yes." Sound continues to carry through the door. It's so fucking hot hearing her like this, knowing she's worked herself up, hopefully thinking of me.

I've never been so fucking hard.

Unbuckling my belt, I push my pants and boxer briefs past my ass and wrap my hand around my already leaking cock.

We'll work ourselves up together.

We will get off together.

We will think of each other together.

I work myself in tandem to her noises, wishing it was her mouth, her pussy, her ass, anything of hers to replace my own touch. As she reaches her climax, she shouts my name. My fucking name that sounds like it was meant to be spoken from her lips. My body jerks and I look down to see my palm is covered in the sticky substance I so badly want to fill her with.

I know Anna hasn't forgiven me yet. I know I don't fucking deserve her forgiveness. But knowing she's thinking of me gives me hope that what's between us isn't over. That knowledge makes it a little easier to walk away as I head back to my house.

I decided I would head back down to the guest house this morning, bringing with me the gift of coffee and a plan. Just as I make it to the front of her place, Anna steps out, taking my breath away. The warmer day temperatures of the day has her wearing a pink and white striped sundress that accentuates her large chest and hugs her hips. Her shoes are some strappy sandal type things with wedged heels that add a couple extra inches to her height, bringing her mouth even closer to mine. It takes everything in me to stop myself from crashing my lips down onto hers.

"Good morning," I greet her cheerfully, extending the coffee in my hand.

"It was," she mutters. "What do you want this morning, Mr. Fisher?"

"Just Keaton," I say, correcting her and floating the cup around the air to bring her attention to it. She sighs and takes the cup from me, making my smile grow even wider. I'm counting that as a win.

Her deep pink lips sip the warm drink and a slight moan from her sends signals straight to my dick, conjuring memories of how fucking hot last night's events were. She takes another sip, savoring the warm liquid. Never in my life did I think I would be jealous of a cup of coffee, but here we are.

"I wanted to offer you a ride to the office. Since we're both going to and from the same place, I thought it made sense."

"Umm, no, that's okay." I see her face flush slightly at my offer. "I think it's best we keep things between us professional."

I can't help but think of all the naughty scenes we could reenact in a professional capacity. Under my desk. Over my desk. On my desk. My dick twitches, reminding me that Anna and I aren't there yet.

"Professionals carpool to work all the time," I counter. "Besides, think of how much better it would be for the environment."

Anna looks behind me, staring at my vehicle parked in the driveway. "You drive a huge ass truck."

"Ah, this is true. But one huge ass truck is better than one huge ass truck and one sedan." I smile at her cheekily.

Her assessing gaze suddenly has my confidence slipping, unsure if I'll be able to change her mind. Looking at the two vehicles in the driveway, her head darts between them like she's watching a heated tennis match. Anna takes a deep breath and yields. "Fine. For the earth."

It may just be a ten minute drive to the office, but that means I get twenty extra minutes of my Anna's undivided attention today. Operation Get-My-Wife-Back is officially a go.

Chapter Twenty-One

Anna

"So, how was work?" Keaton asks as we drive back to our home. I mean, not *our* home, but the houses we both live in. At his address. Separately. But still also together. Ugh.

"You should know. You were there with me all day," I grumble.

He glances over at me with a smile that lights up his entire face. "I know. Wasn't it great?"

A snort escapes me. "It wasn't bad, really." I fidget my hands in my lap and he seems to notice.

"What's wrong, Anna? Do I need to fire someone?"

"Oh my gosh, no! Nothing like that. I just had a question and, well, it's kind of embarrassing." I look over at him as he stares out over the road, but when he turns his head in my direction, I look back down at my hands.

"You can ask me anything, Anna."

I'm not sure why, but I trust him. "Umm, it's just. Well, I had a question about. Ugh." I decide to just spit it out. "What do you do?"

He laughs. "What do you mean? Did I not appear busy enough for you?"

"No, I don't mean *you* when I say you. I mean, what exactly goes on at Phisherman's Cybersecurity?" I want to hide at the lack of knowledge when it comes to my new place of employment, but my genuine curiosity has me looking at his handsome profile.

Keaton nods his head and hums before speaking. "Let's see where I need to start. What exactly do you know about cybersecurity?"

I cringe. "That it has something to do with security for computers and stuff?"

His laughter fills the cab of the truck, but it doesn't make me feel ignorant, though I am. It's a beautiful sound and I can't help but want to hear it more often. "So, basically nothing."

I shrug.

"Think of the internet like a giant city. Cities are full of tons of people, and most of those people are upstanding citizens, but a few of them are dishonest, unethical, even criminal. The good people just want to do their day-to-day routines of working, shopping, talking to friends and such. But the bad people are working the scene. They're stealing wallets, breaking into houses, and tricking people out of money." He glances over at me. "You with me so far?"

I nod and he continues, "Our job is to be a full-time security team to businesses. We keep out hackers, scammers, and viruses that are trying to steal money or identities."

"And how do you do that, exactly?" I ask.

"We install protections like firewalls and antivirus. Look for cracks in the system. Train their employees so they don't fall for phishing scams. And if one of the bad guys get in, it's our job to take them out."

"So you're like a superhero?" I ask, cheekily.

Keaton's smile is contagious and I can't help but feel my cheeks tighten at the grin spreading across my face. "Fuck, yeah."

A few moments pass between us, the silence growing awkward before he finally breaks it. "I'm really relieved I don't have to fire anyone. I hate that shit."

"No firing necessary," I assure him. "Everyone has been amazing, so far. I met a girl named Amanda. She said she's Lincoln's assistant?" Keaton nods. "Well, she invited me to join her for lunch tomorrow and I think I'm going to go."

"I think that's great, Anna. It will be good for you to get out of the office and see your new town a little bit. Amanda is good people. But you know, if you want to see more places in town, I would be happy to show you around." He looks over at me sheepishly before turning his gaze back to the road.

I want to tell him that yes, I would love to go anywhere with him. That I've missed him and being forced into his orbit has only made me realize why I wanted to marry him in the first place.

But then a part of my brain lights up and tells me to run. My heart tightens and reminds me of how hurt I was that morning in Vegas. "I appreciate it, but I really did mean it this morning when I said we should keep things between us professional."

Keaton's shoulders sag at my statement. "Right, professional."

The remainder of the drive is quiet as we make it back to Keaton's house. As I step out to walk the stone path to my place, I fight against the urge to turn back and look at him. I'm not ready to give up on him. Or to give up on us. But I'm also not ready to forgive him just yet.

"Your chariot awaits, m'lady." Keaton bows as he holds the door of his shiny pickup open for me to climb into.

"Bit cheesy, don't you think?" I tease him, but secretly I love the royal treatment he's been giving me this week. He's been so good at keeping our relationship professional, but I can't help but love the little moments we've had to get to know one another. If I'm not careful, I'm going to be falling for my husband.

Once Keaton is settled on his side and backing out of the driveway, I ask the question I've been dying to have answered since our drive home yesterday. "So, what did you do next?"

Keaton smiles and even though it's hidden because I'm sitting to his right, I know his dimple is on full display. "Well, we were in the middle of the Caribbean Sea, and he had just gotten stung by a jellyfish. The only people there to help were me and Cam. So, we did something we saw on a tv show once."

I gasp, "You did not do what I think you did. Did you?!"

He nods, "Yup. We pulled our pants down and drenched Lincoln's leg in piss."

"And did it work?"

"Hell no," Keaton laughs, the sound wrapping its arms around me in a hug. "Apparently that isn't a real thing. So now he's covered in our urine and still screaming like a motherfucker, writhing around the sand in pain."

"So, what did you do?" I manage to ask around my giggles.

"We picked him up and hauled his ass back to our little community where there's a medical clinic. Luckily it was a mild sting, though, I'm sure he would tell you otherwise. They got him fixed up and then he went back to the beach house and took the longest shower known to man."

My laughter gets louder and as it does, Keaton's smile grows wider. He holds the steering wheel with his left hand and moves his right hand, palm up, onto the console. It's a silent invitation and one I want to take so badly that my fingers tingle in need.

Instead, I form a fist with my hands to resist the urge to touch him and look out the windshield. "There she is. Phisherman's Cybersecurity. Are you ready for another day of work, boss?"

A slow sigh ripples through Keaton, and he moves his hand to rest it on the gearshift. "Let's do this."

Unlike every other day when Keaton usually walks out of the office with me, he is already in the truck when I walk out to meet him. His windows are slightly tinted, but I can still see his features tight in frustration. Frustration at me.

I open the door and get myself buckled before looking over at him. His jaw is tight. His knuckles are white from gripping the steering wheel so tightly. I could feel the storm clouds building inside the cab of the truck.

My stomach twists in knots. Of course he's furious. This is his company, and it means everything to him, and I've gone and fucked up with one of his biggest clients. I deserve whatever wrath he wants to bring down on me, but I can't handle the silence any longer.

"I'm sorry I'm late," I whisper, but he doesn't react. I increase my tone slightly in case he didn't hear me.

"And I'm so sorry for everything else, Keaton," I say, my voice still quiet. "I guess I chose the wrong date on the calendar when I scheduled the meeting and I know that isn't an excuse, but I'm just really sorry. I understand that Caruso Enterprises is one of our most important clients and that meeting was very important. I should have double-checked. I should have done better."

He slams his hands against the steering wheel, and I shut my eyes, ready for his anger, but not wanting to bear witness to the disappointment on his face. "You and your damn rambling," his voice was low, but full of heat. "You think I'm mad over missing a fucking meeting I didn't want to attend in the first place?"

My eyes open and I take him in. He's still facing forward, seemingly trying to control his emotions. Even with the rage coursing through him now, he was the most handsome man I've ever seen. Today he has on a solid black button-up tucked into a pair of solid black pants, held up by a solid black belt. His fancy looking shoes match his hair with a salt and pepper effect. I suppose it's the perfect outfit to match his current mood. "I couldn't find you, Anna," he manages to grit out.

I blink at him, confused. "What?"

"When you realized your mistake, and that's all it fucking was, you took off. I looked all around the office and couldn't find you. You wouldn't answer your phone."

The idea of him searching for me while I cowered in the bathroom on the next floor down never occurred to me. I just assumed he would never want to see me again after I messed up.

"I left it on my desk," I cut in softly. "I went back to find it, but it wasn't there."

He sits my phone between us on the console before he speaks. "I thought you were gone. I thought I'd lost you again." Keaton's eyes look up at me, his face stricken with grief. "I thought you left me, Anna. For good."

A strong dose of reality slaps me upside the head. He isn't upset that I messed up his calendar. He isn't mad at me for making his big-ticket clients furious with him for missing out on another one of their lengthy meetings they demanded from him.

He was worried. Worried about me.

I pick my phone up from the console and put it in my purse. I replace it with my hand, palm up. Keaton's blue eyes question me, and I give the slightest nod of an answer. Then he puts his hand in mine and squeezes our fingers together. He huffs out a sigh and brings our hands up so that our elbows rest on the barrier between us. Placing a kiss on the back of my hand, he whispers, "Thank you. Thank you for not leaving me."

The spot where his lips touched my skin pulses and it's then I realize that the walls I had built around my heart were crashing down. And I was in no hurry to rebuild them.

Chapter Twenty-Two
Anna

I t's been two weeks since moving to Cheatham and I love it here. The small town is so welcoming and seriously straight off a Hallmark movie set. The downtown square is strung up with lights and with the gazebo in the middle it makes for a real romantic setting. Salons, restaurants, small businesses and the local radio station surround the space, making it the most popular spot in town, and there's always an upcoming farmers market, festival, or car show being advertised.

The hospitality doesn't stop there. Everyone at Phisherman's Cybersecurity has been so nice and I've become friends with Lincoln's assistant, Amanda. I admit that when she first asked me to go to lunch with her and peppered me with tons of questions, I thought Lincoln had sent her as a spy. But now that we've had lunch together practically every day, a full hour of her filling me in on the gossip as though I've lived here all my life and know exactly who she's talking about, I realize she's just nosy. And I love that about her.

So yeah, the town is great. And the people are great. And as much as I don't want to admit it, my boss is seriously amazing. For a solid three days I was proud of myself for providing nothing but some stifled conversations and the bare minimum. But there was no denying the attraction between us. And there is no denying that I'm back to feeling the same way about him now as I did when we met on that plane.

The man brings in a coffee truck every Monday morning and pays for his entire staff to start their day with some much-needed caffeine. When I was struggling with the new-to-me phone system, he was so patient as he walked me through the process. He even fixed me up the cutest little cheat sheet in case I needed more guidance down the road. And when Jackie in accounting found out her mom had been diagnosed with cancer, he gave her a week of paid time off to help them adjust to their new normal.

Being his passenger princess has become my favorite part of the day. I had forgotten how easily this man could make me laugh and smile. It felt nice having these normal conversations with him and made me long for the relationship I once thought could have been a possibility. The time together has also given us time to get to know each other, since we were practically strangers when we decided to sign up for forever. I've learned that he has an allergy to mushrooms, had his first kiss at age twelve to a girl named Delilah who now owns a bakery here in town, how he had originally planned on going into engineering, but then stayed home to take care of his family after his dad passed. Even when I've seen firsthand how much his brothers can annoy him, there is no doubt that there's a ton of love amongst them. No matter how much they bicker, and it's an impressive amount, they maintain a standing lunch date every Friday at Pizza Papa.

That would explain why I see a younger version of Keaton heading this way. I'd bet money that Camden is closer to my thirty than Keaton's forty. There's definitely a family resemblance, but where Keaton's face features a sharp, lickable jawline, Camden's is fuller. His dark hair is longer and dips below his ears in little curls. Glasses sit on Cam's face and his cherub cheeks raise them slightly as he smiles at me. I notice the dimple Keaton has is missing from Cam's face, too. Those striking blue eyes are the same, though.

"There's my favorite sister-in-law," Camden teased as he sauntered up to my desk.

I shush him and he laughs. "Got it, we're still keeping that under wraps. How are my big brothers today?"

"I haven't seen Lincoln yet today. You're here before he is, which is pretty impressive since you're traveling from across town instead of across the office." Lincoln's office is identical to Keaton's but is located on the other end of the building. According to Keaton too much togetherness can be a bad thing with them, so they decided on that layout early in the planning days. I've gotta admit, from the way I've seen the two interact, it probably is for the best. Camden has his law office downtown, closer to the courthouse.

Camden leans down closer to me to avoid eavesdroppers. "How is it working for my brothers? I know Lincoln can be a bit of a grouch. Keaton is usually very laid back and easy to get along with, but the two of you have a history. Just wanna make sure you're hanging in there."

I smile at his sweetness. You can tell Camden is the sweetheart of the bunch and wants to make sure everyone is happy and getting along. "I really love it here," I tell him honestly. "I don't deal a whole lot with Lincoln, but he's nice to me when we do interact. Keaton is, well, he's wonderful."

A soft smile graces my lips, and a hushed sigh breathes out of me. It takes me a few seconds to realize what I just admitted and who I just admitted it to.

"He's a wonderful boss, I mean. Come on? A coffee truck every Monday. Pure genius."

Glancing up, I see the huge smile on Camden's face. "Oh, shut up," I groan, and run my hand down my face.

"Your secret is safe with me sis," he says with a wink, then graciously changes the subject. "Have you tried out Pizza Papa yet? Best pizza in the county. You should join us for lunch."

I shake my head. "I haven't had the chance to try it yet, but Amanda and I already have a date for sandwiches over at Crumb and Get It." The sandwich shop on the square is one of my favorite spots and I have visited it way too often in the short time I've lived here. It's the pickles, I swear.

"Solid choice. Well, if I can't get lunch out of you, why don't you join us tonight at Kalli's?"

"Kalli's?"

"Yeah, Kalli's Corral. It's the only bar we've got in this town, but it's a good one. I can't promise they have the fancy drinks from the big city, but you can definitely get something to wet your whistle."

A night out sounds much needed, and I decide I'll ask Amanda her thoughts about it at lunch. "I might see you there."

"Good news, girl!" Amanda comes dancing to our table after stepping outside to make a call. "Jason is gonna take care of the kids so we can go out tonight. I'm so excited! I haven't been to Kalli's since before my youngest was born."

When I had asked Amanda what she thought of the place and that Camden invited me to go, she insisted I would have a great time there and then offered to tag along to be my wing woman. She just had to check in with her husband to make sure her three children were taken care of before she could commit. I didn't have it in my heart to tell her I wouldn't be needing her assistance in landing a man. There was only one man I had any interest in, and he was one I had firmly put in the off-limits zone, though these past couple of weeks have me reconsidering.

Panic begins to set in as I think about another drunken night with Keaton. "Maybe it's not such a good idea to go out tonight," I try to think of an excuse. "I don't have anything to wear."

Amanda snorts, "Just wear you a pair of jeans and a sexy top to show off those huge knockers you have. Since your boss can't help but stare at them, you may as well flaunt them in his face."

"Amanda!" I hiss, but my new friend just shrugs and takes another bite of her sandwich.

Dressed in the sexiest pair of jeans I own and a scoop neck black top that does flatter my chest quite nicely, I throw on my black kitten heels and look at myself in the mirror. My first thought is whether Keaton will like the way I look or not. Even when furious with him, my heart flutters every time that man crosses my mind. These days that's an awful lot.

On our way home this afternoon, I mentioned that Amanda and I planned on being there tonight and he offered me a ride. There was nothing I wanted more, but I decided some space between us was much needed, so I opted to have Amanda pick me up.

Anxiety has a firm grip on me as I consider for the first time that he may be there with another woman. Even if he isn't, the man is a fucking catch and there's no way someone won't come up and hit on him. Jealousy boils my blood at the thought of another woman talking to him. What if it's even more than that and she touches him?

My freak out is interrupted with Amanda letting herself in and calling out, "Knock, knock!"

"Most people knock before they let themselves in, ya know?" I say with a laugh.

Amanda ignores me as her eyes dart around the guest house. "Dang girl, this place is nice! I knew Keaton had money, but you're living in luxury."

I must admit that I was equally enamored with it when I had moved in, noting the quartz counter tops and high-end appliances that filled the spacious kitchen and opened up into the living room adorned with high ceilings. Everything was neutral except for the pops of color I had added with throw pillows and blankets. It looked like a place out of a magazine.

"It's just temporary," I remind her, and myself. "I'll have a much less impressive place of my own soon enough."

"A place like this and a neighbor like Keaton Fisher? I'd be doing everything possible to stay if I were you, girl. Now speaking of our boss, let's go see if we can catch him getting drunk. I bet he's a giggly one."

I don't tell my new bestie that I know exactly what Keaton is like when he's drunk. Giggly? No. Charming and sexy enough to end up in a chapel with him? Abso-fucking-lutely.

Walking into Kalli's Corral, I need a moment to adjust to a sensory overload. Live music pumps throughout the place that features a dance floor among several high tops with stools. The smell of beer and peanuts waft through the air and while the overhead lights are off, there's track lighting at the bar and several spotlights in the place. I can already tell tonight is going to be fun.

As I take everything in, Amanda leads us to a large table where several people from work are already seated. "Fancy meeting you here," Keaton says, that dimple popping and making me weak in the knees. "I saved you a seat." He pulls out the stool right beside him. Sitting down, he leans over and whispers so only I can hear him, his hand placed on the small of my back. "You look fucking stunning tonight, Baby."

That damn nickname has me melting as electricity shoots through my body at his touch. I don't hide my gaze as I allow myself to drink him in. He changed out his slacks for a pair of jeans, but he's still wearing his daily button-up with the rolled sleeves giving me delicious access to eye fuck his arms. There are a lot of places on a man to love, but the arms get me every time. And Keaton's are the very best. "Back at ya," I say with a grin, appreciating how natural it feels to flirt with him.

Did I just fucking flirt with my boss? Yes. Yes, I did. And it felt amazing. It felt right. My mind pulls out a projector and shows me stills from our time together in Vegas. Being with Keaton is so easy and I'm really tired of life being hard. Maybe a night of flirting and fun is what the two of us need.

Our table fills up quickly and we are easily the loudest and rowdiest in the place. As I glance around, I see Camden but notice Lincoln's absence. "Linc didn't want to join?"

Camden answers on behalf of his brother. "He's staying in with Charlie to watch a new movie. She's been really big into My Little Pony lately."

"That sounds like so much fun for Lincoln," I smile cheekily. "Does he miss out on nights like this a lot?"

This time Keaton answers. "We include him the best we can, but it's the life of a single dad. Mama watches Charlie pretty often but here lately she's not, um, been feeling well." I note the sadness in Keaton's expression as he mentions his mom. I'm eager to learn more about that, but I won't push the subject tonight.

"Let's dance!" Amanda shouts and most of the table gets up to head to the dance floor, including myself and Keaton.

The bluegrass band on the stage has been playing popular hits with their touch of twang and I laugh as I dance to renditions of Genie in a Bottle and I Want it That Way featuring mandolins, banjos, and fiddles. We've been out here for close to an hour and although I'm having the time of my life, I can feel sweat beading at my forehead and rolling down my spine, so I excuse myself to go back to the table for a break.

Drinking down my hard cider, others come back to the table for some rest, and I notice Keaton in the mix. He smiles at me, and I can't help but return it.

"You looked like you were having a lot of fun out there."

"Were you watching me?" I ask, my eyebrows raised in curiosity.

He takes a drink before giving me a smirk that just barely conceals that left cheek dimple. "May have been."

My heart and pussy flutter with desire. I love knowing his eyes were on me as my body rocked to the beat, writhing around the way it would as though he and I were a tangled heap of passion.

"I haven't danced like that in years," I confess. "The atmosphere here is amazing."

"The company is even better," he replies, leaning in so I can feel his breath brush against my face. His lips look so damn good and if I'm being honest with myself, working with him has completely thawed my icy heart. We both lean into each other, but are interrupted before things can get too far.

"Shit, no. Of all the dadgum nights," Amanda huffs coming up to our table.

"What's going on?" I ask, genuinely curious and concerned. She's been having so much fun and I'm sure with being a mom to three little ones, these types of nights are few and far between.

"I am so sorry, girl, Jason just texted. Apparently, Sadie started throwing up and well, he's a good dad, but he's pretty helpless when it comes to that stuff. I hate to cut our night short, but I need to head home."

Completely understanding, I go to grab my purse, but Keaton wraps his arm around my waist. I see Amanda's eyes track the interaction. "You head on home and take care of your sick kid, Amanda. I'll make sure Anna makes it home safely."

My friend looks at me, her eyes lit up and a knowing smile spread across her face. "You okay with that, Anna?"

My voice is caught in my throat at both Keaton's touch and someone's knowledge that there is clearly something happening between us. I don't know what that something is just yet, but certain parts of me sure know what they want to be happening. I nod and Amanda heads out of the bar. Everyone else is back on the dance floor, leaving me and Keaton alone at the table.

"I have a few confessions to make, Anna."

I look up at him but say nothing. The heat in his eyes is a good indication of what at least one of those confessions might be.

"Number one. Our car rides together are the best part of my day."

"Mine too," I confess, making a small smile pull at his lips.

"Number two. I've been hard all night with the way those jeans hug your curves and those fucking perfect tits of yours are on display."

I bite the inside of my cheek to stop myself from whimpering out loud.

"And number three," his words are breathy, "I have so many regrets about how I handled certain situations with you. But I will never regret the two of us standing in that chapel together and vowing to be together forever and always."

My own breath catches as the familiar chords of Elvis Presley's "Can't Help Falling in Love" begin to play. Keaton leans in to brush a kiss against my lips and I melt into him. It's nothing compared to some of the heated moments we had in Vegas, but it sets my very soul on fire. "Dance with me?"

He holds my hand as we navigate through the crowd to find a place on the dance floor. Holding me tightly against him, we sway back and forth to the song that was played during our wedding.

My head rests on his chest and despite the large crowd in a small town, everyone else seems to fade away. I've missed this. I've missed him.

"Keaton?" I say his name softly.

He hums in acknowledgement.

"Will you take me home?"

Chapter Twenty-Three
Keaton

Being able to hold Anna in my arms as we sway to the song that played during our ceremony was totally worth the hundred bucks I gave Kalli to bribe her into playing it.

It hasn't been easy tearing Anna's walls down. The walls she put up because of me. The first week she was here, I had to keep checking the thermostat to see who was messing with it. Turns out it was just the icy blasts of her cold shoulder. She spoke when necessary and nothing more, but it didn't stop me from talking.

I shared with her about my family, my company, and my weaknesses. Finally, by the end of the week she was responding, and even starting the conversation all on her own. Those moments in my truck were the highlights of my day, but tonight, holding her like this with her head against my chest, nothing has ever felt so right.

As the King croons out the classic line about being unable to help falling in love, Anna looks up at me.

"Keaton?" Her sweet voice is soft so only I'm able to hear it.

I hum to let her know I'm listening.

"Will you take me home?"

Those words snap me out of the dream I was having that my girl wanted me back. That she trusted me again and was ready to pursue our marriage. But she's biting that bottom lip of hers and I know she does that when she's overthinking. Defeated, I let out a heavy sigh.

"Yeah, Baby. Let's go home."

We drive in silence and it's killing me inside. I replay every word I said and every action I made to see if I scared her off. Maybe that kiss was too much too soon, but I wasn't imagining things when she pressed her lips against mine and kissed me back. Before I'm ready to call it a night I'm pulling into the driveway and the girl I am falling so fucking hard for is about to pull away from me again.

"Thanks for bringing me home," she says, unbuckling her seat belt.

"Well, ya know, it was on the way." I give her a small smile and am grateful for the one she gives me right back. "Just a sec and I'll get your door."

She tries to protest, but I've already hopped out and made my way around the truck. I open her door and place my hands on her hips to help guide her out of the tall vehicle. When her feet hit the pavement, I should let go, but I keep my hands where they're at, not wanting to say goodnight just yet.

She feels so good in my hands. I pull her into me and wrap my arms around her back, hugging her in a way I don't think I ever have with anyone else. I could stand here all night like this, but instead, I release her, and we walk hand in hand down the stone path to her temporary residence.

"Do you want to come in?" Her beautiful emerald eyes look up at me as she tucks that pouty bottom lip of hers back between her teeth.

Do I want to come in? Yeah. Yeah, I fucking do. But I want her trust and love even more. I want her to know without a doubt that she wants what's between us to work out. So, I piss my dick off and run my mouth.

"Anna, there is nothing more I want to do than go inside your home with you. I want to push you through that door and kiss you until your lips ache. I'd only give them a reprieve because I want to focus on those tits that have been teasing me all fucking night, spilling out of that top. Once I've left bite marks all over the flesh and your nipples are so hard they hurt, I want to undress you so my eyes can explore every beautiful inch of this incredible body. Next, I want to bring you to orgasm by tossing one of your legs over my shoulder and consuming that delicious pussy that's haunted my memories. And finally, after I've gotten you so fucking wet you've made a mess of my face and your thighs, I want to sink so fucking deep inside you over and fucking over again until you can't fucking talk tomorrow because you lost your voice from screaming my name."

I watch her throat bob as she swallows thickly. She shifts in a motion that has her thighs rubbing together. God why am I being such a dumbass right now?

"But more than any of that Anna. More than the desire I have for your body. I want your heart. I want it so damn bad I'm in physical pain from the ache in my chest. I want you so bad that when I drop you off after work, all I want to do is go to bed and sleep so I can see you in my dreams because any moment I'm not with you is absolutely fucking miserable. I want your pride. I want your trust. I want your love."

I stare at her openly, letting her see all of me and all that I want to be for her. "And that's why I can't come inside tonight, Anna. I need to deserve you. I need you to want this marriage to work. I need you to take a chance on me. A chance on us." I place my thumb under her chin, tilting her head and placing the softest of kisses on her cheek. "I can't have you, Anna, until you're ready to have all of me. I can't have you until you love me the way that I love you."

I didn't plan on saying those words to her tonight, but I don't regret letting her know exactly how I feel about her. The only thing I do regret is that speaking those words into existence is making it even fucking harder to walk away from her. Again.

Chapter
Twenty-Four
Anna

M y feet are frozen to the stone beneath me as I watch Keaton retreat to his house. I'm trying to process everything he just said.

Keaton loves me.

Me.

The girl who has been told that men who look like him don't want women who look like me.

Me.

The girl who has been called chubby since her toddler days and then made fun of all through school for being larger than everyone.

Me.

The girl people make stupid bets on as a joke.

Me.

He loves me.

My breaths pick up and my heart pounds inside my chest as I realize that his feelings aren't one sided. I am so fucking in love with my husband. But he left and as I hear the click of the door shutting behind him as he enters his mini mansion, it feels like a dagger piercing my heart.

Keaton loves me and I love him and fuck that door for thinking it can stand between us. Stumbling over the stones, I race down the path to his house. When I reach the door, I hesitate for just a second. I've never entered his home before, but I suppose there's no time like the present and there's no better reason to break in than to tell the man I love just how much he means to me.

Stepping inside, I immediately freeze. Keaton is nowhere to be seen, but holy fucking hell, this place is stunning. I find myself standing in my absolute dream kitchen. A large island with wooden cabinets and a marble countertop sits in the center with lantern-style lights giving off a soft glow in the middle of the night. Wooden beams are spaced perfectly across the ceiling providing a rustic elegance, which is exactly how I would describe Keaton.

Keaton. The man I'm here for. The man I love. I dash around his house, finding myself in rooms more stunning than the last. He's not in the dining room, living room, office, or bathroom. Climbing the stairs, I'm out of breath and take a moment to hunch over and catch my breath. That's when I hear it. The spray of the shower.

I follow the sound of the water to the master suite, and I can't help but whimper at how perfect it looks. It's like Keaton was inside my head when he designed this beautiful home. The Alaskan King size bed is centered on the wall and if things go the way I want, I will definitely be exploring it later.

My lusty dreams are halted when I realize the sound of running water is no longer filling the space. I turn and face the door of the master bedroom. The door that's slowly opening. The door that my husband is stepping out of. With nothing but a towel around his waist and water droplets dripping down his chest.

I want to lick them off him.

I want to snatch that towel and sink to my knees in front of him.

But more than I want that right now, I want him to know how I feel.

When his head comes up to see me, he startles and jumps back. "Fuck, Baby. You scared me."

"I'm sorry," I whisper, but secretly I'm not sorry at all because what a fucking view.

He shakes his head. "No Baby, I'm sorry. I'm so fucking sorry. I'm sorry for leaving you in Vegas. I'm sorry for ruining the job you were so excited about. I'm sorry for wanting you when I know you don't feel the same."

"You're wrong," I cut him off.

He cocks his head and looks at me, crushed and confused.

"You're wrong about me not wanting you the way you want me. I want you so much it hurts. I've always wanted you. Even when I tried so fucking hard to hate you, I couldn't. Do you know why, Keaton? Do you know why I couldn't hate you?"

He doesn't answer. He just stares at me, so I tell him. I tell him the truth.

"Because I fucking love you. I love you so much, Keaton." My breath escapes me as I choke on sobs, not having realized that tears are streaming down my face. I wipe at them furiously, mad that they're interrupting my moment. When I regain my composure, I speak again to the man who is just standing there staring at me.

"You said you couldn't have me until I was ready to have you. You said you couldn't have me until I love you the way you love me." I wipe away the rogue tears once more. "Well here I am, Keaton. Wanting you. Loving you. So have me. Take me. I'm yours."

My chest heaves as I take in the beautiful man across the room from me. He stands there motionless for several moments before the corner of his lip curves up into that sinful smirk of his.

"Fucking finally."

Chapter Twenty-Five
Keaton

"Keaton Fisher." Mr. Scottsdale, the high school principal, stepped into my biology class at the end of the day. "Can you collect your things and come with me, please?" The "oos" of my classmates didn't bother me as I did what the principal asked. I know I hadn't done anything wrong, but when I stepped out in the hallway and saw my younger brother Lincoln standing there, I had no doubt he did something wrong. I swear if he jeopardizes my scholarship because he pulled some dumbass prank, I'm gonna kick his ass. "What did you do?" I accuse him and he holds up his hands. "Don't come at me like that, I am just as confused as you are." We follow our principal to his office, where the sheriff and the guidance counselor are seated. The door clicks behind us as we step in, the space suddenly becoming a lot smaller. "Boys, we brought you in here because unfortunately we have some bad news." My brother and I look at each other unsure what the hell could be going on. "Earlier today there was a bad accident out on the interstate. Unfortunately, that accident involved your father." "Is our dad okay?" Lincoln asks. Mrs. Grimes, the guidance counselor, begins to cry and shakes her head. "Boys, I'm so sorry." "Where's our dad?" I ask and the sheriff

*looks over at us. "Your dad didn't survive the crash, boys. He's passed.
I'm so sorry for your loss."*

I scrub at my skin until it's raw, trying to erase the painful
memory from my mind. Instead, another one crashes into me.

*"Hey, Mom, I'm home!" I call out to the house where we all live.
For now, anyway. The company my brothers and I have started
together is slowly building and I see big things for our future. I walk
further into the house, but my mom isn't perched on the couch in
her usual spot. Hmm, maybe she's taking a nap. Heading into her
bedroom just to make sure she's okay, I find my mother in her bed,
pale and breathing shallowly, covered in her own vomit. Was she
sick? Is it a bug? "Mama, you feeling okay?" There's no response from
her. I walk over and place my hand against her forehead and she's
burning up. Fuck. She was fine this morning. "Mama," I say again,
but she doesn't react. That's when I see it. The empty prescription
bottle in the bed next to her. I call 911 and then Lincoln. Cam is
hours away at law school, so I'll have to catch him up later. It feels like
hours before the ambulance shows up, even though my phone shows
that I only called six minutes ago. I stood back to let the paramedics
take over. Lincoln was on his way and as soon as he arrived, I hopped
in his car, and we followed the emergency vehicle to the hospital in
the next town over. They pumped her stomach but ultimately sent
her to Lexington where she spent several weeks in recovery and we
found out what happened. She had gone into town that morning for
her monthly hair appointment down at the Clip n' Curl, followed
by lunch with some ladies in town. Apparently, she had complained
about not being able to sleep without my dad beside her anymore, so*

one of them offered her some pills to try and help. What had actually happened was she overdosed on them as she tried to take the pain away, and then when we finally got her better and discharged from the hospital, we brought her home and she never left it again.

A roar comes out of me as I blink back the tears that burn in my eyes. I try to remind myself of the positives. Mama is here. She's okay. She made it.

Anna sits beside me on the plane, her thick thigh brushing against mine, and all I want to do is reach out and touch her so badly. I want to tell her that I'm sorry and there was nowhere else I wanted to be than with her. But the look of hatred on her face has me keeping my hands and words to myself. "I don't want to speak to you." Her words sliced my skin, sharper than any blade ever could. "I don't want you to speak to me." Another cut, deeper this time. "We are going to fly home and go our separate ways." Knowing I had lost the only woman I ever felt this way for was the final blow. I open my mouth to say something, anything to make her believe me. But she's right. I hurt her. I'm the problem. I don't deserve her.

Physically and emotionally exhausted from my memory-laden shower, I turn off the water, ready to get in bed and try to sleep off the pain that has crept up in my chest. As I step out of the bathroom, a figure stands in front of my bed. I jump back but then see it's the curvy goddess I'm head over heels for.

I listen to her confession, holding my breath the entire time she tells me what I've longed to hear.

She loves me.

"Fucking finally," I say and take pleasure in the gasp that sounds from perfect lips as I rush to her, palming the back of her neck and crashing my lips to hers in a fierce, fiery passion. It's not enough. I need more of her. I need all of her. And I need it right fucking now.

I tug off the tease of a top that has showcased her perfect tits. I ought to give her a whipping for wearing that out in public and allowing eyes other than mine to linger at her beautiful display. I snap her bra off so fast that teenage me would be hooting and hollering with applause if he were here to witness it. Her plush lips feel so good against mine, but I rip them away so I can suck her nipple into my mouth.

She writhes and moans against me as my tongue flicks over the bud, bringing it to a hardened point. I pull back to blow a cool breath over it and a shudder runs through her. God, I love how responsive she is to my touch. I repeat the motion with her other breast, making sure I give them both the equal attention they deserve.

"More, Keaton. More, please." A growl escapes me as I swap our positions. I move her over the bed, pushing her back until her front side is flat against it, then I lean down to her ear. "More?" I ask. "What do you want more of, Baby?"

"You, please," she whimpers and I'm about to explode from the sound alone.

"Where do you want more of me?" Teasing her may be my new favorite thing to do with this woman that drives me absolutely crazy with need and desire.

"I..." she stammers and it's the cutest fucking thing. "I want you in my pussy, Keaton. Please."

Sliding her jeans down her legs, I notice she upgraded her panties tonight from her white cotton briefs to a lacy, black thong. I run my finger up and down the scrap of fabric making her squirm. "Beg me, Baby."

She groans at my demand. "Please, Keaton. Please touch my pussy."

Pulling her panties down and off her, I bring them to my nose and inhale her intoxicating scent. "That's strange. This doesn't smell like *your* pussy, Anna."

"What?" she shrieks. "Those are mine. You just fucking pulled them off me. What are you talking about?"

I take the flimsy fabric, soaked in her arousal, and bring it to her nose. "Breathe that in, Anna. Does that smell like *your* pussy?" I trace my fingers around her, faintly brushing where she wants me, but not giving in just yet.

"It's mine, Keaton. Those are mine." Her voice is crying out and she's trying to lift herself off the bed, but we can't have that. I crack my palm against her ass, taking in the beautiful shade of red that blooms across her cheek.

"Stop lying to me, Anna. That doesn't smell like *your* pussy at all." I lean over her, allowing her to feel my hard cock underneath the towel that's failing to conceal how I feel about this gorgeous woman.

I reach down and use my fingers to spread her lower lips apart. "This doesn't look like *your* pussy, either, Anna."

She trembles and I can feel her cunt pulse against my fingers. I swipe one of them inside of her, collecting the arousal that's dripping from her. Sucking the taste off my lips, I hum. "It doesn't even taste like *your* pussy."

"Keaton, please," she whines and I get a sick pleasure from the torment I'm putting her through.

"You gave that beautiful speech and have already forgotten what you said."

"What are you talking about? Please. Please Keaton, I need you."

"I believe the words you said were 'I'm yours.' So, let's try this again. Where do you want me?"

"My pussy," she repeats, and I slap my palm against her left cheek this time, causing her to cry out beautifully. "Your pussy. Yours. It's yours. Please touch your pussy, Keaton. Please, it's yours."

"Fucking right it is," I mutter, spreading her legs apart and lifting them at her thighs so I can explore what's mine. Her tangy taste floods my mouth and I can't get enough. I chase her wetness with my tongue, then insert a finger inside before slipping in another. She clenches around me so tight I could explode right fucking now, but I won't allow myself that particular pleasure until I'm balls deep inside her.

I'm relentless, pumping my fingers in and out of her as my tongue swirls around her clit. I can feel how close she's getting, and I want at least one orgasm from her before I sink my cock inside this delicious cunt.

I take my time licking over her clit before sucking it into my mouth, refusing to stop until she's a complete mess. I push a third finger into her, and she comes undone. "Fuck, Keaton, yes. Yes!" My girl isn't quiet as she rides through her orgasm and I fucking love it. Scream the house down, Baby. Wake the whole fucking neighborhood. Let the whole world know that you belong to me.

When her breathing begins to regulate and she finally begins to settle against me, I pull my fingers from her, sucking her sweet taste off each one. Her eyes track my movements, and I smirk at her, knowing she loves every dirty action I make. "Tell me what you want now, Wife."

A sexy smile blooms on her face. "I want you to fuck me, Husband."

Chapter Twenty-Six
Anna

K eaton wastes no time flipping me over, grabbing my hips and maneuvering me on the bed so I'm in the position he wants. I'm laying with my legs spread, eagerly waiting for him to undress so he can fill me up in the way only he can. But as I wait, he begins to retreat.

"What's wrong? Where are you going?" I try not to sound needy, but I can hear the panic in my voice as doubts and insecurities begin to creep over me.

He takes a step my way, running his hand up and down my leg soothingly. "Well, I was headed to get a condom, but if you're that eager to start growing our family, I'm more than happy to oblige." He gives me that dashing smirk of his and I'm torn between wanting to kiss it and slap it.

"We should probably get the husband-and-wife thing figured out before we add kids to the mix, don't you think?" I sass. "Besides, I'm on birth control and I'm clean."

"I'm clean, too. So, are you saying you want me bare, Baby?"

I nod and Keaton growls. He fucking growls and it sets me on fire.

My husband strips down, showing off his amazing abs he's worked so hard to create and maintain, as well as the thick, long shaft that hangs between his legs. The image makes my mouth and the space between my legs begin to water. Fuck he's so hot.

And he's mine.

He climbs up on the bed, but before he touches me, he stops and stares. Normally I'd be trying to hide under the intense gaze, but there's nothing but desire in his crystal blues as his eyes rake over my body.

"You take my breath away, Anna. The way your golden curls are splayed out makes you look like an angel. These fucking lips could tempt me into doing anything, giving you everything you could possibly desire." His fingers begin to trail over my breasts in the tenderest of touches, teasing my nipples delicately to the point I let out a tiny whimper. "I love these so much. The way they look, the way they taste, the way they fill my hands like they were made just for me. Like you were made just for me, Baby."

My breaths are staggered as I watch him align his cock to my entrance and I jerk my hips forward trying to speed up the process. Keaton chuckles, "I love how eager you are. I hope you're ready, Baby."

He thrusts into me, and my breath catches at the fullness. He's so big and thick and I'm floating in a painful bliss right now as my body adjusts. "Feels. So. Good," I manage to choke out as he relentlessly pumps into me.

When he hits that special spot inside of me, I let out an embarrassingly loud moan, but I'm too far gone to care. Every doubt and insecurity floats away as Keaton fucks it out of me.

I can tell he's close and trying to wait for me. "Be a good wife and come for your husband, Anna."

And I do.

I wake the next morning with a delicious soreness between my legs and smile at thoughts of the man who loves me. The man I love in return. Rolling over to curl beside him, I notice the absence of his body, but my hand feels the roughness of paper.

Good morning, Wife. I know last night was a lot, so I didn't want to wake you, but wanted to leave you a note so you didn't worry. I'll never leave you again, Baby. I hope you know you're stuck with me now. Take your time, but I'm eagerly awaiting your arrival downstairs so I can see that gorgeous face of yours again.

Love you,

Keaton

I can't help the smile that spreads across my face so large it starts to make my cheeks ache. There's not a time I can remember being this happy and it makes me eager to share this news with my favorite people.

Anna

I have a confession…

Skyla

Please tell me it is what I think it is!

Anna

I think I'm in love with my husband. Scratch that. I'm definitely in love with my husband.

Skyla

Pay up, bitches! I accept cash, check, Venmo, PayPal, coffee, diamonds, or that adorable pink sweater in the window in the boutique downtown.

Anna

Did the three of you seriously make a bet on my love life?

Jasmine

Ugh. Skyla did. But I didn't verbally agree, so there's no contract holding me to it. I'm not paying you shit, Sky.

Penny

Just sent money your way, Sky.

Penny

Thanks a lot, Anna. I was really hoping you would stay strong for at least one more week.

Skyla

Got it, Pen!

Skyla

Okay, Anna. Spill. I need all the dirty deets about the silver daddy.

I leave a voice message going over all of last night's events, from the dancing at Kalli's to his confession outside my house, to finding him stricken with grief, and finally to the spasm-inducing orgasm that left me so satiated I had my best sleep in years.

Skyla

Loooooove this! Anna, I am so happy for you. Are you going to have another wedding? Can I be a bridesmaid this time? Or you know, at least get an invite?

Penny

I'm happy for you, Anna, but just be careful. The two of you have sped through some major life choices and it might not be a bad idea to slow things down a bit.

Anna

Don't worry, Pen. We rushed into things last time, though we were intensely intoxicated. I think I'll hold out at least an entire weekend this time around before I do

> something crazy like renew our vows or have kids with the man.

Penny

> Don't even joke about that!

Jasmine

> Well, when his dumbass screws up, just know I'm ready with the papers.

Skyla

> Oh, Jaz. Always so willing to stick it to the man. Maybe you should try having a man stick something in you.

I toss my phone to the side so Jaz and Sky can bicker with one another, then head to the bathroom so I can take care of things before I head down to see my man. I learned today how incredibly difficult it is to brush your teeth and floss when you have the biggest smile on your face.

Picking up Keaton's rumpled shirt from last night off the floor, I slip it on and pick up my phone to check it before making my way to the kitchen.

Daniel

> I miss seeing those curves of yours every day, Anna. You can't ignore me forever. I'll be seeing you soon.

Yesterday I would have been shaking as I read Daniel's words. I would have spiraled into an episode of fear and nausea. But not today, Satan. Doing what I should have done as soon as I quit my job, I block his number and head down to say good morning to my husband.

1 1 0 0 1 1 0 0 0 1 0 1 0 1 1 1 1 0 0 1 0
0 0 0 0 0 0 0 1 1 0 0 1 1 0 0 0 0 0 1 0 1
1 0 1 0 1 0 1 0 0 0 1 1 0 0 0 1 1 0 0 1 0
0 0 0 0 1 1 1 1 0 0 1 0 0 0 1 0 0 1
0 1 0 1 1 1 0 0 1 0 0 1 1 1 0 1 0
1 0 0 0 1 0 1 0 0
0 0 1 1 1 0 0 1
0 0 1 1 0 0 0 0
1 0 1 0 0
1 0 1 1
0 1 0

Chapter Twenty-Seven

Keaton

The pancakes have been flipped. The smell of bacon lingers in the air. And my smoke show of a wife just entered the kitchen. She's wearing the button up I wore last night. And she fucking looks like mine. My cock springs to life and I'm prepared to let the breakfast I just fixed for her spoil so I can consume her instead.

"Good morning," she says, wrapping her arms around my waist and tilting her head up like she's asking for a kiss. Strongly believing in the phrase "happy wife, happy life." I oblige. It takes a lot of control to keep myself from moving any further so she can get some calories in her after last night's workout session, but I need her reenergized so we can have a repeat performance later on. "Mornin'. I've got pancakes, bacon and coffee ready. Or if you'd rather, there's orange juice and milk in the fridge."

"Mmm, coffee sounds perfect. You didn't have to go to all this trouble, Keaton, but I appreciate it."

"Taking care of you is no trouble at all," I admit, fixing her up a plate as she pours herself a cup. I note how she only fills it halfway before she finds the sugar bowl and scoops a couple of spoonfuls.

Then she heads to the fridge and takes out the milk to fill up the rest of the cup. She seems to be making herself at home and I can't get over how good that looks.

"No wonder you're such a sweet girl, with the way you doctor your coffee up like that," I tease her, wrapping an arm around her waist. I can feel her body tense under my touch.

"Baby, what's wrong?" Total panic sets in as I think of every single thing that could possibly have caused her discomfort. Is the milk sour? I don't drink it often, so it does expire on occasion. Is she sore from last night? Maybe I bruised her, and it hurt when I touched her.

I immediately drop my hands and apologize. "No, Keaton. It's fine. It's just," she takes a deep breath in and lets it out heavily. "My old boss used to call me that, and it just gives me the creeps. I know you didn't mean anything by it, but I'd much rather you call me Baby."

I press a kiss to her forehead, breathing her in while thinking that I may need to pay her former boss a visit if he ever made her the least bit uncomfortable. "Alright, Baby, I think I can manage that."

We dive into our pancakes, both of us opting to drown ours in syrup. It's really the only way. When she bites into a piece of her bacon and lets out a seductive moan, my pants tighten to the point of discomfort. "Keaton, if I knew you could cook like this, I'd have stopped in for breakfast ages ago." I smile at her compliment, and we continue our conversation until our plates are clean. Leaning back in my chair, I'm eager to ask Anna what she wants to do today, but she's biting her lip like she's upset about something.

"Baby, I really am sorry. I would never have said it if I had any idea that it made you uncomfortable."

"Oh, it isn't that. I'm just still a bit hungry," she confesses, standing up and walking around the table.

"Oh, well I can make some more pancakes. Or there's cereal in the pantry you could..." Words escape me as Anna is suddenly on her knees in front of me. Her small hands run up my thighs as her tongue flicks out to lick her lips.

"I don't want more pancakes or cereal, Keaton. I just want you." She reaches into the sweatpants I tossed on this morning and pulls out my cock, already hard just from being in the same room as her. "You think you can just parade around in these gray sweatpants of yours, showing off that impressive erection, and I'm not going to do anything about it?" She runs her tongue up my length, and I about fall out of my fucking chair. "Well then you don't know your wife very well, do you?"

Her mouth works its magic, licking and sucking like I'm her favorite piece of candy and her hunger is insatiable. She flicks her tongue over my tip, catching the precum that's built up and then makes a show of swallowing. "Mmm, Keaton, you're the best thing I've ever tasted."

I pull her to me, crashing my lips to hers and exploring her mouth. I pick up a hint of my own taste, the maple flavor of the syrup, but it's her sweetness that consumes me. My hands find themselves under the shirt of mine she has on, finding her completely bare underneath.

"Are you fucking telling me that you were sitting across from me this entire time with nothing covering this sweet pussy of yours?" I slap my hand against it, making her buck in my arms and releasing a moan that has me slapping against her again. "Do you like when I spank this pussy of yours, Wife?"

Anna's head falls into my shoulder and her head bobs against me.

"Thought it was your pussy, Husband."

I smile at her cheekiness as I push two fingers inside of her soaked entrance and groan. "You're right, this is my pussy, and it's fucking drenched. Did you enjoy sucking my cock? Is that why you're so wet for me, Baby?" I feel her nod again as I add a third finger inside, pumping in and out in a rhythm that has her grinding against me.

"Unbutton that shirt for me, Baby." She does what I ask as she continues riding my fingers, exposing her breasts and then moving her hands to them to explore. She's so fucking hot like this with her head thrown back, seeking out her pleasure. I pull my fingers from her and the whimper she releases makes me grin. Anna loves it when I'm inside her, and I'm willing to give her everything she wants.

Sucking off her taste, I don't hold back how much I enjoy it. I want her to see how much I desire her. "So fucking sweet, Baby." Her tongue darts out and wets her bottom lip and I drink the movement in. When she shifts on my lap, I catch a glimpse of something behind her, and I smile as an idea begins to form.

I give her no warning as I lift from my chair, pushing Anna back against the table in the process and then slamming my cock deep inside of her. "You taste so fucking good, Baby, but let's see if we can sweeten you up." I grab the syrup bottle, and she tracks my movement as I drizzle the sticky substance over her nipples. Leaning down I suck the left one into my mouth, completely coating it with my tongue so I don't leave any of the sweet liquid behind. I repeat my actions with the right one, all the while pumping my dick in and out of her.

"You're the best fucking thing I've ever tasted, Baby."

Her eyes roll back into her head, and I know she's close. I bring her right nipple back into my mouth and suck it, pressing my teeth into it slightly and sending her over the edge.

"Oh my god, Keaton. Oh my god," Anna cries out, the most glorious sound I've ever heard in my life.

"Oh my god," a deep, grumpy voice growls from behind me.

"Oh my god!" Anna cries, but this time it's not in pleasure. I use my body to cover the delectable curves of her body that are currently on display.

Why the fuck is my brother standing in my kitchen this morning?

"Who's that, Daddy?"

And why the fuck did he bring his daughter with him?

Chapter Twenty-Eight

Anna

"A re you homeless?" The small child sitting next to me on the couch looks up and asks. Lincoln's daughter is adorable, with his same honey brown locks braided into pigtails, freckles dotting her cheeks and the bridge of her nose, and those beautiful blue eyes all the Fisher men were blessed with.

"Excuse me?"

"Are you homeless? If you are, Daddy and I make blessing bags to keep in the car. We hand them out when we see people who look like they could use a little help. I can get you one, if you want." I smile at the thought of grumpy Lincoln building these bags with his daughter and handing them out to others. Sometimes the biggest grumps have the biggest hearts.

"Oh, I'm not homeless." I assure her.

"You sure? You were wearing one of Uncle Keaton's shirts and you're in his home. If you don't have your own clothes or house, then you're probably homeless. And that's okay. Daddy says sometimes people get down on their luck and go through trying times, but it doesn't mean they're bad people. They just need a little help, is all. Do you need a little help?"

I think I love this little Fisher with a huge heart.

"You know what, I could use your help with something." She straightens up, trying to make herself bigger, prepared for any task I throw her way. "I was trying to decide what to watch, and I just can't figure out what would be good."

Those blue eyes of hers light up and she begins to bounce. "My Little Pony! It's the best. Here, I know how to turn it on. Uncle Keaton showed me." She grabs the remote from the coffee table and works the system like a professional. "My name is Charlie. I'm six. Your turn."

It takes me a second to process what she's said, so she stops her search, staring at me with raised eyebrows and a "get on with it" expression. This kid is funny. "Oh, I'm Anna. I'm thirty."

"Whoa," she takes a second to process the information, her lips making a perfect circle. "That's so old. Is that why your boobies are so big? Because they've had so long to grow? I asked my Daddy when I would grow boobies. He said we don't talk about boobies. What was it like when you were a kid? Were there dinosaurs? Were all your tv shows in black and white? Sometimes my Grammy likes to watch tv shows in black and white. They're real boring."

"Charlie." Lincoln's gruff voice startles both of us girls as he and Keaton walk back into the room. I can't find it in me to look at my brother-in-law. After he caught us in the kitchen, fortunately shielding Charlie's view from seeing the sticky situation Keaton and I had gotten ourselves into, I went back upstairs to make myself a bit more presentable to hang out with the kid. I have no doubt that he saw a few things before I managed to clean myself up and I have no idea how to act normal around him now.

"We're heading home. Let's go." Charlie wasn't having it.

"Why? We just got here. Anna and I were going to watch My Little Pony, and Daddy, guess what..." She pauses for dramatic effect, "She's thirty."

He snorts, clearly amused by his offspring. "Is she now? That's all fascinating, but we've got to get back to Grammy and make sure she's okay. Uncle Keaton and Anna are going to come over to our place."

I stare at Keaton. Apparently, he's made plans for us today. And apparently those plans involve me meeting his mother.

"But Daddy, this is the bestest episode, and Anna needs to watch it. We're best friends now."

"Best friends, you say?" Lincoln asks. "Guess I'll just have to let Uncle Cam know that when he comes over, too." Charlie's eyes grow wide, and she tosses the remote before leaping from the couch and bouncing over to her dad, who lifts her upon impact.

"Uncle Cam is going to be there? He's my favorite!" Lincoln shoots a smirk over at Keaton.

"Thanks, Pip. What about me?" Keaton asks, his hand over his heart as though he's wounded. The look on his face tells me this isn't the first time Charlie's broken this news to him.

She just shrugs at him and then fires a million questions at Lincoln as he walks them out the door. "Can we do the fire pit tonight? I want marshmallows. But can you not catch it on fire this time?" As her voice trails off, I turn to look at Keaton, who has his hand on the back of his neck and a sheepish look on his face.

"So, umm, how would you feel about meeting my mom?"

We pull up to the incredible farmhouse that Keaton grew up in. The white board and batten siding has been well maintained and is crisp and striking with the black trim, accents, and roof. Natural wood posts flank the large, covered porch where a set of black rocking chairs are featured. Beautiful blue hydrangea bushes and hostas in the front, welcome you to the home. You can just feel that this is a happy place to be and I'm so thankful Keaton is sharing it with me.

"This place is stunning."

Keaton snorts in confirmation, "It wasn't always like this. Lincoln has really fixed it up and it's come a long way. He's trying so hard to make it a perfect home for Charlie and every time he feels he strikes out in one area, he makes up for it in another."

"What do you mean?" I ask.

"Lincoln feels guilty for Charlie growing up without her mother. He's been in the dating game for a long time, but when you live in a small town, you exhaust your options pretty quickly. Women from out of town know his name because of his bank account, and well, he gets a lot of first dates, but they show their true intentions and rarely get a second. Every time he goes on a bad date, the house gets a nice little addition. That's how Charlie got a pool last year."

"What happened to Charlie's mom?" I ask hesitantly. I don't want to pry into Lincoln's life, but I guess he's technically my brother now, too, so I'm genuinely curious.

"She took off when Charlie was born. When they were discharged from the hospital, Lincoln was prepared to take them both to his place, but she insisted on driving her car. Nicole said she'd meet him and Charlie there, but she never showed up. He was a mess, worried she had wrecked, or something awful had happened to her. She finally texted him the next day and said she just wasn't ready to be a mom, but knew he'd be a great dad." Keaton looks over at me. "He is, you know? He loves her so much and I know if I'm ever lucky enough to have a child of my own, Linc will give me the best advice."

Seeing how much Keaton cares for his family makes me love him that much more. My voice is quiet. "So, you want kids?"

He chuckles lightly. "I know it's something people usually talk about before they get married, but yeah, I really do. I turned forty this year, so I'd like to start sooner rather than later, but I'd wait if you weren't ready yet, Anna. And if you decide that's not something you want, I'd respect that, too."

My heart is pounding in my chest as I realize what this beautiful man just confessed. "You want kids with *me*?"

"I want everything with you, Anna." He leans over and places the softest kiss on my lips. It isn't enough, so I wrap my arms around his neck and pull him closer, strengthening the kiss between us until he pulls back and lets out a laugh.

"As much as I would love to start on the baby making, Baby, can we maybe not do it in the car right outside my mom's house?" I let out a laugh and allow him to escape my hold. Then we head inside so I can meet the first woman he ever loved.

Chapter Twenty-Nine
Keaton

Nerves build in my gut, knowing I'm about to have the two most important women in my life meet one another. I just hope my mom is the incredible woman I got to grow up with and not the shell of the broken one we've had these past several years.

While I was initially furious with my brother for barging into my house and seeing parts of my wife no other man should ever see, I couldn't blame him after I heard what was going on.

"She won't get out of bed, Keat. She's soiled herself multiple times these past few days because she refuses to move. She won't talk to me. She won't even talk to Charlie. I clean her up. I feed her. And I'm tired. I'm so fucking tired. But I do it anyway because I can't lose her. We can't lose her, Keat."

He may be a complete ass most of the time, but I admire the hell out of my brother. Lincoln moved back into our childhood home the same month that Nicole had skipped out. At first Mama was amazing. We still couldn't get her to leave the house, but she took care of Charlie when Lincoln had to work and made sure he knew how to be the best father. Things were great for a long while, but when Charlie started Kindergarten this past year, Mama took a turn for the worse. It's been hell on all of us, but Lincoln bears the brunt of it.

I realize it isn't fair to let Anna walk in without knowing what she might see on the other side of those big double doors. "Anna," I begin to warn her as we step up on the large wraparound porch, but I don't have the chance to give her a heads-up thanks to the tiny spitfire who has now joined us.

"It's about time you show up. You're old and slow." Charlie quips and I can't help but smile at my filter-lacking niece.

"Charlene Elizabeth Fisher," Lincoln bellows from inside the house. "Don't be fucking rude."

"Ooo you just got full-named, Pipsqueak." I snatch her up and dangle her in my arms, holding her upside down. "You better behave. In fact, you should be extra nice to Anna because she's extra special." I smile over at Anna, and she looks at me curiously.

Charlie squirms in my arms, but her giggles let me know she loves our interaction. "What makes her extra special?"

"Well, you see, Pip, Anna is my wife." I look between my two girls as both of their jaws drop. Charlie shocks me with a hell of a lift to right herself and then demands I let her go. She runs off to the kitchen hollering out for her dad, no doubt giving him the news I just dropped on her. Secret keeping isn't a strong suit of hers.

"Keaton," Anna hisses, "you really think this is the time to announce to your family that we're actually married?" She looks so cute with her brows furrowed and her I can't help but give her scrunched up nose a kiss.

"I think it's the perfect time. I want everyone to know who you are to me, Anna."

"Well, I personally think the timing is a bit late." I turn and can't help but feel my face light up as I take in my mother. Today is a good day.

She's not only gotten herself out of bed, but she's showered and done her hair and makeup. She's wearing white pants with a hot pink top and her signature earrings she always used to wear. It was always a highlight of our day growing up to see which pair Mama chose for the day. Today she went with a pair of sparkly flamingos.

"Mama, I want you to meet Anna Keith, my wife. Anna, this is my mom, Sharon."

"Keith?" She raises her eyebrows and looks between the two of us. "You kept your last name?"

"Oh, it's just," Anna stumbles over her words, "you see, we didn't really plan on getting married and so, well, I just didn't, I mean, I haven't..."

Mama smiles at Anna and goes over to embrace her in a hug. "You have every right to keep your name as it is, take his, or change it to something like Glitter Shimmertits. I was just teasing you a bit to properly welcome you into this family." Mama steps back from the hug and loops her arm with Anna's. "Now, come sit down with me and let's chat long enough to make my son squirm."

Anna smiles over at me and then follows the woman who raised me into the living room.

Nothing good can come from the two of them talking about my childhood, but I decide it's best to leave the two of them to chat and get to know one another. I go off to the kitchen, finding my brother making burger patties. I head over to the sink to wash up and help him. "Mama looks good."

Lincoln nods, "When I came back home, I walked into her room, and she looked like she was on her deathbed. About made a call to the damn coroner. I told her you and Cam were gonna come over for dinner and she didn't move or open her eyes. Nothing. But then I mentioned you were bringing a woman along. She blinked up at me but didn't speak. So, I added the little fact that you had gotten married out in Vegas to this woman, and I couldn't cover my ears in time for the shriek that woman let out. I don't know where her strength came from, but she pushed me off the damn bed and told me to get the hell out of her room so she could get ready to meet her daughter-in-law."

"I'm glad Anna's magic works on someone other than just me. Seriously though, I hope she lasts like this for a while. It's so good to see her up and moving around. I've missed her."

"Holy hell," Cam moves into the kitchen, sitting grocery bags of chips and buns on the counter. "Mama looks good."

Lincoln nodded, "Who knew it just took one of us fuckers getting married to do the trick?"

Lincoln fires up the grill as Cam and I set everything else up for tonight. Charlie is running around the backyard darting between the Halloween inflatables they recently set up. Mama and Anna continue to talk like they're the best of friends. This feels really fucking good.

"Supper's ready!" Lincoln hollers out. I run inside to the kitchen to grab the jar of pickles I know Anna will be looking for and Mama stops to give me a kiss on my cheek.

"You and Anna seem to have been getting along," I say to her.

"Oh, she is just the sweetest thing. And so pretty, too. No wonder you had to get her drunk to marry you." Mama's teasing is one of the things I've missed most about her, and I can't help the huge grin at having both my mother and my wife back in my life.

"It just took a few lemon drops and a quick trip to Paris and I had it in the bag," I wink at Mama.

"She's really lovely, Keat, and I think you somehow managed to find the one woman put on this earth just for you." Her sweet face grows serious. "But she has demons, Keaton. Be prepared for them."

Chapter Thirty

Anna

1 0 1 0 0
1 1 0 0 1
0 0 1 1 0 0 0 0 0
1 0 0 0 0 1 1
0 1 0 1
0 1 0 1

We've been sitting around the fire pit after a delicious meal, sipping on ciders and beers as Charlie catches lightning bugs around the backyard. Everyone's been telling stories, mostly at Keaton's expense, and I laugh for what must be the thousandth time tonight. It has been the most incredible evening being here with Keaton' family. My family now, I suppose.

"Well," Camden stands up and stretches, "I'm gonna head on home. I have a case that I need to try and work on some before I call it a night." We say our goodbyes as he leaves, and Sharon excuses herself to head to bed, too.

"Come on, Little Bit," Lincoln hollers at Charlie. "Time to wash up and get in bed." Charlie bounces over to him with her little mason jar full of the critters she's managed to catch tonight. Once Lincoln's convinced her to release them, which is mighty impressive after that bottom lip of hers stuck out the way it did, he picks her up to pack her inside for the night.

"You headed out?" he asks his brother.

"We will be in just a bit," Keaton says while taking my hand, "I think we're gonna sit and enjoy the fire a little longer."

Lincoln gives a scowl before he shakes his head and goes inside with his daughter, leaving me and Keaton alone outside.

He tugs at my hand he's holding, pulling me closer to him. "I need you closer. You've been too far away from me all night."

I stand up and walk over to him, still holding his hand. "I've been sitting beside you this whole time. Just how much closer do you want me to be?"

Keaton jerks me harder until I'm straddling one of his legs. "Sit," he commands, and I do as I'm told. "You can never be close enough, Anna. I've watched how amazing you've been all night. I know you weren't prepared to meet my entire family today, but you completely captivated every single one of them. Mama, well, she's not like that most days. In fact, we haven't seen her like this in years. You helped her shine tonight, Baby. I'm so thankful for that. I'm so in love with you." He pushes on my thighs so I'm pressed into him.

The movement feels so damn good. He isn't wrong. I may have been beside him all night, but I've missed the nearness we've had since last night. A rush of desire comes over me and we need to get home. Now. "Keaton, take me home. I need you."

"Ride me, Baby." He grips my hips, thrusting me against his thigh and I somehow manage to hold back my whimper.

"Are you crazy?" I whisper-shout at him. "Your mother, brother, and niece are just inside."

"I'm crazy about you." He kisses me, all the while pushing me so that I'm rubbing in just the right way against him, sending tingles throughout my entire body. "Now fucking ride me. Get that cunt of yours, the one I know is dripping for me, and ride my fucking thigh. I want to see you take your pleasure."

When he takes that demanding tone, this man could convince me to go grocery shopping naked on a Sunday after church. I start to rock back and forth against him, unable to keep my noises contained as pleasure begins to coil its way through my body. Why is this so fucking hot? I haven't dry humped anybody since high school and I know it didn't feel this damn good.

"That's right, Baby. You want to come so fucking bad, don't you? Then be a good girl and chase that orgasm. Grind that clit against me." His dirty words spur me on and I pick up my pace.

"Keaton, this feels so good. I'm so close." I continue rocking over him and reach down to grab the bulge that's formed in his pants. He lets out a moan that almost brings me to orgasm from the intensity of it.

"Fuck, Baby, you look so hot like this. That wet spot you're leaving on me is gonna make me come in my pants like I'm a fucking teenager." I grind harder, hitting my bud against him so perfectly that I'm about to tip over the edge. "That's it, Baby. Keep going, Anna. Be a good wife and come for your husband."

My orgasm rips through me and Keaton kisses me to quiet my sounds. He shudders beneath me and when I look down, I see the evidence of his pleasure on the crotch of his army green britches. We sit like that for several moments, me still straddled over his leg with my head resting on his shoulder, and him with his arms wrapped around me and his head resting against mine. The fire crackles behind us as it dies down.

"Sounds like the two of you both finished," we hear Lincoln's voice from somewhere in the house, "so be sure to lock up before you leave."

"You and Mama seemed to have a lot to talk about." Keaton glances over at me in the truck on the way home. His face is only lit by the dim lights of the dash and it's still enough to take my breath away.

"She's amazing," I gush. "We talked about how we met, of course. Then she asked questions about me and my family. I told her how I enjoyed photography and would love to take some pictures of her place, and she welcomed me to come out anytime. Things got a bit sad when she was telling me about how much you're like your dad and I thought I lost her there for a moment."

Keaton lets out a heavy sigh. "My senior year of high school, my dad died in a car crash. Just some random accident and a case of being in the wrong place at the wrong time. To say Mama was devastated is the understatement of the century.

"She mourned just like the rest of us where she had moments of rage and moments of sadness. But on the day of the funeral, it's like she went numb. She detached from us. Disconnected. My dad was the only one in the car when he passed, but it was like we had lost both of them."

"That's awful," I say quietly. "And you were all still children. You still needed her."

He nods in agreement. "We would speak to her, but the conversations were always one-sided. She would occasionally have friends over, or would meet them out, but then she started canceling her plans. She stopped taking their calls or responding to their messages. One day it was all too much for her, and we ended up in the hospital. After that, it was like a world without my father was a world she didn't want to be a part of, so she went home and never left."

"What do you mean?" I ask, confused.

"I told you earlier that Mama isn't typically like the way you saw her tonight. The truth is that she hasn't left the house in years. Hell, the reason Lincoln was over at our place this morning was because he couldn't even get her out of bed."

He looks over at me before turning his eyes back to the road. "Tonight was the first night in forever we've seen her look like herself."

"So, what was different about tonight?" I ask and he smiles.

"You."

Chapter Thirty-One

Anna

I try to imagine a world in which Sharon Fisher doesn't light up the way she did tonight. She's stunning and there's no wonder how she managed to birth three of the most handsome men I've ever laid eyes on, particularly the one with several flecks of silver running through his hair and beard. But I saw the darkness Keaton was talking about. I saw it ripple through her when she spoke of her late husband. And I know she saw it in me, too, when a message came through on my phone. Even though I had blocked him, Daniel managed to find a way around that.

Unknown Number

> Oh, stupid Anna. You thought blocking my number was going to keep me away from you?

Unknown Number

> I was looking forward to seeing you at the golf event today. Imagine my surprise when dear old dad said you had something else to do instead.

I had been looking for an excuse to give my parents for skipping out on my dad's annual charity event and when Keaton had asked me to meet his family tonight, it was the out I needed. Those events are boring as hell. The men go out to the greens and blame their clubs or caddies whenever their game is off. Meanwhile, the women stay in the club drinking tea, while spilling it, too. Nobody likes to gossip quite like the wife of a golfer. They love to whisper about who is having an affair, whose company is struggling, and who has gotten fat. Then they barrage me with backhanded compliments to make themselves feel better in their bodies.

Oh, Anna, your face looks a bit thinner. You must tell me about the diet you're on.

You and I both know I'm not on a damn diet, Patty, now leave me the hell alone.

I pull up my phone and see he left multiple messages. Typically, he stops at just one or two, getting a dig in about my size or stupidity, or leaving a crude and vulgar message that has my stomach turning. Tonight my stomach is turning for different reasons. Of course he calls me stupid and sends a dick pic, but it's the threats that come in this text chain that have me squirming in Keaton's passenger seat.

Unknown Number

> I sure hope that new boss of yours isn't overworking you. I can't imagine why else you wouldn't want to come see me today.

Unknown Number

> Maybe you just need to see what you're missing. Do you miss having my fat dick

pressed up against you? Wait until it's shoved down that ungrateful little throat of yours.

Unknown Number

[Image]

Unknown Number

I'll see you soon, sweet girl. And this time you won't be able to come up with some stupid excuse to get away from me.

Unknown Number

Oh, and don't try to be cute again and block this number, stupid girl. You're already owed multiple punishments. We don't want that fat ass of yours too sore, do we?

"Everything okay?" Keaton asks and I realize my breathing has become ragged. There's a tightness in my chest and the taste of bile is creeping up my throat.

I want to tell Keaton what's going on. He's so understanding and surely would listen to what I have to say. He would believe me when I tell the truth about the messages and Daniel's actions. But a part of me can't help but think he may be like my dad and the thousands of other men who would blame me in this situation. The men who would say I was asking for it because of the way I dressed or whatever fucking bullshit reason they give to defend their beloved predators. So I keep quiet, give him a small smile and tell my husband the first lie in our marriage.

"I'm fine."

Monday mornings and I are not typically friends, but I can't complain about waking up in Keaton's arms. "Good morning, beautiful." His sweet words have me snuggling into him and I hate that the workweek is so much longer than the weekends. Staying in bed with Keaton sounds like a dream day, but alas, responsibilities call.

"I wish we could just stay like this. Do we have to go in?" I whine.

"Well, fortunately I know the boss. So maybe we can be a little late." Keaton captures my lips in a sweet, steamy kiss before pushing me onto my back. His lips trail down and pepper me in kisses down my neck and to my breasts where he gives plenty of attention. I knew from the moment we met that Keaton was a boob man, and since I have plenty to offer, I'm not complaining.

His tongue grazes over my nipples as his hands explore my soft stomach. Maybe it's the fact that I feel so damn good right now, or just the fact that I trust this man and believe him when he says he loves my body, but I don't try and pull away from his touch.

His hands reach down and spread my thighs apart and he moves lower to place delicate kisses along my thighs. Sleeping with Keaton is amazing, but waking up with him is fucking fabulous.

"Keaton!" I gasp just as he slips his tongue into my cunt, teasing it with his movements. My hands find the back of his head and make fists in his hair, bringing him closer to where I need his attention, then rocking my body to quicken the pace.

"Mmm, yes!" I cry out. "That feels so good, Keat, please give me more."

"Yes, Baby. Tell me what else you like." Keaton purrs, bending his head back down to resume his position.

"That right there feels so good." He slides his tongue back inside me. "And when you flick your tongue over my clit it feels amazing, too." Keaton moves his tongue the way I described, and I realize he's handing the reins over to me this morning. I've always been more submissive in bed, believing that if I do as I'm told it will make up for my body not being what he really wants. But Keaton allowing me to be the dominant one this morning gives me a rush, and I can't wait to see how far I can take us with me in charge.

"You're such a good boy, making my pussy wet like that. Push a finger inside, then show me just how wet I am." Keaton groans against me, the bristles of his beard brushing against my pussy in a way that sends vibrations up my body. Slowly he pushes his thick finger inside me, and just as gradually pulls it from my core, bringing it up so that it glistens in the sunlight streaming through the window. Keaton brings my wetness closer to my face and then brushes his soaked finger against my lips. My curious tongue explores the taste, but then Keaton crushes his lips against mine to devour the rest.

"You're doing so good, Baby. Keep telling me what you want," he whispers in between kisses.

I want this. I want him to keep ravaging my mouth until neither one of us can breathe. But I also want him, I need him, inside of me.

"I want you to take that glorious cock of yours and fuck me so hard I soak the sheets."

He gives me a wicked grin. "As you wish, wife."

My previous position on Monday mornings has been extinguished. They are infinitely better when they're kicked off with a sweaty sex session with my husband.

The past two weeks have been incredible. Each night I make love to my husband and then I wake up in his arms every morning. We finally decided it was time to officially move me out of the guest house and into his place, and we're down to the last of the things that need to be transferred.

"I just have a few things hanging up in the closet I want to be sure to grab. Do you mind getting those?" I stuff the last of my clothes from the dresser into a box.

"What the fuck?" Keaton growls before walking out of the small space with a box in his hands. A black box with a gold bow.

Shit. Fuck. Shit. I forgot all about that stupid box from that stupid man who still won't leave me alone.

"I can explain." I try to say, but before I can provide an explanation for what he's holding in his hands, pain settles in my chest, and I can't breathe.

"Fuck, Baby, sit down." Keaton crosses the room, pushing lightly against my shoulders until I'm forced to have a seat on the edge of the bed. "Breathe, Anna. Deep breath in. 1. 2. 3. 4. 5. Now out. 1. 2. 3. 4. 5. Good job. Just keep breathing." He runs his hands up and down my arms, relaxing me as I attempt to mimic his breaths.

"That's a good girl. Calm down for me, Baby. It's okay. Everything's going to be okay."

But I shake my head. It's not okay. The things Daniel has done to me are not okay. The fact that he still won't leave me the fuck alone is not okay. "You know how I told you my former boss gave me the creeps?" My words come out shaky, but Keaton must understand because he gives me a nod. "Well, he sometimes messages me things. Like, really bad things."

Keaton's nostrils flare and his face turns red, but he doesn't say anything. He waits and he listens, so I continue, "And the night before I moved here, my dad invited him over for family dinner.

When we left, he gave me that box. I didn't know what to do with it, so I just shoved it in the closet. I'm so sorry." I begin to sob, and Keaton softens.

"Anna, you have nothing to be sorry for. You did nothing wrong." He holds me as I cry into his chest. "He's going to stop, Baby. He's going to leave you alone. For good."

I let the words of the man I love sink in and it feels so good to believe him.

"I'm going to kill him. I'm going to fucking murder Daniel Brenner." I'm pacing back and forth in my home office. After sending Anna upstairs for a bath followed by bed, I called my brothers and told them what was going on. Lincoln had Charlie and couldn't come over, but Cam lives next door and showed up in under five minutes.

"As your attorney I'm gonna need you to not say shit like that in front of me," Camden says and I glare at him.

"Am I just supposed to let him get away with this? He's a fucking pervert and he's harassing her." I fall into the chair behind my desk, furious with what Anna has had to deal with and feeling completely helpless about it all.

"With the messages he has sent her, there's enough here for her to press charges. If she wants, I can get the paperwork ready for her to file for a protective order. But I'm just going to let you know that with a man like that, this is gonna get messy. And it's gonna go public."

Fuck. The last thing I want is for Anna to have to deal with any of this shit. "Wait, she mentioned that this guy is best friends with her dad. What if we told him what was going on?"

"I think that's something you should probably discuss with your wife." I run my hand down my face in frustration.

"Listen Keat," Camden continues, "it's late and it sounds like you and Anna have both had a rough day. Let me investigate this and see what I can come up with. We'll start fresh in the morning."

I walk my youngest brother to the door and lock things up for the night. Then I head upstairs and crawl into bed where Anna has already passed out for the night. She looks so peaceful, and I can't help but think she doesn't deserve to be dealing with the shit that she's been through. *You were part of that shit.* I kiss the top of her head and settle in beside her. As sleep begins to pull me under, I remember what Mama told me. Maybe Daniel Brenner is the demon Anna is dealing with. It was time to decode my wife's secrets and make sure they couldn't hurt her anymore.

Anna woke up before me, and I met her in the kitchen before work. It's been a week since I discovered that fucking box in her closet and we're not any closer to taking down the asshole causing a disruption in Anna's life. Now that I know about it, I see the way she hesitates when checking her phone. I hate that she's been living in fear of him and I want nothing more than to see it go away for good.

"It smells delicious in here," I say, sniffing the cinnamon in the air. I grab Anna's waist and pull her into me. "It must be you." I bring her lips to mine and taste the sweetness I constantly crave. She kisses me back before playfully pushing me away.

"I woke up craving cinnamon rolls, so I made some." She says, explaining the strong aroma in the kitchen. Wait. Did she say craving?

"Umm, you were craving something? And you have buns in the oven?" I stare at her in disbelief. I know she said she was on birth control, but the way the two of us have been going at it lately, I wouldn't be surprised if one of my swimmers went for the gold.

"What are you talking about?" She asks as I slide my hand to her stomach and press in. "Oh! No! No, not that. This is not an announcement, I swear." I can't say that I'm not a little disappointed she isn't currently carrying my child, but I can't say I'm not relieved either. Even though we've officially been married almost three months, there's still so much I need to learn about my wife.

"But," she says, biting that fucking bottom lip of hers. "Maybe one day."

I smile at my gorgeous girl. "Definitely one day, Baby."

She gives me one more kiss before going over to the oven and pulling out some sinfully delicious looking cinnamon rolls. As she sits them on the counter, she grabs her camera that was sitting on the counter. I notice how she's staged the island with a simple white plate that has a dusting of cinnamon sugar. It sits on one of my plaid flannel shirts and there are some wooden beads that flow around it.

Carefully extracting one of the hot rolls from the pan, she sits it on the plate gently as though she's performing major surgery. She steps back, angles her camera, and clicks. She snaps a few pictures before going through and seeing her work, a smile spreading on her face. Anna happy is the most beautiful thing I've ever seen.

"Let me see, Baby." She passes the camera over and pride swells in my chest. She's good. Like really fucking good. I can see her being able to make a career out of her passion, and I would fully support her if that's what she wanted.

"You made these look even better than in real life. And they look really fucking delicious." I pluck a hot roll out of the pan with my fingers, instantly regretting it as the hot icing drips down my hand. "Shit, that's hot."

Anna puts her camera back down on the counter and rushes to my side, grabbing my hand and assessing it like she has a medical degree. "Hmm," she hums. "It doesn't appear to be burned too badly, but I think I have a remedy that will help take that pain away."

She pulls my hand closer to her, then her tongue flicks out and licks the icing from my middle finger. "Oops, missed some," the seductress whispers breathily before sucking the same digit into her mouth. Her movements have my cock standing at attention, begging for it to be next in line. But all too soon, Anna pulls away and smiles up at me.

"Oh, Mr. Fisher. We keep getting ourselves into these sticky situations."

Chapter Thirty-Three

Anna

Anna

> Keaton knows.

I've been on edge all week waiting for Keaton to go off the rails and hunt Daniel down. I know he was furious when I told him about the messages and why that fucking box was in my closet, and it's awful to think this, but my goodness was he hot as hell in that moment. Knowing he was mad for me. That he wanted to avenge me. That he would do anything for me. It got me all kinds of hot and bothered to see how much he genuinely cares. But now I need some advice, so I turn to the girls who help me through it all.

Jasmine

> Oh good, Keaton knows. I'm so glad HE knows. Do you mind letting the rest of us know?

Skyla

> Calm down, Jaz. Grab a Snickers. You sound hangry.

Penny

Everything okay over there, Jaz?

Jasmine

Ugh, sorry guys. It's just that I've been dealing with this new client who is absolutely driving me insane. I didn't mean to take over your conversation with my problems, Anna.

Penny

But now you've got us all curious. What does Keaton know?

Anna

About Daniel. He found something that Daniel gave me and I told him everything.

Well, not everything. I haven't told anybody about my last day in his office and that's a memory I want to completely block out and forget it ever happened. Denial may be a river in Africa, but it's also my current residence.

Jasmine

Wait, other than the creeps, what did Daniel give you?

Anna

Let's just say it was a goodbye "gift" I definitely didn't want.

Penny

Omg, how did Keaton take it?

Anna

He was livid.

Jasmine

What? Let me see the earliest flight I can get so I can come dickpunch that son of a bitch.

Penny

I cannot believe he got angry at you for what that creep was doing. Get me a ticket, too, Jaz. Sounds like I owe him a dickpunch, too.

Anna

What? No! He wasn't mad at me. He was livid with Daniel.

Anna

And stop with all the dickpunching. Nobody is getting near my husband's dick but me.

Skyla

Yes! Those are the spicy details we want. Tell us what you're doing with your husband's dick!

Jasmine

For the love of Dolly Parton, do not talk to us about your husband's dick.

Anna

Absolutely not.

Penny

No thank you!

Skyla

Party poopers.

I shake my head at my friend's silliness. God, I miss them so much. One big trip and a handful of get-togethers throughout the year is just not enough time with these ladies.

Penny

So, is there anything he can do to help you stop him? Did the two of you talk about solutions?

Anna

Well, Cam told us that we could press charges, but that Daniel is likely to blow things up and cause a scene. So now we're looking for strategies that won't have everything blowing up in my face.

Skyla

Is Cam the grumpy, tatted Daddy? Or is he the Clark Kent looking one?

I smirk at the description she gives Keaton's brothers. She's not wrong.

Anna

Clark Kent

Skyla

Ooo, smart and sexy! Hook a girl up!!

Jasmine

For crying out loud, Sky. Can't you keep it in your pants?

Skyla

> Ugh, that's the only place it's been. I'm in a dry spell because I'm cute, but chubby and nobody wants to love me. So, leave me alone and let me daydream about Superman.

I'm once again shaking my head at my friend when Keaton walks by my desk. "What's so funny?"

"Just talking with my friends, I answer. "By the way, have you ever noticed how much Camden resembles Clark Kent?"

"Huh. I've never thought about it, but I guess I can see it. Good to know that I'm the superior superhero."

I crinkle my nose at him. "Oh, and who is that?"

"Isn't it obvious?" He lowers his voice and puffs out his chest. "I'm Batman."

Ugh. It's been a long ass week and even though it's Friday, there doesn't seem to be an end in sight. Keaton has had to work late the past two nights and has let me take his truck home early while he caught a ride with Lincoln. I've dozed off before he has made it home both nights now, and I miss him. It looks like another late night is in store for us, though.

My phone buzzes on my desk and with a yawn I pick it up and flip it over.

Unknown Number: It's been weeks, and I can't get your taste off my mind, sweet girl.

My mouth goes dry, and a rush of nausea comes over me. I make it to the bathroom just in time for my lunch from Pizza Papa to come up. Thankfully we have private bathrooms here, so nobody can see what a mess I am right now. Walking over to the sink, I wet a paper towel and put the cool, damp cloth on the back of my neck.

It's one thing for Daniel to send me the messages he does. But why did he have to send one that reminds me of the worst moment in my life? It takes several minutes for me to regain my composure and be ready to go back out and sit at my desk, but just as I'm about there, I literally run into my husband.

"Anna, Baby, what's wrong?" He whispers, a reminder that the staff doesn't know about our nuptials yet.

I sport a fake smile and in a high pitch I don't think has ever left my mouth before, I shriek that I'm fine. It's clear Keaton doesn't believe me, and I can't say I blame the man, but before he can demand the truth out of me Lincoln comes up behind us. "Keat, we need to go over these numbers."

My husband looks at me with a pained expression and this time I give him a real smile, albeit a very tiny one. He motions for his brother to go into his office and then he shuts the door. I sit at my desk and delete the vile message before blocking the new number. *Soon.* I tell myself. *This will all be over soon.*

"Miss Keith, can I see you in my office, please?" Keaton's voice is a bit louder than usual, and I note a few of our colleagues, well my colleagues, his employees, giving me the *ooo girl, you're in trouble* look.

When I hear the click of the door closing, horrible memories pop up. *He isn't Daniel. He won't hurt you. He loves you.*

I repeat the words I know are true in my head, but it doesn't stop me from jumping when Keaton's voice booms in the small space. "Bend over, put your hands on the desk and pull that skirt up, Baby."

"What? Why?" I ask, confused about what's going on.

"It's been too long since I've been inside you. I've missed you so much. I can't wait until we get home. I need you now."

I can hear the desperation in his voice, and any other time this would be hot as hell, but after the message and the memories, I can't help but see myself in Daniel's office.

"I...I can't." I stammer out. "I want to, but I can't do this, Keaton." Tears get stuck in my throat as I choke out his name.

"Hey," he comes over and pulls me to him in a hug. "Baby, shh. I'm sorry. I just wanted you so bad, but I didn't know trying something here in the office would make you upset like that. If you're not into public sex, that's fine. I'll wait. I'll wait for you, Anna."

His sweet understanding has me crying harder, drenching his crisp shirt that fits his impeccable body just right.

"Is something else wrong, Baby? Do you want to talk about it?" His hand strokes my hair as I cling to him like a fucking koala that can't be bothered to leave the tree. I shake my head and the incredible man I married just continues to hold me and tell me everything will be okay.

God, I hope he's right.

Chapter Thirty-Four
Keaton

A nna and I are a couple of hours later than usual when we pull into the parking lot of Phismerman's Cybersecurity, and I have no regrets. She has been extra emotional these past few weeks and I can't imagine the hell she's going through internally. Making love to her this morning was cathartic for the both of us and the need for each other was so strong we had to go for another session in the shower.

I look across the truck as she paints her lips with her signature dusty pink color. It may have just been moments ago that I was inside of her but if she'd let me, I would hike up that navy dress she's wearing and go for another round right here in the cab of this vehicle. The way she reacted in my office the other day tells me that's not going to go over well, so I adjust myself and try to calm the fuck down.

"What if we just go back home and stay in bed for the rest of the day?" I'm only half joking, but she grants me a smirk.

"It's a little late for that now. We're here, so we may as well go in. Besides, you have that meeting with Caruso Enterprises in ten minutes and they will not take kindly to being rescheduled."

I groan at the mention of our latest acquisition and the biggest pain in my ass. We're bending over backwards to provide them with every possible security measure they can dream of, but nothing we do is ever enough.

Giggling, Anna leans over and gives me a kiss. "Come on, hubby, let's go to work. As we walk into the office, I realize our hands are linked together and she's not pulling away. She isn't trying to run for me or hide that there's something between us, and this is the happiest I've been since our night in Sin City.

"It's about time the two of you showed up," Lincoln huffs, his permanent scowl is deeper today than usual. He runs his hand over his dark military cut and shakes his head, the motion allowing me to catch a glimpse of the tattoo on his neck peeking out. When he's at work, Lincoln wears long sleeves and long pants, but the man is completely covered in ink. "You seem to forget every time we have a meeting with this fucking company."

"I didn't forget. We got here just in time. Besides, what do you need me for? You could hold this meeting on your own."

He shakes his head at me. "Nope, you're the boss man. That's why you get paid the big bucks."

When I told my brothers about the business I wanted us to go in on together, it was my goal to split things amongst us equally. Camden was in college at the time and said he didn't deserve that since he couldn't afford to put into it. Lincoln claimed that since this company was my idea and I'm the one that brought them on board and provided them career opportunities, that I deserved to be the main shareholder. Technically I own forty percent of the company while each of my younger brothers owns thirty. Still, I have made it clear since day one that we are all equal, no matter what the numbers might say.

"You're just as much the boss as I am, Linc."

"And you *all* make the big bucks," Anna adds.

Lincoln rolls his eyes at us. "Just get your ass into the conference room." As he turns and walks away, I lean into the woman standing next to me.

"So glad he's in a good mood today," she giggles adorably and it makes me want to claim her right here in front of the entire office. Janine would be so fucking pissed. So instead of dealing with my chief people officer, I boop Anna on the nose and we go our separate ways.

"I'm so fucking done with them. Let's just cut our losses and tell them we can't work with them anymore." Usually Lincoln is the grump, but for some reason this fucking company gets under my skin. We've installed next-generation firewalls with intrusion prevention built-in. We've encrypted every single piece of data they've thrown at us. We even provided online training for their staff to prevent falling for phishing scams. Nothing we do is enough for Caruso Enterprises and it makes me wonder what exactly they're trying to keep hidden.

"They're the hottest thing in Vegas right now and that place is a fucking desert. If we can put up with their bullshit demands a while longer, you'll see it's all going to be worth it." I hate it when my brother is being reasonable. Sometimes I think he was meant to be the oldest of us siblings.

"Is it too early for bourbon?" I ask, needing something to calm me down after hearing about how our firewalls are inadequate and being told how we should run our business. If they think it's so fucking easy, why didn't they choose this field over their fucking slot machines?

Lincoln pours each of us a glass of Basil Hayden and sits in the leather chair beside me.

"How's mom?" I ask, feeling guilty that I haven't been out to see her in a few days.

"She's doing better, but still not great. Would probably love it if Anna came out and saw her again." I nod at that and smile, remembering how well the two of them got along.

"We can definitely do that. Anna's been itching to go out there and take some photos."

"I forgot she's into that. I may have to have her take some photos of Charlie. My Little Bit isn't so little anymore."

"How's the nanny search going?" I ask and he heaves out a stressed sigh.

"I'll admit that I'm extremely hesitant to just open the door for anyone when it comes to who is gonna spend the day with my girls, but it's slim pickings out there. To find someone who will sit with a reclusive woman and take on a rambunctious six-year-old is not proving to be easy. But Janine called me this morning and said she thinks she found the right one."

"That sounds promising," I say, straightening in my seat at the positive news. But Lincoln shrugs.

"I don't know about her. She's real young and fresh out of college. Mama might eat her alive." He takes a sip of his bourbon. "Janine did ask me if I had any secret wives out there that she needed to know about before she hired someone, though. Know anything about that?"

My brother smirks at me as I flip him the bird like the mature adult I am. We shoot the shit for a few more minutes, finishing up our drinks and genuinely enjoying each other's company. I really like my brother when he isn't being a grumpy asshole. Fine, I like him then too, but I like him more when he's like this.

"How are things with you and Anna?" he asks.

I can't help the smile that spreads across my face. "We're really fucking great. Things have been pretty awesome. She told me she loves me, ya know?"

He raises his glass at me in congratulations. "And you feel the same?" I smirk in his direction. "Yeah, I know you do. Happy for you, brother."

I make my way to the bathroom before heading to my office, but when I look at Anna, there's an older man standing in front of her.

Overall, he's got a slender frame, but there's a bit of a gut that's formed from either beer or age. His hair is slicked back and that dye job ain't fooling anybody. I look back at Anna's face and when I see it covered in fear, I know instantly who the man is that's way too close.

Daniel. Fucking. Brenner.

He reaches over her desk and runs his hand down her cheek.

"Get your fucking hands off my wife."

Chapter Thirty-Five
Anna

I saw Keaton step out of the conference room about thirty minutes ago looking like he'd gone ten rounds with Rocky Balboa. He and his brother were walking in the direction of Lincoln's office, presumably to complain about what happened on that call. I don't know many details about Caruso Enterprises, but I know they've been a pain in his ass since day one.

As I finish typing up the minutes I took during a meeting from earlier in the week when my desk phone rings.

"Hey, Anna. I hope you're having a good day so far." Chelsea, the receptionist at the front desk, is always so sweet. "I just wanted to let you know that there's a man on his way up to see you."

"Oh, well I hope he doesn't mind waiting. Mr. Fisher is currently in a meeting."

"He isn't here to see Mr. Fisher," she explains. "He clearly stated that you were the one he was looking for. Anyway, I just thought I'd give you the heads up. Have a great day, Anna." She ends the call and I hang up my phone wondering who in the hell would be here to see me.

"Hey, sweet girl." My spine stiffens at the sound of that voice. That name. I look up and standing directly in front of me is Daniel Brenner. "I told you I'd be seeing you soon."

I want to scream. I want to run away. But fear has me frozen in this fucking desk chair that digs into my sides. "I thought I told you not to block my new number, but you just had to go and disobey orders. Tell me, does your new boss know you're such a naughty girl?"

Keaton. I need Keaton. I shout his name over and over in my mind as though I have telepathic powers. Why are he and Lincoln taking so long? Why isn't he here already?

"Have you missed me, sweet girl?" Daniel asks, his voice sending a tidal wave of nausea crashing into me. Memories of being trapped in his office surface and I start to tremble. I shake my head, and Daniel reaches across my desk, running his hand down my cheek and catching my chin, squeezing to stop my motions. His spit lands on me when he says through gritted teeth, "Don't lie to me, you fat whore."

"Get your fucking hands off my wife."

I feel instant relief at the sound of my husband's voice. It's going to be okay. He's here and it's all going to be okay. But when I see that Daniel has only grown angrier, I should have known better.

"His what?" He roars, then lifts his hand and slaps me across the face so hard that all I can hear is a ringing in my ears.

Pain radiates through my face at the unexpected assault. A flash of dark hair and business attire is all I see before I hear the sound of bones crunching. Needing to know Keaton is okay, I pop up from my seat behind my desk to look down at the violent scene between my two bosses on the ground. There's blood on Daniel's face and on the tile floor, so I rush around to the other side of my desk. I need my eyes on Keaton. I need to know if he's okay. There's a river of blood flowing from Daniel's nose and I can see there's blood on Keaton's knuckles, but I can't make out if it's his own. The way he has Daniel in a hold and punching him repeatedly makes me think it isn't. Other than a look of fury that would send Attila the Hun running for his mommy, Keaton appears to be okay.

A few people in the office have gathered to see what the commotion is all about and I hear someone call for security, but my focus is on my husband. He doesn't need his employees to see him like this. He doesn't deserve Daniel to wreck his life the way he's done everything he can to wreck mine.

"Keaton!" I cry out, hoping to gain his attention, but he's lost to his rage, hitting Daniel relentlessly. "Keaton, please. It's Anna. Stop. Please." My voice must finally get through because he releases Daniel's shirt that he has grasped in his fist, and staggers back. I rush to him, tugging his hair with my fingers, running my hands up and down his arms, trying to ground him so he's back with me.

"Are you okay? Please tell me you're okay." His breathing is heavy, and Keaton doesn't say a word, but he wraps me in a hug and for the first time in a long time, I feel safe around the bloody mess of a man on the floor.

I cling to Keaton but say nothing, hoping he can feel how much I love that he fought for and protected me. I want him to feel how much he loved me. Everything is silent for a few moments until a villainous laugh bubbles out of Daniel.

"Oh, sweet girl, you really fucked things up. You fucking married him? When you knew you were mine? Knowing that sweet cunt of yours belongs to me." I flinch at his words and when I look at Keaton, his brows are furrowed in confusion.

When I glance back at Daniel, an evil grin is fixed on his face. "Tell me Anna, does your husband know that I had you first? That I felt you first? That I tasted you first?"

Keaton tenses under my touch before he drops his hands from holding me. Gasps sound from the crowd behind me. Daniel's crude words make me sound like I'm some kind of workplace hussy. There's no telling what my coworkers think of me, but there's only one opinion that matters to me at this moment. I stare up at my husband, but his gaze is averted, looking anywhere but at me.

"Keaton I didn't. I never..." Daniel cuts me off before I can explain why my former boss knows such intimate details about me.

"Did you forget to tell your husband about how you would wear sweet little skirts just to tease me? How I had you up against the counter in the workroom? And the way I sank myself into you while you stood there in my office?" Keaton backs away, no longer within my reach.

"You didn't tell him about all those late nights and weekends we spent together? Oh, sweet girl, I can't believe you hid all that from him."

My body began shaking at the way he was twisting his words. He knew I didn't want any of that, but Keaton didn't. "Daniel, stop. Just stop and leave. Leave now or I'm pressing charges."

Daniel's laugh sends disturbing chills down my spine. "Pressing charges? You really are such a stupid, fat fuck. Your caveman of a husband broke my fucking nose. I'll be the one pressing charges. And you better believe I will take every last fucking cent from him." Daniel, who has managed to get to his feet by this point, turns to face Keaton. "Be prepared, Fisher. I'll take your fucking company, and then I'll take your fucking wife."

I watch my husband, expecting him to be furious at Daniel's callous words. I expect him to lunge in Daniel's direction, tackling him to the ground. I expect him to yell and tell Daniel to get the fuck out of his office. What I don't expect is for him to do nothing.

He stands there, expressionless. Then, without so much as a glance in my direction, Keaton walks into his office and closes the door.

"Anna, you have to come out of the bathroom." Amanda has been trying to summon me for the past hour, but I haven't been wallowing in self-pity long enough to surface from the harsh fluorescent lights and the powdery air freshener that fills the small space. After security escorted Daniel off the premises and Keaton went into his office, I took in the hushed whispers that were circulating and the look of disdain from my previously super friendly colleagues. It wasn't until Lincoln bustled through and told everyone to get back to fucking work before I bolted to the staff bathroom, where I've been hiding for some time.

Amanda's voice sounded on the other side of the door mere moments later, and she's been trying everything in her power to get me to emerge. I've tried to tell her I'm never coming out. That I'll die in this bathroom. I haven't decided yet if it will be from thirst, starvation, or if I'll just drown myself in the toilet. I've tried to tell her that people can shit somewhere else, when she says other people need to use the facilities. I've tried to tell her all those things, but I can't. Every time I open my mouth I choke on my sobs. This perfect little life in this perfect little town with this perfect little man is no longer a reality.

Because there's no perfect little me.

"Shit, fuck, damn," Amanda curses. "Listen Anna, I know that life seems really shitty for you right now, but things are a helluva lot worse for Keaton right now. You have got to come out of the bathroom. Now."

Somehow knowing that Keaton is in trouble has my voice returning. "What's going on with Keaton?"

"I don't know," she admits, "but the police are here."

I escape my fetal position from the floor and make my way to the door. I deserve the wrath that comes from Daniel showing up, but Keaton doesn't deserve any of this. He is the most generous, caring, loving, selfless man I've ever met. He defended and protected me when I didn't deserve it. He loves me despite me being completely unlovable.

So, when I open the door and see him being escorted through the office with two police officers, I feel the pain of the sharp shards my heart has broken into.

Keaton stops as he passes us. "Amanda, call Cam and explain what happened. Tell him to meet me down at the police station."

He looks over at me. "Is it true? Does he know how you *taste*, Anna? Does he know how you fucking *feel*?" His words are like ice and his glare at me sends sharp pains as I nod.

"But it's not what you think," I try to explain as he stands there, cutting into me with those bright blue eyes.

I wait for him to ask what I mean. To yell at me. To spit at me. To tell me to get the fuck out of his office and out of his life. But instead, Keaton doesn't say anything. He hardens his features and walks away.

And that's so much worse.

Chapter Thirty-Six
Keaton

"How much longer?" I've been pacing the tiny interrogation room for what's going on centuries. No wonder people confess all sorts of things in here. It feels as though the concrete walls are caving in on you and knowing someone is on the other side of that window is unnerving.

My hand is bruised and throbbing, but the pain is nothing compared to the one in my chest where it feels like my fucking heart has been ripped out. Normally when I've had a bad day, I can't wait to hold Anna in my arms and let her make all the problems go away. But what do I do when she's the fucking problem?

"You're being questioned for assault, Keat. They're trying to determine if the damage you did to that asshole's face is worthy of a misdemeanor or felony. It's not gonna be a quick process."

Amanda followed through and Cam was here waiting before we even made it to the station. It helps that his office is close by, I suppose. He's already spoken with the officers and the prosecutor and now I'm just waiting to hear that I can go home.

The word home cuts me like a knife. Home is where Anna is. Home is where all of her things are. Home is where she told me she loves me. Home is both the last place and the only place I want to be right now.

"Gotta say, I'm pissed I missed the show. I would have helped you take down that asshole." Lincoln cracks his knuckles before throwing punches into the air.

"Yeah, and then I'd be trying to bail out both of my big brothers for being complete idiots," Cam rolls his eyes.

"You're right," I say with a heavy sigh. "I am a fucking idiot."

"Keaton, stop. I didn't mean it like that."

"Whether you did or not doesn't make it any less true. I've been an idiot since the first moment I met her." A vision of Anna in the airport has my heart aching and my teeth clenching. "I was an idiot when she dragged me into that chapel. I was an idiot when I told her I love her. And I was a fucking idiot for believing her."

"You know what, when you say it all out loud, you are a fucking idiot."

"Lincoln, stop," Camden says. "Keaton, he doesn't mean it."

"Oh, I fucking mean it alright. But you're not an idiot for marrying the girl you're so obviously in love with. You're not an idiot for believing what she said about the guy we could instantly see was harassing her.. No, you're an idiot for being so goddamn willing to throw all of it away."

"She fucking slept with him, Linc!"

"Did she say she slept with him? No. This deranged guy with a hard-on came into your office and started making wild accusations about the woman you say you fucking love. And you're choosing to believe him before talking to her and setting the record straight.

And that is what makes you a fucking idiot." Lincoln kicks at my cell and my fists tighten, apparently not finished throwing a few punches.

"Guys, you're gonna make Officer Guthrie come over here and if I have to listen to him give you a speech about what will and will not go down in his cells, I'm going to strangle the both of you and then we'll all be on that side of the bars." I look over at my usually passive brother, but Cam appears to be on edge.

"Sorry, Cam. Tell it to me straight, how much shit am I in?"

He lets out a heavy sigh and shakes his head. "I don't know, but things don't look good right now, Keat. You struck him multiple times and witnesses say he never even raised a fist in your direction. I know you said he touched her, but if Anna doesn't come forward and say that touch was unwanted or that there was a threat or something with it, then this could be a long ass road in front of us."

My chest tightens at the thought that maybe I interrupted something she was wanting in the first place. "You really think she wanted him to touch her like that?"

"You really are a fucking idiot," Cam mutters. "I think Anna loves you more than I've seen anybody love someone before. I think you did the right thing putting that guy on his ass. I think you need to talk with her and genuinely listen to what she has to say because there's more to all of this than what we currently know."

"Fisher, bail has been posted," Officer Guthrie interrupts before I can take in what my brothers both have told me. What Anna has told me. She may love me, but I can't help but wonder if there was once a time when she loved him, too.

"Time to gather your belongings and head home. And Keaton," I look at Caden Guthrie, the man I played football with all through high school, as he twirls his wedding ring around his finger. "Stop being the idiot your brothers say you are and talk to your wife."

I can't fucking be here. Every surface of this house is covered in Anna's scent. Every corner is haunted by a memory we made with one another. Her things are everywhere. The coffee cup she drank from this morning sits in the sink. Her clothes are hanging in my closet. I want to believe she loves me and only me, but every time I close my eyes, all I can see is that jackass on top of her.

Fed up with the pacing I haven't been able to stop since I got home, I decide the best way to get rid of the thoughts that won't let up for even a second, is to numb them with alcohol.

"Let's go to Kalli's," I holler at my brothers who are busy watching the Cats play on tv.

"The game is on," Lincoln states.

"And it will be on at Kalli's."

"Maybe a drink isn't the best idea," Camden suggests.

"I don't plan on a drink." *I plan on about fifty.*

"Can you just fucking man up and call her already? Talk to Anna and find out what's going on. You sitting here worried about something that may or may not have happened isn't doing anybody any good."

It doesn't take much for Lincoln to get on my nerves, but today he is being an exceptional pain in my ass. I don't need a fucking therapist right now. I need my brother. And some bourbon.

"Listen Linc, I'm about tired of your shit. I'm not in the right headspace to talk to her right now. The thought of that asshole with his hands on her has fucking ripped my heart out of my chest. I want to go to the bar with my brothers and get out of this house where the only thing I can see no matter where I turn, is her. I don't want to talk about her. I don't want to think about her. And I sure as hell don't want to feel anything about her. Now are you coming with me or not?"

Begrudgingly, they stand up and we head out to Lincoln's Bronco and off to drink my problems away.

"Thought you weren't going to have a drink," I hear Lincoln mutter, "you've had like fifty."

I can't help but smile happily for the first time since this morning. "It makes me feel good. I felt bad. I don't want to feel bad. Good beer makes for a good mood."

"That's bourbon you fucking idiot," Lincoln says, but even his bad mood can't bring me down after the several drinks I've consumed.

"Same thing."

"It really fucking isn't."

"I like the way it looks when you hold the glass up in the light. It's so pretty. Like her. She's so pretty." I take a sip and then look back over at my brother, my good mood slipping a little. "Why does she have to be so pretty? Have you seen her? So. Fucking. Pretty."

"Thought you didn't want to talk about her?" Lincoln drawls, taking a drag of his beer.

"I'm not talking about nobody. I didn't say who I was talking about." I lean in and whisper to him, "But in case you were wondering, I'm definitely talking about Anna."

The motherfucker rolls his eyes at me, and I whine at him, "Don't do that."

"It'd be a helluva lot easier to stop if you could stop doing and saying stupid shit. You ready to go home?"

I shake my head. "Can't go home. Nope. Can't be there."

"And why the fuck not?"

"All her stuff is there. That's why I came here." I wave down Kalli to let her know my glass of bourbon is empty and she shakes her head, denying me more of the sweet liquid.

"Please, Kalli. Just one more?" I plead, but her face is all scrunched up at me. She walks down the bar and stands there with her arms crossed. "Oh, no. Are you mad? Did someone here say something? Did I say something? Why are you looking at me like that?"

"Wanna tell me why you're drinking like it's your last day on this earth?"

I snort. "Nope. I'm fine."

"When people say they're fine that means they're anything but. Pretty sure you're working your way to polishing off an entire bottle all by yourself. So try again."

I don't want to share my pain, but the words slip from my lips regardless, "Broken heart, Kal. Broken heart."

"Get the fuck over yourself," Lincoln growls.

"Stop being mean to me. I'm sad and drunk."

"If you would just talk to her, you might not need to be in this state right now." Camden tries to convince me. I could have sworn he wasn't here just a minute ago. In fact, he entered the bar with us and then poof. It's like he disappeared. Maybe I have had too much to drink.

"Where the hell did you come from?" I ask.

"I had to make a quick phone call. He can have one more, Kalli. Give him one more pour and then we're taking him home."

My favorite bartender fills up my glass again and I smile at my baby brother. "I knew I always liked you the best."

A hand reaches up and slaps the back of my head. I turn to look at Lincoln. "That just further proves why Cam is the better brother."

He snorts a "whatever" at me and focuses back on the game. I pull out my phone. If my brothers want me to talk to Anna, then I'll talk to Anna.

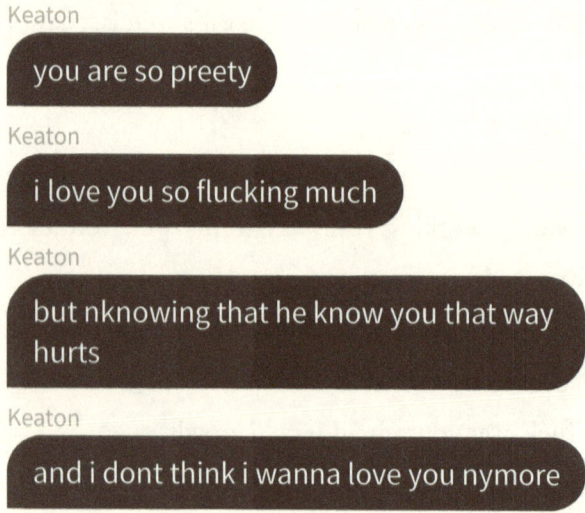

Keaton

you are so preety

Keaton

i love you so flucking much

Keaton

but nknowing that he know you that way hurts

Keaton

and i dont think i wanna love you nymore

Chapter
Thirty-Seven

Anna

"Spill," Amanda demands.

She had brought me to her home after calling Camden like Keaton had requested. I assumed I was no longer welcome at Keaton's place, and even if I were, I didn't have a way to get there since I rode with him, and he had the keys.

"When I was between jobs, my dad recommended that I go to work for his best friend, Daniel. I was his executive assistant and for the first few weeks or so things were going really well. Then he started sending me texts. Nothing inappropriate, not yet anyway, but little messages here and there. Things like 'I miss you' and 'You look so pretty today,' but it was almost every single day. I told myself it was in my head. I said, he's just being friendly. But then they became even more frequent. And that's when they became more suggestive.

"Soon after the messages started, he began finding little ways to touch me in the office. A hand on my hip. Brushing an imaginary piece of fuzz off my shoulder. Swiping away an eyelash from my cheek. Again, I just thought maybe he was a touchy-feely kinda guy, and I tried not to read into things. He has been involved with my family for so long, and he had always hugged me before, so I thought I was making a big deal out of nothing. He wasn't making advances. He was just comfortable.

"But then one day the messages turned from fairly innocent to downright obscene. His touches became more frequent and migrated to areas he had no business venturing toward. One day he cornered me in the workroom and implied that I had been teasing him and wanted what he was trying to give me. Then the day before I left for Cheatham." I sob, and my sweet friend reaches out to hold my hand, "The day before I left, he called me into his office. He locked the door and then," my sobs grow heavier. "He touched me. He touched me, Amanda, and I tried to fight. I tried to push him away, but he had me pinned and I couldn't stop him. It was just his fingers, but..."

"'Just' nothing, Anna. That is still crossing the line. Hell, touching you in the first place was crossing the line. I am so sorry, sweetie. Please tell me you told someone about this. Your parents?"

I shake my head. "You're the only person who knows. I haven't told anyone about what he did. I was about to start this new life in a new place, and I just wanted to forget everything that happened. Besides," I sniff, "I didn't think anyone would believe me."

"I believe you. And Keaton will believe you." Her words feel like a fist squeezing my heart and I sob a little harder.

"Speaking of Keaton. Do you care to explain the whole 'wife' situation?" Her lips tip up in a smirk and I can't help but let out a small laugh. I tell her about the drunken wedding that took place with Keaton, the plane rides, the reconciliation, and how fucking in love I am with my husband.

"You have to tell him, Anna. You have to make him listen."

I groan, "What if he doesn't believe me? He hates me."

"He does not hate you. That man loves you more than life itself." She scoffs, "He would do anything for you. He's just hurt and confused right now. Once he learns the truth, he will be kicking himself for all the hurt he's caused you."

I hope she's right. I hope Keaton will believe me and help me fight Daniel. Maybe not in a way that lands him in jail this time. But I know he needs some time. So, I wait. I wait for him to want me back.

"Hey Anna," Camden says in a tone that holds so much pity it has me wanting to find a shovel and bury my own grave.

"How is he, Cam?"

"He's in a rough place right now," Camden admits. I can hear guitars and fiddles in the background, the loud voices, and the clanging of glasses. Knowing he's at Kalli's, a part of me is crushed that I've driven him to drink the pain away. Another part of me is terrified that he might find someone there to help him forget all about me.

I can't help but sob into the phone, and the bleeding heart of the three brothers continues, "He just needs time, Anna. I have no doubt the two of you will work it all out. You're meant to be together. But for now, well, it may not be the worst idea to give him some space. I called the local bed and breakfast, and they have a vacancy. I've booked you a room there for the week."

I gulped. A whole week? A week away from Keaton? A week of him thinking the worst of me?

"Oh, okay. I understand. But all my things are at his place."

"I know, and I can't guarantee I can get everything, but I will get as much as I can and bring it to you as soon as I'm able. It may not be tonight though, so maybe you could stop at the dollar store and grab a few things? I can cover the cost."

"You don't need to do that, Cam. I got myself into this mess."

"Anna, I highly suggest you let me start on the papers to file for a protective order. Keaton told us awhile back about the messages and the creepy ass gift. Then, with him showing up like he did at your place of employment, well, it should be enough for the judge to grant."

I never imagined I would ever be in such a mess. In need of a lawyer. Filing a restraining order. Losing the love of my life.

"That sounds good, Camden. Thank you. For everything."

"Hang in there, Anna."

I'm curled up under the covers of my bed in the dark at Sheets & Sweets Bed and Breakfast. It really is the cutest little place and while I'd much rather be at home tucked into Keaton's arms, I can't help but be grateful Camden booked me a room here.

The cozy bed and breakfast has a total of four rooms, not including the owner's suite, and the older woman I met when I checked in told me her boyfriend owns the place and makes the best breakfast spread across five counties. While the grief has taken away my appetite, I smiled at her and promised to be down in the morning.

It took going to both the Dollar General stores in town to find an outfit in my size, along with the basics I needed until Cam could bring me some of my things. Amanda was kind enough to haul me around and then drop me off here, making sure I made it to my room alright and giving me the hugest hug and prayer of hope before she headed home.

Her generosity and love made me realize how much I truly love it here in Cheatham and that just makes me hurt so much more. If I lose Keaton, I lose everything. My home. My job. My new friends. And the stranger I met who became the man I love.

My phone flashes, the only light illuminating the surprisingly spacious room, and I pick it up to see it's just the people I needed.

Jasmine

> Anna, we haven't heard from you in a while. You alive?

Skyla

> If not, I hear death by dick is a good way to go.

Anna

> I fucked up, guys.

My phone rings immediately, "Hey, Sky."

"What's going on?"

The sobs start again, and I find it hard to breathe. I can't seem to gain control of myself to calm down. "He...hates...me..."

"Who hates you?"

"Keaton." I can't control the tears any longer. Huge drops fall on my phone, my lap, and the beautiful handmade quilt on the bed.

"There's no way," Skyla insists. "I haven't even met the man and know he is head over heels for you. What in the world could have happened for you to think he hates you?"

"Daniel showed up."

"Shit. I'm on my way." The call ends, and I glance back at my phone.

Jasmine

> Seems unlikely. But how?

Penny

> Are you okay, Sweetie?

Jasmine

> Anna? Where did you go?

Anna

> Sorry guys. Sky called.

Skyla

> I sure did. I will land in Kentucky soon enough and together we're going to tackle whatever the hell is going on. Mama Sky is on the way.

Jasmine

> Mama Sky?

Skyla

> Don't hate on my nickname.

Penny

> Literally nobody calls you that.

Skyla

> Well they really should start.

Penny

> How bad is it? Do we need to book flights, too?

Jasmine

If you need me there, Anna, you know I'll be there. But I have a big contract I'm doing stuff for and it's going to be difficult for me to miss. But I can. You let me know.

Anna

I'm going to be okay. Don't worry about me. And Penny, you have to be there for your first grade babies, so you stay put, too. Honestly Sky, I'll be alright. Nobody needs to make a special trip just for me.

Skyla

Who says this trip is just for you? I just read me a small town romance where the main male character had a pierced peen and I can't wait to get to Kentucky and find myself one of those. Plus, I just so happen to love special trips.

Jasmine

You're ridiculous.

Penny

But I need the title of that book.

Skyla

What do you know? I'm already headed to the airport now. See you soon, Anna Banana!

The first smile in hours starts to spread across my face. Everything is going to be okay. My friend is going to be here soon to help make me feel better. Camden is going to help me with my whole former boss situation. And I'm going to find a chance to talk to my husband so that he can still love me.

My phone flashes in the dark and when I see Keaton's name on the screen, butterflies begin to flutter in my chest. But those butterflies quickly become boulders as his drunken words weigh down my heart.

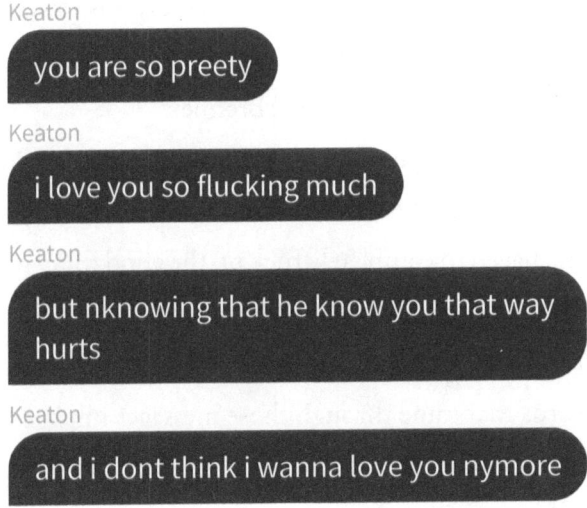

Keaton

you are so preety

Keaton

i love you so flucking much

Keaton

but nknowing that he know you that way hurts

Keaton

and i dont think i wanna love you nymore

Chapter Thirty-Eight
Keaton

E verything about me feels like total shit. How was I so happily
married and in love yesterday only to be in a total state of
misery today? Oh, that's right. Daniel Brenner.

Somehow that asshole managed to not just hurt Anna with his
fucking creepy messages he sent her and that damn box of weird
shit, but he managed to completely fuck up the good thing we had
going here. The love that we both shared for each other.

Did she really let him touch her? I know he can't be trusted. I
know the words that came through those messages imply that he
wanted something she didn't reciprocate. But I fucking asked her.
I asked her if he was telling the truth.

And she nodded.

Before I know it, I'm sending my pillow flying across the room.
I can't stay in this fucking house where the memory of Anna
is surrounding me. I head out to my truck and drive to see the
woman I know who once lost the love of her life.

"Uncle Keaton!" Charlie flings herself into my arms the second my feet touch the porch of the old farmhouse. I give her a big squeeze and then put her back down.

"Hey, Pipsqueak. Where's Grammy?"

Charlie wrinkles up her nose. "She's inside watching one of her old shows. She says there's only so much My Little Pony she can take in one day." My petite niece gives me a once over like she's a private detective. "You have a bellyache or something? You don't look so good. You're not gonna blow chunks or anything, are you? I don't think I can handle that. If you're cantankerous you need to go back home."

I can't help but chuckle. "The word is contagious, Pip. And I'm not sick. I just need to talk to Grammy about something real quick."

"Well good luck. When she starts watching those old shows of hers, you can't tell her nothing." Charlie runs back into the house, headed straight for her room to play with one of the hundreds of toys she's been blessed with over the years. I follow her inside and find Mama sitting on the couch.

She isn't dolled up today like she was the last time we were here, but she looks a lot better than I've seen her in the past. There's color in her cheeks and she's wearing pajamas, but at least they match and aren't threadbare.

"Hey, Mama." I sit down beside her and it gains her attention.

"Well, hey yourself. What are you doing here, Keat? Where's that pretty wife of yours?"

I let out a deep sigh and she instantly understands the reason for my visit.

"Ah. Her demons have come out, haven't they?"

I nod, but stay silent.

"I don't know what kind of secrets she has, but I know that you're a strong man who can handle them."

Shaking my head, I confess my fear. "I don't know that I can, Mama. I know the things he's done and that she is legitimately afraid of him, but what if he gave her something I can't? What if she finds someone who gives her more than I can give?"

"Keaton, you have so much to give. You're a good man. A good son. A good brother. Charlie adores you and so do your employees. I met Anna. She adores you, too." Her face lights up with a smile I haven't seen in years. "And don't think for one second the two of you were quiet when you were outside by the firepit. It sure sounded like you were giving her a whole lot."

"Mama," I groan.

"Where are these insecurities coming from? They seem unlike you."

She isn't wrong. I can't remember the last time I felt like I wasn't worthy of the things I wanted and worked hard for. I've always been confident and sure of who I am and then that carried over to the company I built.

"We were drunk when we got married, Mama. We didn't even know each other a full twenty-four hours. I knew she was the one the moment she held my hand on that plane. But what if it wasn't as quick for her? What if she doesn't care the way I do? What if she doesn't love me as much as I love her?"

"Well then, I'd say she's a fool. But I've met the girl, and I believe her to be far from that." She sighs heavily and squeezes my arm. "Sounds like you need to have a talk with your wife."

I match her sigh with my own and run my hand through my hair. "I know. You aren't the first to tell me that. She deserves to tell me about her side of things, and I owe it to her to listen. But that's an uncomfortable conversation I just really don't know that I want to hear."

"Keaton, I would have a lifetime of uncomfortable conversations if it meant I got to speak to your father just one last time."

I look over at her and for the first time in over a decade I see the strength inside my mother that used to be there all those years before my dad passed away. I see the woman who raised me and is still doing the job even when facing her own battles. "I know you miss him, Mama. We miss him, too. But we've missed you more."

Tears well in her eyes. "You're a good man, Keaton. And a good husband. You'll do what's right. Take the time you need, but don't wait too long. The ones you love won't be around forever."

"What the hell are you doing here?"

After talking with Mama, I've been playing Barbies with Charlie in her room to take my mind off things for a bit. Absentmindedly, I run a brush through pink hair with shimmers for what is probably the thousandth time when Lincoln walks in the room.

"Am I not allowed to come over and see my niece?"

He snorts. "You can come take my place and play Barbies any time you want. But you're deflecting. What's going on? Is this about Anna?"

Charlie's head pops up. "Anna? I like her! Is she coming back? Did you make her mad, Uncle Keaton? My friend Tucker says that his dad made his mom mad and so his mom cut holes in every single one of his shirts so that now when he puts them on you can see his boobies. But I guess they're not really boobies because he's a boy. Can boys have boobies? What do boys have?"

"Charlie," Lincoln groans out.

"Sorry, Daddy. I know I'm not supposed to talk about boobies, so that's why I'm just trying to get the facts. What are boy boobies called?"

"We aren't talking about boy boobies or girl boobies or any boobies," Lincoln grits between his teeth. "Go back to playing with your dolls while I talk to your Uncle Keaton."

"Here ya go, Pip." I pass my pink-haired Barbie back to Charlie and get up. Leaning in so my words aren't overheard by little ears. "Are you in a bad mood because you haven't seen any boobies in a while?"

"Out!"

Chapter Thirty-Nine
Anna

"Chocolate, strawberry, mint chocolate chip, regular chocolate chip, chocolate chip cookie dough, brownie fudge, and cotton candy. Pick your poison."

I stare at the mountain of ice cream my best friend picked up on her way to Cheatham. She's so extra and I absolutely love that about her. I grab a spoon and the pint of cookie dough before settling back in my bed. "Thanks, Sky. Though, I'm not sure ice cream is going to be the answer to all my problems."

She shrugs, "Maybe not, but it will make the regret taste better going down. Now, tell me everything."

I go over everything with Skyla, feeling guilty that I withheld some of the pieces, but when I look at her there's no judgement or disappointment to be found. "And now he's not speaking to me and says he doesn't want to be in love with me anymore."

Skyla sits her pint of strawberry ice cream on the nightstand with her spoon on top. She turns her body to face me, takes a big gulp, and then blows the biggest raspberry I think I've ever seen come from someone's mouth.

"Eww, Sky, you got strawberry spit all over me," I complain, but can't help but laugh at her crazy antics.

"Sorry, not sorry, Anna Banana. That's the biggest load of crap I've ever heard. He sent you a drunk text when he was hurting, but that man is so far gone for you he may as well be on Jupiter. Have you tried reaching out to him?"

I shake my head.

"Sounds like you're both being idiots if you ask me."

"Gee thanks, Sky. I'm so glad you flew from who knows where just so you can tell me how dumb you think I am."

"Maine."

"What? Why Maine?" I'm frustrated with her, but genuinely curious. Skyla's travel stories are always the best.

"Well, I went to Connecticut and tried their lobster rolls and it was delicious. Then someone asked me if I had ever had one from Maine. Said they were completely different. So I figured I needed to try it out for myself."

"And?"

"Very different. Very delicious. Though, you can't really go wrong with lobster." She grabs her pint of ice cream again. "And I don't think you're dumb, Anna. But I do think you and Keaton are both avoiding a conversation with one another and that right there is dumb. The two of you need to talk about this. You need to tell him that you never wanted Daniel to touch you. He assaulted you, Anna."

I'm listening to her words, and they make sense, but I'm not ready to hear Keaton say it's over. "What if he doesn't want me anymore, Sky? I was in way over my head with him from the very beginning. Now he knows I'm damaged goods. Why would he still want this?" I motion to my body and involuntary sobs begin pouring from my mouth. I grab a napkin and sit the ice cream down, so I don't make an even bigger mess.

"What in the world are you talking about? How were you in way over your head?"

"You haven't seen him, Skyla. He's so handsome and successful and funny and smart and everything that every woman could ever dream of. The man's abs have abs for crying out loud. Let's face it, the only reason we are even together is because we both got way too drunk, and I talked him into committing to me in a sham of a marriage."

She scrunches up her nose. "So he was drunk on the plane?"

"What?"

"On the plane on the way to Las Vegas. He was drinking those little mini bottles of liquor?"

"No. He wasn't drunk on the flight at all. Though, in hindsight it probably could have helped with his nerves."

"So, he was drunk in the car then? When he drove you to the hotel?"

"What? No! He would never be reckless like that," I defend him.

Skyla just nods, but she still looks frustrated. "So you're telling me that he was completely sober on the plane when he kissed you. And still sober when he offered to have you stay with him for the night. He hadn't had a drop to drink when he told you he wanted to have his way with you. And yet you still think you had to get him drunk to want you?"

I consider what she's saying. "Well, when you put it that way..."

"Anna, I know that you have insecurities when it comes to your body. I know what people have said and done to belittle you just because you're bigger. I know because I hear the same things. But the fact is that regardless of your size, regardless of your doubts, that man wants you.

"You are such a fucking catch, Anna Banana, and I wish you could see what Jasmine, Penny and I see. I wish you could see what Keaton sees in you. You are funny. You are beautiful. You are smart. You are talented. You are worthy, Anna. You are worthy of the love of a man who wants you so much that he's in pain every second he's without you."

"Then why doesn't he want to love me anymore?" I ask meekly.

"I don't know the answer to that. That's a question you will have to ask him. Hell, he probably has his own self doubts, too. But the fact is that whether he comes to his senses or not, you're coming out of this with your head held high knowing that anybody out there on this planet, and even the planets beyond, would be complete fools to not see how much you have to offer. And you're no fool, Anna. So see it inside yourself."

I nod slowly as I process my friends' words. Keaton did nothing but praise my body and worship my curves. He never once looked at me like he didn't desire all that I am. Even if he never looks at me like that again, it's time I start seeing myself in that way.

"I hear you, Sky. I will try to do better. I'll try to love myself."

"This place is incredible, Anna. Do you really have to leave?"

Skyla and I have managed to explore every inch of the tiny town in the past couple of days, and I am completely convinced she has introduced herself to every single one of the just over a thousand people who inhabit it. I rub my hand over my chest as the ache forms knowing I will no longer be a part of that small number.

"I just don't see how I can make it work. There's no way I can continue working for Phisherman's and in case you didn't notice, there aren't a whole lot of employment options around here aside from that. Plus, things with Keaton were going so well that I didn't even think of starting to look for a place."

My best friend steps over and gives me a hug I didn't know I needed. I swear a hug from Skyla is like a beam of sunshine being transferred to your soul. "Thanks, Sky. I needed that."

When she steps away from me, I see the sparkling gleam of a dream in her eyes. "You know," she draws out, "this bed and breakfast has a for sale sign on it."

I raise my eyebrows at her.

"Can't you just imagine?" She squeals. "We'd be like Lorelei and Sookie with our own inn. The two of us would make this place so stinking cute and you could capture photos of it that will have everyone wanting to visit. Incredible breakfast spreads just like Walter does of French toast, fruit, sausage, and bacon would be available on the weekends, but throughout the week it would be more of a grab and go option. We'd greet people the way Hazel does like we've known them all of our lives. What do you think?"

I want to give Skyla the answer she's looking for. I want to tell her that her dreams sound like possibilities. I want to know that there's still a place for me here in Cheatham.

"I think neither one of us knows how to cook, so those incredible breakfast spreads aren't going to happen. And I think that there's no place for me here in this town without Keaton." I sink onto the mattress and Skyla comes to sit beside me, a sad, knowing look on her face. She wraps her arms around my shoulders, and I lean over into her, tears beginning to fall.

"I love this town, Sky. But I love him, too. Even if he doesn't feel that way about me. There's no way I can be here and risk seeing him every day. There's no way I can be here knowing that he might move on and fall for some other girl. There's no way I can be here knowing it was my fault. I'm the reason we're over. I'm the reason he doesn't want me anymore."

My words come out as sobs as she holds me tighter. I bask in the comfort of my friend for a little while longer before I pack up my life and head back to the city.

There's pounding on my door and I glance over at my phone to check the time. But it's not just the time I see filling my screen. My last message from Keaton, his damn heart shattering words, are pulled up. I was going to say something to him last night, but the words never came. What was going to fix this mess that I got us into? How was I going to convince him to believe me?

Nobody ever believes me.

The never-ending knock on the other side of the door wasn't about to allow me my pity party. I don't know who the fuck would be here at seven in the morning, but clearly they don't realize I'm currently residing in heartbreak hell.

I climb out of bed, but it's apparently too slow for the person demanding my presence so early in the morning. A familiar voice calls out.

"Anna Laura, you open this damn door right now."

Shit.

Why is my dad here?

How does my dad know I'm here?

I unlock the door and before I barely pull it open, he's shoving himself into the small space.

"Pack your things, Anna Laura. We're going home."

Going home? He drove all this way to tell me to come home? My stomach sinks. Why is my mom not here with him?

"Is Mom okay?"

"She's fine, but clearly you've lost your ever-loving mind."

Shit. "Daniel told you."

He's been darting around the sweet but small room, picking up the dirty clothes I threw on the floor and piling them up on the bed. But he stops his movements, and when he turns to face me, I think I may crumble under his look of utter disappointment.

"Yes, Daniel told me," his voice is sharp, tight. "Because apparently my daughter was either too ashamed or just too damn selfish to let her parents know that she married her boss the second she moved to this town."

"Technically I was married to him before I moved here," I say softly.

His eyes narrow in disgust.

Way to go, Anna. Just make things worse.

"What did you say?" His voice is like sandpaper, scraping against every raw part of me.

I don't want to tell him. I really, *really* don't want to. But I've already stuck my foot so far in my mouth it's gonna take a crowbar to extract it, so I might as well go ahead and take the plunge. "Remember my trip to Las Vegas with the girls?" I wait for his response, but when he doesn't so much as offer a head nod, I continue. "Well, I met this man on the plane. And we hit it off.

And then we went out for drinks. And then we kinda, sorta, got married a little bit."

"How the hell do you get married a little bit?"

"Well, I guess we didn't get married just a little bit. We got married a lot a bit. I mean, the marriage is legal and binding," My words come out rushed.

"And that's why you moved to Cheatham? He is why you left home?"

I shake my head. "No, I left because," my words trail off. I left because his best friend is a bastard who violated me. But I'm not ready to tell him that. I may never be ready to tell him that. "I left because there was a great job opportunity, and I'd have been crazy not to take it up. Keaton being the owner was just a strange coincidence."

"Do you have any idea how insane all of this is, Anna Laura?"

I flinch at his cruel tone.

"And I'm supposed to believe that life is so great for you here? That you love your job and your husband and that everything is just so much better here in Cheatham than life was back in the city?"

I bite my lip. Until Daniel showed up, everything truly was better here. But now, I'm not sure anymore.

"So tell me, why is it that when I got to this small town and popped in and asked people about you, they told me I'd find you here at a bed and breakfast instead of at the home you were supposed to be renting? Why aren't you with this so-called husband of yours?"

Damn. News in a small town really does travel fast.

Since I haven't withheld the truth from him yet, I give my dad another dose of honesty. "Because he's pretty mad at me about something right now."

My dad snorts, "Well that makes two of us."

"He expects me to get my things and be at their house in the morning. I'll go over to Keaton's place while he's at work today." A part of me breaks to know that the final memory between Keaton and me is our relationship breaking because of a sick man's lies.

"I'll go with you." Shortly after my dad left, Skyla came to my door demanding to eat at my favorite place in town. She reaches over to grab my hand as we sit at Crumb and Get It. I'm really gonna miss this place. And their pickles.

"No, Sky. I think," I choke back a sob. "I think I need to do this on my own. I won't be great company."

"Anna, I am so sorry everything sucks right now. But I came to be here for you. I'll do whatever you need."

"I appreciate it, Sky. I just think I need that moment to myself."
I look at my sweet friend with her red fiery curls framing her
beautiful face covered in freckles.

Understanding, she nods, "But do you think maybe before you
head that way you could point me in the direction of some of the
single men in this town? If I'm not going to spend the day with
you, I may as well spend it under someone else."

Chapter Forty-One

Keaton

I roll over to press myself into Anna's soft body, but the cold side of the bed is just a reminder of what I've lost. Everything from the past few days comes rushing back into my brain. I really am such a fucking idiot. I should have talked to her, but instead I chose to believe that she betrayed me.

Groaning, I move my sluggish-from-too-much-bourbon body to the bathroom and get ready for another rough day at work, knowing the woman I love won't be there. I've been working in Lincoln's office this week to avoid seeing her empty desk. I don't want her to quit. I don't want her to leave. But I don't know if I want to see her right now, either.

"I can't be the assistant for both of you. And I refuse to be his,"
Amanda complains to Lincoln, jerking her thumb in my direction.

"What did I do?" I ask, but I know what I did. I fucked up. I
didn't talk to Anna when I had the chance. I pushed her away with
drunken lies I only typed to try and protect myself.

Amanda glares at me. "You sit here playing the victim, when you
have no idea what that poor girl has been through."

"I do know. She told me about the messages he sent. But she
didn't tell me about the fact she slept with the man."

"Because she didn't, you idiot!" Amanda shouts at me, making
Lincoln smile so big I want to slap it off his face.

"I asked her if it was true and she said yes. You were standing
right there, Amanda."

"You asked her if he touched her. You asked her if he tasted her.
Did you ask her if she wanted it?"

Her question leaves me frozen and sick to my stomach. I knew
the man was a lot of talk and she even told me that he would
occasionally touch her back or run his hand across hers. But is the
man so evil that he would force himself on her?

"What do you mean?"

Amanda shakes her head, "It's not my story to tell. You need to
ask her."

I grit my teeth. "Well, she won't fucking talk to me, so if you
know something about Anna, then you better fucking tell me or
you're out of a job."

"The fuck you will. She's my assistant, asshole," Lincoln
interjects.

"And I own the majority share of the company. I'm the CEO. I can fire her if I damn well want to."

"Now you're playing that card? And people think I'm a dick," he grumbles,

I take a deep breath and try to calm my tone, "Amanda, please tell me."

She looks at me with heavy eyes and sighs. "I can't Keaton." I go to say something, but she holds her hand up to stop me. "Not because you're being a massive dick right now, and the fact you threatened my job when we both know your brother wouldn't be able to function without me," I look over at Lincoln and we both shrug, "But because I promised Anna. If you want to try and hear it from her before she leaves, she texted me earlier today asking if you were at the office. She's going to your place to get the rest of her things before she leaves."

"Before she leaves?"

"She's moving back in with her parents for now."

"But that's where he is," I say, stating the obvious.

Amanda's next words slice right through my heart, "But it's where you're not."

November air nips at the back of my neck, and I can smell that rain is coming. It doesn't matter. It can pour sheets down on me for all I care. Nothing will stop me from having the opportunity to talk to Anna. I need to convince her to stay. Convince her she still loves me. Convince her that I still love her. That I never stopped. That I never will.

I think back to all the signs she gave me that Daniel had taken things too far. The box. That time in the kitchen when I called her "sweet girl." The way she tensed up in my office when I tried to have my way with her. Why wasn't I able to decode these things sooner?

Heavy drops begin to fall, but I don't mind. The only thing I care about is that Anna is here and I desperately need her to hear me out before it's too late. I storm into my house and call out her name but am only answered by silence. "Anna!" I shout again, darting between the rooms, but finding the house completely empty.

Defeated, I walk outside and take a longful look down the road, but that's when I see it. Her small, white sedan sitting in my driveway. She's here. I turn and find myself racing down the stone path to the guesthouse where I pray she's double checking to make sure she has the rest of her things.

Please be there. Don't be too late. You can't let her leave believing you don't want her.

When I reach the guesthouse, I knock on the door. "Anna," I call out. She steps into the living space, and I see her for the first time in days. Fuck, she's gorgeous. Her blonde hair is in a ponytail, putting her full cheeks on display. She's wearing a pair of black loungers with a light blue scoop neck shirt that lets me steal a peek at her incredible cleavage. I give her a smile and raise my hand up in a greeting. But she turns to her bedroom. And she shuts the door.

It's been ten minutes since I knocked. Ten minutes since I shouted her name. Ten minutes since I laid eyes on my girl. Ten minutes of standing in the pouring rain. Ten minutes to regret everything I've said and done since Daniel Fucking Brenner showed up at my company and wrecked our world.

Then the door opens.

She stands there in the doorway, arms crossed like she's holding herself together. Her eyes are tired. Guarded. Not angry. Empty. She doesn't say anything. She doesn't ask me in.

I deserve that.

"Hey, Baby." She goes to shut the door on me, but I reach out and catch it.

"Anna, I'm sorry. I'm not here to ask you to forgive me," I say, the words catching like gravel in my throat. "I just couldn't let the last thing I said to you be a lie."

She doesn't move. Doesn't blink. Just stares at me like I'm some stranger who used to wear the face of someone she loved.

"When I sent those messages to you, I was in a dark place. All I could picture was you with him and it broke me."

"You broke me," she barely whispers.

"And I'm so sorry for that, Baby." She crosses her arms at me, and I correct myself, knowing I deserve the right to lose the endearment. "Sorry, Anna. If you never want to see me again, I'll walk away. But I need you to hear the truth, even if it's too late to matter. The truth is that I didn't mean it when I said that I didn't want to love you anymore. I lied. I lied because I was hurting. I lied because I wanted you to hurt, too."

Her eyes flash at me, furious and wounded. "And I did. Congratulations."

I flinch but continue, "I lied when I said that because the truth, Anna, the truth is that there's not a moment since you crashed into my life that I haven't been in love with you. The moment I saw you at the airport, I knew you were perfect for me. When you helped me overcome my fear of flying."

She lifts her eyebrows at me.

"Okay, maybe overcome is too strong a word. But when you were there offering me comfort, I was in love. I was in love with you when I saw you glowing in the lights of the fountains at the hotel. And when you had us racing down to the sidewalk so you could experience Paris. I was in love with you when I said 'I Do' in that chapel. I was in love with you when I woke up the next morning and had to leave. And I was in love with you even when I knew that you were very much not in love with me.

"And if that's still the case, I still want you to know. I want you to know that I love you so much that I reach out for you when I wake up in the morning. I love you so much that I've had to work out of Lincoln's office this week because your empty desk and your absence is all that consumes me when I'm in mine. I love you so much that I'm standing here in the pouring rain begging for you to listen to me. Even though I don't deserve it. Even though I didn't offer you the same respect. I'm standing here because I'm so fucking in love with you, Anna Keith."

She stares at me as the rain continues to pour down. "I don't know if I can forgive you."

"That's okay, Baby. I wouldn't blame you if you couldn't. But if there's even the smallest part of you that still feels something, still wants to believe in what we were, I'll spend the rest of my life trying to be worthy of that."

She stands there, contemplating me and my words as the rain continues to bead down my face. Then she turns and walks away.

But she leaves the door open.

Chapter Forty-Two
Anna

When I arrived at Keaton's place, I could hardly pack up the first box. Every piece I picked up was like a fragment of the life I was losing. My heartache was slowing me down until I let the grief completely consume me and I curled up in the bed we once shared and shed tears over the life and love I was losing.

But then the anger set in. Why am I the one blaming myself for something a cruel man did to me? I didn't ask for Daniel to touch me. I didn't ask him to show up here in Cheatham and detonate a bomb on my life. And who the hell did Keaton think he was? He didn't want to look at me. Didn't want to speak to me. Didn't want to love me anymore if his drunken words were true. Like I was the one who somehow orchestrated this whole fiasco.

So when the handsome man I drunkenly married showed up at the guest house as I was packing the last of my things, I let him stand there. And when it started raining, I let the rain soak his stupidly attractive body. For a little while, anyway. And when I opened the door it was only to give him back his key and tell him goodbye.

But I needed his words. I needed to hear what he had to say. I needed him to know that I was angry and hurt. And I needed to hear that he didn't mean what he said. That he still loves me.

So, I leave the door open. The literal one at the front of the guest house and the metaphorical one to my heart.

I tell myself it's the rain.

Or pity.

Or closure.

But when Keaton steps inside, dripping and hesitant, I don't stop him.

Walking over to the bathroom, I grab a towel from inside of the closet. I cross back over the small space and sit it on the arm of the couch in front of him. I can't hand it to him directly. I can't risk touching him. If I touch him, I know I'll crumble. And I have to be strong to say what I need to say.

"I can't keep doing this, Keaton," the words are soft as they pass my lips. "I can't keep feeling like I'm not enough for you." I whisper the next part, "You promised you would never leave me again."

He rubs the towel through his hair and down his face. "I know. I know that I fucked up. I know that you hate me.

"I should hate you," I release a sigh of defeat. "I should, but I don't. I want to, but I can't. Because I love you too, Keaton. From the moment I watched you grip the armrests on the plane to this very moment where you're being a complete dumbass. I still love you."

He walks around the couch until he is standing directly in front of me. He reaches out his arm, but I hold my hands up. "I love you Keaton, but I'm still insanely pissed at you."

Taking a step back, he nods. "I know. And you have every right to be." He hesitates before speaking again. "Amanda mentioned earlier that I didn't have the full story. When I asked you if what that fucker said was true, you said yes. I'm just really confused, and I know I have no right to it, but I want to know. I need to hear the truth from you, Anna. What happened with him?"

He looks like a man ready to watch his world fall apart and it makes me want to run over and throw my arms around him in comfort, but I remain where I am. I stay strong and hold my head high. Because it wasn't Keaton who had his body violated by a man he was expected to trust his entire life.

But he is the man who protected me.

He is the one who showed up for me.

And he is the one who loves me.

So I tell him.

I tell Keaton about the worst day of my life.

Keaton is standing in the middle of the guesthouse like the air has been knocked out of him. He hasn't said a word in nearly a minute, probably because he's got his jaw so locked tight I swear I can hear his teeth grinding.

"I'm sorry," I whisper, apologizing for not telling him sooner. For causing the pain that's written all over him.

He lifts his eyes to mine and the look in them has a soft gasp escaping my lips. Not pity. Not revulsion. Fury.

"Don't do that," he says, his voice tight. "Don't apologize for his crimes. You did nothing wrong, Anna."

I nod, but tears sting anyway. "Keaton, I promise I wasn't trying to keep a secret from you. I was just so humiliated. So disgusted. So, ugh, I don't even know. I just wanted to put it behind me and pretend like it never happened."

"I'm not upset with you. Not even in the slightest. Fuck, Baby, I'm so damn proud of you."

My nose crinkles. He reaches out to run his thumb over to smooth it out. And it feels so good that I find myself leaning into his touch.

"I'm so proud of you for getting out of that situation. For getting away from him the best way you knew how. I'm proud of you for telling someone what happened. You did good, Anna."

"But he isn't gone, clearly," I whine. "Him showing up here in Cheatham was one thing, but he's always going to be around. He's my dad's best friend and has been since before I was even born. He's always there. At every holiday. Every cookout. Every event you could think of."

"Then you tell your dad what you just told me. You tell him about his best friend's crimes."

"But what if he doesn't believe me?" I can feel myself crumpling, but Keaton pulls me into his arms. I breathe in his scent, and it brings instant comfort. I've missed this. I've missed him.

"Daniel told him about the two of us being married. I've never seen him look more disappointed in me than at that moment. What if he thinks I'm just trying to ruin Daniel because of mistakes I made?"

"Our marriage is not a mistake," Keaton presses his lips to my forehead. "And we have the proof. You have messages from Daniel. He had no reason to be at our office, other than the fact he was there to see you. We show that to your dad, and well," he releases a breath, "if he still takes his side over yours, then maybe your dad isn't the man you think he is."

I nod, but my whole body is shaking.

"I'm here, Anna. I believe you. I love you. And you don't have to do this alone anymore. I'm not going anywhere. Not now. Not ever again."

I let his words settle me and I realize I believe him.

"Then let's take him down. Together."

Chapter Forty-Three

Anna

My confessions have left me mentally and physically exhausted. I look at Keaton, and he doesn't seem to be much better off.

"Stay with me," I say. He looks at me with hope in his eyes and my heart melts. "Please, stay with me tonight."

He nods. "I can sleep on the couch if that makes you more comfortable."

It wouldn't. Being in his arms again has me realizing I don't want to be apart from this man for another night. "No. Stay with me. Beside me. Please."

A soft smile has the dimple on his left cheek just barely making an appearance. "I will always be beside you, Baby."

We get ready for bed in a peaceful silence, and when we climb into bed, he wraps his arms around me and I drift off to sleep knowing that no matter what happens, Keaton will be there beside me.

Anna

So while I was packing things up in the guest house last night, Keaton came over…

Jasmine

And you told him to go to Hell?

Penny

Did he grovel? He better have groveled.

Anna

I did not. And he did. In fact, he said a lot of things that made me want to give him another chance. Give us another chance.

Skyla

Woohoo! More newlywed adventures!!

Anna

Well this next adventure is about to royally suck. I hate to leave you while you're in town, Sky, but there's somewhere I need to be today.

Skyla

Don't you worry about me. I made a *really* good friend last night and now he's following me around like a sweet, little puppy dog. I'm sure he would like to hang out some more.

Penny

Sky, be nice to that boy.

Skyla

Oh, I was very nice to him. And he's no boy. This guy is all man.

Anna

You'll have a lot more fun with that than where I'm going.

Jasmine

Where are you going?

Penny

Is everything okay?

Anna

Today is the day Keaton gets to meet my parents.

My parents were expecting me today since my dad demanded I return, but they probably expected me to bring luggage and not the handsome man I married. Keaton turns into the paved driveway, and when he turns off his truck, he looks over at me.

"You ready for this?"

Nope.

But I nod anyway, and we exit the vehicle. I smile at all the decorations on the front porch. My mom is an avid lover of Christmas and firmly believes that the first Christmas tree goes up as soon as curfew ends on Halloween. I've always shared the love of the holiday, but something tells me today's visit isn't going to be so holly jolly.

Before I can turn the knob, Keaton's hand grasps mine and I wonder if he is as nervous about this as I am.

He's a stranger to my family.

He's a stranger who married me while we were both drunk in Vegas.

He's a stranger who stayed married to me in secret.

He's a stranger who beat the shit out of my father's best friend.

But as I look at him, he seems calm.

"This isn't going to go well," I say to him.

He nods. "As long as we go through it together."

Taking a deep breath, I open the door, and we step inside, ready for whatever awaits us behind it.

"Mom? Dad?" I shout out to the empty foyer. Keaton and I walk further into the house as we hear my mom's voice.

"Oh, honey! You're here." Footsteps are headed our way from the kitchen, and I wonder if she's already started her holiday baking. No matter how badly this day goes, one of my mom's chocolate chip cookies will make any day better.

When she comes around the corner, her kind eyes meet mine, then immediately take in the man holding my hand. She fixates on where our hands are joined, then looks up at me again. "And you brought a friend."

"No, Mom." I straighten my posture. "I brought my husband."

"Like hell you did," I hear from behind us and turn to see my father. His expression is pure fire, and I can't help but squirm under it. Keaton's grip on my hand grows tighter and I remember that no matter what, he's with me in this.

"Mom. Dad. This is Keaton Fisher. My husband."

"It's nice to meet you both. You've raised an incredible daughter," Keaton says politely, but it just fuels the fire already radiating within my dad.

"Is it? Is it nice to meet us after you married my daughter without permission? Or is it nice to meet us after you assaulted my best friend?" My dad spits his words in our direction as he steps closer.

The two most important men in my life are sizing one another up. The man who loves me so much that he pushes me to be the best version of me he thinks I can be. And the man who loves me so much that he accepts me as I am. They're about the same height, but Keaton has maybe an inch on my dad, but also a solid fifty pounds. Whereas my dad is lanky, Keaton's fit frame is muscular. "Tell me, Mr. Fisher, you think attacking another man makes you strong?"

I look at my husband, who is somehow still calm. "No, sir. But I do believe standing up for my wife makes me strong and worthy of being here."

"Standing up for her, how? Against Daniel? He's known her since she was born and would never hurt her."

"But he has," Keaton and I answer in unison.

"The day he showed up to my office, he called Anna some of the cruelest names and then slapped her," Keaton explains.

My dad's eyebrows furrow in confusion and I can hear my mom gasp from somewhere in the room.

"What did you say to him to make him react that way?" My dad turns to me, his arms crossed and chest puffed believing I'm the problem. Just like always.

My voice cracks as I let the truth spill from my lips. "I didn't do anything, Dad. Daniel has been harassing me for almost the entire time I've worked for him. And on my last day at work, he called me into his office, and, Dad," I force myself to say the words that don't want to come out, "he touched me."

Sobs sound from somewhere in the room, and I reach my hand up to my cheeks, surprised to find no tears. I turn and look at my mom, her beautiful face streaked. "Oh, honey. Why didn't you tell us?"

"Because it's not true," my father barks. "I've known Daniel for over thirty years. He wouldn't do that. Especially not to my daughter. You can't just make accusations like this, Anna Laura. You can't try to ruin someone's life in retaliation for letting your big married secret slip."

"She's telling you the truth, sir," Keaton says strongly, tightening his grip on my hand.

"What do either one of you know about the truth? This man," my dad points to Keaton, "is causing you to be erratic. He's the reason you left home in the first place. Left a good job with Daniel. He's the reason you're making these false accusations against a man I've known and called my best friend for decades. And this man isn't welcome in my house."

"Dad, if he goes, then I go," I say, attempting to stand my ground.

But my dad's words cut me like a knife. "Then so be it."

He chose Daniel. He chose his friend over his daughter. He chose not to believe me.

"No." My mother's firm voice shocks me out of my emotional spiral.

"What did you say, Kara?" My dad's icy tone is directed in her direction, but she's been married to him long enough to not care.

"She and Keaton are not going anywhere."

"You can't tell me you believe this?"

"I believe our daughter, Craig." My mother walks over and wraps me in her embrace. She whispers in my ear, "I believe you, honey. I love you. I'm proud of you. And I'm so sorry that the son of a bitch hurt you. I'm so sorry I didn't step in when I saw what was happening that night at dinner."

"I oughta drive you all over to Waverly Hills and see if they're still accepting patients. The lot of you are crazy if you think for one second that man hurt Anna."

"And you're crazy if you choose him over her," my mom jabs in his direction. "She's our baby girl, Craig. She's telling you something painful, hoping you can help. And you're pushing her away."

I don't know if it's the pain from my dad's rejection or the strength of my mom's support, but my tears are falling freely now. My voice comes out in sobs, "I'm so sorry, Dad. I never meant to be your greatest disappointment."

His face drains of color.

"My entire life I've never been good enough for you. I just needed to lose a few pounds. Or make better grades. Or I n,eded to get my head on straight and get a degree in something more practical. I needed to make more money. I needed to work where you wanted. I needed to marry someone you chose," I swallow, "I've only ever wanted to make you proud, but I guess I'll take being your disappointment if it allows me to finally be me. A *me* that is completely loved by a man for the first time in my life"

My dad staggers back like he's taken a bullet to the chest. "That's what you think?"

I straighten, my mom and my husband standing tall beside me. "Anna Laura, you have never been a disappointment. I know I've said I've been disappointed with some of your choices, but you, you are the most important thing in my life. And I'm so sorry you ever doubted that."

"Then why can't you believe me?"

He plops down on the tawny brown leather chair beside him, his eyes scanning the floor. After several moments his voice comes out with barely a whisper. "He really did it, didn't he?"

My mom goes over to kneel in front of him. "He really did it. And we're not going to let him get away with it."

My dad nods, "So, what do we do?"

Chapter Forty-Four

Keaton

My heart is full not just with the love, but the pride, that I have for Anna. It's one thing to try and take down your enemy, but standing up against your family is a game I hate she had to play.

"We need him to confess. Pulling a confession out of him is going to be the fastest way to end all of this."

"You're right. And I think I need to hear him say it. I need to know the man I called my best friend is actually the awful man you're telling me he is." He looks over at Anna. "I believe you, Anna Laura, I just need to hear it from him."

She nods because she's so fucking perfect and understanding. "And you think you can get that confession out of him?"

"I can do that," Craig says. "I can invite him over. Act like the two of you are officially filing for divorce. See if I can't get him to admit what he's done. But I don't know how I'm going to handle hearing it."

His wife rubs a hand over his shoulder. "You're going to do great, because you're doing this for our daughter. I can put something together and maybe we could pull it off this weekend."

"No," Anna's dad says, looking up at his wife then over to where Anna and I are standing. "We do this tonight."

"If Anna's dad consents to being recorded, and he's the one with the device, then it can be used as evidence in court," Camden explains. I called my brothers and shared today's events but also needed help carrying out our plan.

"Got it. He can do that." I'm so thankful that Anna's dad is on our side. It's going to make taking down this fucker so much easier. "There's something else I need help with, though, and this is probably going to be more of a conversation for Lincoln."

"If it's anything illegal, I need to hang up." I stay quiet on the line. "I'm hanging up."

When we hear the click that disconnects Camden from the call, Lincoln speaks up, "Alright big brother, tell me what you need me to do." There are so many different sectors of the IT world that so few people know about. Most people believe it's simply fixing computers, but they don't exactly know what that means. When I started taking classes, I loved learning how to build firewalls and protecting people online. That's why I started the cybersecurity business. But it doesn't mean that I didn't learn a few things that were less about protecting, and more about finding information people try to keep hidden. Then I passed all that knowledge over to Lincoln, who took a few courses of his own.

I'm good. Lincoln's better.

I give my brother his orders to infiltrate the IT systems at Brenner & Associates, then hang up. Between Lincoln's skill set in both finance and tech, I know he's the perfect guy for the job to do some digging into the accounting world Daniel Brenner has built.

I walk back into the living room where Anna sits with her parents. Craig speaks first, "I called Daniel and told him that I was grilling out in honor of Anna being home. He'll head this way in a couple of hours." He rubs the back of his neck like he really doesn't want to say this next part, "It's probably best if you're not here."

That's not fucking happening.

"I will stay out of sight, but there's no way I'm leaving Anna." I look at my wife and the smile she gives me makes me feel like some sort of superhero.

"I figured as much," Craig grumbles. "But just know if shit goes down, it's my turn to throw the punches. You already had your chance."

Kara wraps her arms around her husband, "Oh, you're so sexy when you're protective."

"Mom!"

"Tell me what you've got."

Lincoln had something for me within an hour. I had no doubt he was going to find something unethical about this creep.

"We've got him. And shit, it's bad."

He explains to me about the set of files he found behind a firewalled alias, one of which had an unusual name. Accounting firms don't usually store cash transaction transcripts, so why would there be a file for it?

When he decrypted the files and cross-referenced them with the official client ledgers, it was clear that Daniel had been moving client funds between shell accounts. He hadn't just cooked the books. No, Daniel Brenner deep-fried them in grease and wrapped them in offshore shell corporations.

The scope was staggering. Millions of dollars over a handful of years. Inflated valuations. Falsified audit reports. A silent partnership with an overseas consulting firm that never actually consulted.

Daniel Brenner was committing fraud.

He was going fucking down.

Chapter Forty-Five
Craig

The recording device was in my pocket. I would never be ready to hear my best friend confess that he touched my baby girl inappropriately, but I needed to hear it. And I would. For her.

Knowing Anna truly believed I had only ever seen her as a disappointment completely gutted me. I never meant to cut her down, but to push her into being the best I know she can be. Still, my words made an impact on her that she's going to need time to heal from, and it hurts me to know that I've hurt her all these years. I believe in my daughter and tonight I'm going to prove that.

Standing at the grill, flipping some sirloins, I hear my best friend before I see him. "Mmm, smells good out here. This retirement thing is working out really well. You should grill for me more often." He slaps my shoulder as he comes to stand beside me.

"I really do enjoy it. Kara claims it's become my whole personality, but I had to remind her I still golf." I smile at Daniel, but it doesn't feel right. It feels forced and it must look it, because his eyebrows bunch up as he looks at me.

"Everything okay, Craig?"

No, everything isn't okay. You assaulted my daughter, you asshole.

I step back from the grill and shove my hands in my pockets, secretly pressing the button to have my phone start recording. I shake my head and let out a fake, heavy sigh. "I'm just worried about Anna. She doesn't seem like herself."

Daniel shrugs his shoulders, "But hey, she's back home. That's great news."

"She is, but at what cost? I think that guy did a real number on her. Still can't believe she got married in Vegas." When my friend doesn't reply, I continue, "He's just not the type of man I thought she'd end up with, you know? I imagined her sticking around the city with someone more mature. Someone who would come over for cookouts and go to the club to play a round of golf with me."

"Aww, buddy, sounds like you wanted Anna to marry me," Daniel jokes.

"You know, it wouldn't be the worst thing. It might be kind of nice for my best friend to become my son-in-law," I tease him, but his face looks like he's sincerely considering it.

"I'd do it, you know. I'd marry Anna."

I swallow down the glass stuck in my throat at what I'm about to say. It would hurt her, but I'm only saying it to help her. I hope when she hears the recording, Anna knows I don't mean any of what I'm about to say. "Oh, you don't mean that. First of all, she's too young for you."

Daniel scoffs.

"And you can't be attracted to her. I've told her for years she needs to try and lose weight, but she just won't listen. I'm afraid she's at the point she doesn't care, and you don't want some woman who has just let herself go. You want someone who can still get your dick hard."

"Oh, she gets my dick very hard." I catch him adjusting himself and I have to conceal my face when I can taste the bile creeping up.

I clear my throat before speaking, "I didn't realize you were attracted to my daughter."

He lets out a chuckle, "Now you can't go getting mad at me about being attracted to your daughter after you go and say you wish she was married to me. But yeah, I like her curves. I like the way she feels."

"Wait a minute," I need a little more, "has something already happened between the two of you?"

He smirks at me, like the question amused him. "She didn't say anything to you?"

I shake my head. "No."

"Then maybe it's best you don't know about what I did to her in my office." He winks at me like we're talking about anyone other than my only child. I don't want to know. I *really* don't want to know. But I ask. I ask because my daughter deserves justice.

"So, the two of you have kissed?" His smile is pure evil, and I don't know how I've never witnessed it before.

"You could say I know what her lips taste like."

He licks his own lips and I think I'm going to be sick.

I suck a deep breath in and blow it out. "Wow. I had no idea she felt that way about you."

"Oh, she may not yet, but I have ways of making her come around."

My hands create fists and I'm mere seconds away from laying my best friend out. I had no idea he was a predator. I had no idea he was hurting my daughter.

Before I can show up my son-in-law's punches with a few of my own, the devil himself walks out of the house and into the backyard.

"Did you get what we needed?" Keaton asks.

"What is this asshole doing here?" Daniel demands, but I ignore him.

I pull my phone out of my pocket and stop the recording. I hold it up and shake it. "Yup. His confession is all on here."

"What are you talking about? What confession?" Daniel looks between the two of us like he's completely innocent and I wonder how I was friends with such a dumbass for so long.

Keaton speaks before I can open my mouth, "Just the one where you admit to violating my wife."

"My daughter," I grit between my teeth.

"Wait a minute. You knew? You said she didn't tell you that something happened between us. You lied to me," Daniel accuses.

"And you fucking assaulted my daughter," I yell.

He throws his hands up in front of his chest, "Hey now, assault is a strong word. There's no way Anna doesn't want me. Hell, she would probably take any attention she can get from a man. Have you seen her?"

I look over and see my daughter's husband marching over, ready to throw yet another punch at Daniel's face.

Not this time, kid.

I curl up my fist and land it straight into Daniel's gut, making him double over and gasp for breath.

"That's for hurting my baby girl."

He straightens and I can't help but punch him in the same spot again.

"That's for breaking my trust."

Daniel is wheezing but still manages to pull himself to standing. He schools his features. "Craig, we've been friends for too long to let a misunderstanding come between us. How about we just drop the issue and move on, okay? I touched her. You touched me. We're even."

"We are far from even," I growl at him.

"Listen, it's my word against hers. You know this won't hold up in court."

"Maybe the recording isn't strong enough to hold up on its own, so it's a good thing I have another piece of information. You see, when you fuck with someone who works in the technology field, you may want to do a better job at covering up your secrets," Keaton says to Daniel.

"We happened to uncover some interesting accounts at Brenner & Associates. Accounts that reveal what appear to be quite a bit of fraudulent activity. As a businessman myself, I think it's important to share anything we find untoward with someone at the SEC. We wouldn't want any corrupt companies to be taking advantage of unassuming folks."

Daniel's eyes grow wide in fear.

My son-in-law is a mastermind.

"So here is how things are going to go down," Keaton continues. "Let me know which option works best for you."

"Is this a threat?" Daniel says, straightening and popping his shoulders back.

"It's a choice, Mr. Brenner. And I advise you to choose wisely."

I would never admit this to my wife or daughter, but I think I'm actually starting to like my son-in-law.

"Option one. You resign from your company. You sell it and leave town. Quietly. You don't contact this family, and you sure as fuck don't contact Anna ever again."

Daniel huffs out a laugh, "And if I don't?"

"Well, that's option two. That's the option where I hand everything over to the SEC, along with the FBI cybercrime unit. You'll be prosecuted for wire fraud, embezzlement, and securities violations. And once that hits the press, we follow it up with civil suits for harassment, stalking, and sexual assault."

Damn. Did my daughter marry Batman?

"So, what's it going to be, Mr. Brenner?"

My former friend looks over at me. "Craig, come on. What do you want from me?"

Years of friendship should have made me feel something. Remorse. Loss. Anger. But when I look at Daniel, I feel nothing. "I want an answer. Will it be option one? Or option two?"

Chapter Forty-Six
Anna

The sound of squealing tires has my head snapping up from the potatoes I'm whipping together. I hear the kitchen door to the patio click and see my husband walk in, my dad following behind him.

"It's over, Baby. You never have to worry about Daniel Brenner again." I collapse into Keaton's arms, the feeling of relief taking over me.

"He took the quiet option. He will be selling the company and leaving the state, hopefully by Thanksgiving."

"But what if he doesn't," I whisper quietly.

"Then we expose him for fraud. I contact the SEC and FBI, and they hit him where it hurts. His pocket. We can also move forward with the civil suit. Press charges for the crimes that he committed against you."

I reach up and run my hand over the hair covering his jaw. "I don't ever want to see him again. I just want him to disappear from our lives. If we press charges, there will be hearings, and I don't know that I can stand being in a room with him again for as long as I live. So, let's just hope he moves far away and leaves me and every other woman on this planet alone."

Keaton presses a kiss to the top of my head. "I love you, Anna. Thank you for giving me another chance."

I smile at him. "Thank you. Not just for what you did, but for believing me. For choosing me."

He turns his head to press his lips to my hand on his face. "Always you. From the very beginning."

Across the kitchen, standing with my mom, I meet my dad's gaze. He looks tired. Hollow.

"Anna Laura, I owe you a thousand apologies, but I'll start with this one. I'm so sorry for allowing my friendship with someone to hurt the thing that matters the most to me in this world. You."

"Dad, you don't," I begin, but he holds a hand up halting my protest.

"I owe you so many more, but I also want to let you know how incredibly proud I am of you. You stood your ground. You told me your truth. You believed in yourself."

My dad's arms are open for me when I reach him from across the kitchen and we pull each other into an embrace. "I love you, baby girl. And I promise to prove it for the rest of my life."

Keaton and I walk into his place, and I glance around. It doesn't look any different than the last time I was here. I have to remind myself that it's only been a couple of days even though the weight of the events have felt like years had dragged on.

I texted Skyla to check in and see how things were with her and if she minded me spending the night with Keaton instead of hanging with her. I feel bad about ditching my friend who flew all this way to see me, but apparently, she's already become a regular down at Kalli's Corral and was planning to meet up with someone there. She was, however, very eager for the details of mine and Keaton's reconciliation.

"Are you hungry? Thirsty?" Keaton asks, but I shake my head. It's late and all I want is the comfort of my husband.

We walk up the stairs slowly, neither of us speaking. The need for one another is so strong that you can feel the desire in the air around us. When we walk in the bedroom, I realize the only thing I need is him.

I reach up, threading my fingers in his hair. "Thank you. I know I said it earlier, but it's not enough."

"Baby, you're enough." His mouth found mine before I could continue expressing my gratitude for the way he protects me. The way he believes in me. The way he loves me.

The fear, the fury and the ache of the last few days are poured into that kiss as his hands move with purpose tracing the curves of my body. He breaks the kiss, his hands at my waist. "I need you."

"Me too," I breathe out.

Keaton's fingertips skim over my skin with reverence, leaving behind goosebumps in their wake. He takes my lips again, then presses a kiss to my chin. Then to my neck. Then to my shoulder.

"You're safe now," he whispers into it. "You're mine. Only mine."

"I always was," I breathe into him, allowing my own hands to explore his body. The muscles he works so hard for ripple under my touch. A shudder runs through him as I raise his shirt and my skin presses against his. I allow my fingers to outline the muscular set of abs he hides underneath just before I move to his belt.

"Anna, you don't have to do that."

I let out an annoyed sigh.

"I really wish you weren't so against me unbuckling your pants."

Keaton chuckles, "By all means, keep going."

With his permission, I remove the obstacles in my path, then pull his pants and boxer briefs down to release his thick cock standing at attention, ready and waiting. My tongue darts out and licks my lips while Keaton runs his fingers through my hair.

I gently hold him at the base and run my hand up his length, following it with my tongue on the underside of his shaft.

"Fuck. Your mouth feels amazing."

His words spur me on, and I coat his tip with my tongue. When I finally take him into my mouth, the both of us are so charged we could release on the spot. "Baby, please, I want to sink myself inside your sweet pussy, but your mouth is too fucking good. If you don't stop, you're going to be drinking every drop of me."

My clit throbs at his words, wanting the attention he's offering me, but my mouth isn't finished exploring. I continue to move up and down his dick, taking him all the way to the back of my throat, then dragging my lips back up to the tip. With my hands on his thighs, I can feel them begin to shake. A sign that he's close. I break my rhythm to focus just on the head, sucking, licking, tugging until the salty taste of him begins to fill my mouth.

"Fuck. Anna, yes. You are so fucking good at this. At everything."

I'm relentless, not finished tasting every bit he can offer me and the fact that he is losing control just makes my desire that much stronger.

When I'm finally satisfied, I sit back and look up at him, licking my lips to show him how much I love what we just experienced together. "You are way too good to me, Anna." He runs his hands through my hair. "Can I keep you?"

"Hmm, how long are you thinking?" I tease.

"I was hoping for forever."

"Forever sounds amazing."

When Keaton is recovered and recharged, he makes love to me in the house that has become my home in the time I've been here at Cheatham. Just like the man I met that one night in Vegas, he was strong but gentle, assured but sweet, and everything I needed tonight. And in the quiet after, curled against his chest, I finally let myself believe the worst is over and our happily ever after can truly begin.

We are safe.

We are home.

We are together.

Forever.

1 1 1 1 0 0 0 0 1 0 1 0 0 0 0 0 0 1 1 1 0
1 1 0 0 1 1 0 0 0 1 0 1 0 1 0 1 1 1 1 0 0 1 0
0 0 0 0 0 0 0 0 1 1 0 0 1 1 0 0 0 0 0 1 0 1
1 1 0 1 0 1 0 1 0 0 0 1 1 0 0 0 1 1 0 0 1 0
0 0 0 0 0 1 1 1 1 0 0 1 0 0 0 1 0 0 1
1 0 1 0 1 1 1 0 0 1 0 0 1 1 1 0 1 0
0 0 0 1 1 0 1 0 0 0 1 0 1 0 0
0 0 0 1 1 1 1 0 0 1
0 0 1 1 0 0 0 0
1 1 0 0 0 0 0 0 0
0 1 0 0 0 1 1
0 1 0 1 0

Epilogue
Anna

Christmas Day

I wake up as giddy as a child, ready to spend my first Christmas with my husband. Last night we went to Sharon's home and watching the pure joy in Charlie's face as she opened presents and played games with her dad and uncles brought warmth only the Christmas spirit can give.

Today we will be heading to my parents' home and spending the day with them. Keaton and my dad have surprisingly become buddies, bonding over the basketball season and their favorite bourbon. My dad calls Keaton at least twice a week, but it's usually in reference to needing help with something on his computer.

I look over at my husband as he is lying in bed, still sleeping. Somehow this man gets more and more handsome each day. And somehow, I'm the woman lucky enough to be his. Climbing out of bed, I pad over to the bathroom to brush my teeth and get ready for a full day of festivities.

The smell of coffee must have woken Keaton, because he stumbles to the kitchen and immediately pours himself a mug. After taking a sip of his black brew, he walks over and bends his head down to me. "Merry Christmas, Wife."

"Merry Christmas, Husband."

When he kisses me, it makes me want to forget everything we have planned for the day and immediately go spend the day in our bed. I pull him closer and when I wrap my leg around his thigh, he laughs and pulls away. "As much as I would love that Christmas present, Baby, I think there are some things for you under our tree."

I lean up and place an excited kiss against my husband's lips, then squeal as I rush into the living room, eager to start a new tradition with the man I love. We decorated the twelve-foot beast of a tree together. It's dripping in reds and bright greens, looking perfectly festive and perfectly perfect. With it only being the two of us, there are only two gifts underneath. I smile at the hope of one day this space being filled with bicycles and dollhouses.

Keaton sits in his favorite chair with his mug of coffee, and I walk the gift I carefully wrapped over to him. I perch on the arm, and he wraps an arm around me. "I love you."

I smile at him. "I love you too but open your gift!"

He laughs and sits his coffee down. Then, with the speed of a sloth, he unwraps his present.

"What are you doing?" I ask, appalled.

"Opening my gift."

"But why are you being so slow?"

He chuckles, "I don't want to rip the paper. You worked hard on wrapping this and it looks beautiful."

My jaw drops. "Ripping the paper is half of the fun!"

"Do you want to open it for me?" I shake my head but am dying a little inside with how long it takes him to finally get the paper off and open the box.

I bite my lip as he pulls out the pictures. Photos I took of his family. His mom. Charlie. Him with his brothers. Candid shots I managed to capture and show him how beautiful this family he created is.

"Baby, this is beautiful," he says quietly while going through the images. And when he gets to the last one, he looks at me with tears in his eyes. "Is this?"

I nod and let tears flow down my cheeks. Because in my husband's hands is the first picture of what our love created together. He traces his thumb over the ultrasound and sniffs back the tears. "Thank you. Thank you for the best gift I could ever imagine."

He pulls me into him and captures my lips in a kiss that encompasses so much.

Love.

Joy.

Hope.

Promise.

We pull back and he laughs, "You can finally call me Daddy now and it not be so weird."

I let out a laugh myself and push at him playfully. "Alright then, Daddy. What's next?"

He groans, "My gift is going to look so lame now. But it's that one." He points to the only other gift under the enormous evergreen. I rush over to pick it up and shake the box.

"Oh my gosh, you're one of those. A box shaker."

I smile over at him, "I'm a paper ripper, too."

As the paper flies through the air, I get to the box underneath and open it up. Inside is a stunning top-of-the-art professional camera. Much better than my current DSLR. There's also a note typed out on a Phisherman's Cybersecurity letterhead.

I believe in you.

Make your dreams come true.

You're fired.

I turn to my husband to find out what he means.

But he isn't in his chair.

He's down on one knee.

Holding a box.

That's holding a ring.

"Keaton," I whisper.

"Anna, I want you to know that I believe in you. That I will always believe in you. And that I want to see your dreams come true. I'll miss you like hell in the office but knowing you're out in the world pursuing your passion will be worth it. And I want you to do it with my ring on your finger. The one I chose with you in mind and not just what was available at the chapel. I want to give you the wedding of your dreams. I want to make all your dreams come true. And I was hoping you would make all of mine come true, too. You've already got a head start with our baby on the way, but will you promise to never leave me, Baby? Will you promise to marry me again? Can I keep you forever?"

Tears fall as I smile at my husband. My fiancé. The father of my unborn child.

"Forever sounds amazing."

Thank You

I wanted a dedicated place to thank YOU for taking the time to read my book. Knowing you took a chance on me as an author and read my book when there are so many options for you to choose from does not go unnoticed, and sincerely means the world to me.

If you loved the story, I would love your review! Please consider leaving one on Amazon, Goodreads, or your favorite platform. I would love to be tagged!

Want more from the Phishing for Love Series?
Look for them in 2026!
Decrypted (*Lincoln & Sierra*)
Defended (*Camden & Skyla*)

Acknowledgements

There are so many people who have helped me on my path to accomplishing my dream as a writer. Thank you doesn't seem like enough, but I'll give it a try.

To my husband: Thank you for believing in me, no matter what. When anxiety hit and I felt like I couldn't make my dreams come true, you helped me see that I could. No matter what happens on this journey, my words are in this world because you stood by me and told me I could. I love you infinity x infinity.

To my parents: Mom, you always have and forever will be my biggest cheerleader. Thank you for giving me the feedback I needed to hear, and wanting to be with me every step of the way along this journey. Dad, knowing you're proud of me and wanting to share with everyone (literally everyone) about my accomplishments means more than I can put into words. I'm sorry the dad in this book kinda sucked, but I'm so glad you don't. I love you both a bushel and a peck.

To Evie, Raven, Sammi, and Ansley: You women are seriously the best beta team I could have ever conjured up. Thank you so much for the endless rereads, the critical viewpoints, the needed praise, and the overall desire to want to see me succeed. I asked you to help me in creating something I could be proud of, and you definitely pulled through. I appreciate each of you so much!

To my ARC readers and Street Team: Knowing you wanted to be one of my first readers and were willing to support me blindly just proves the kind of rock stars each of you are. Your support, kind words, reviews, and willingness made every tedious day that led to release that much more bearable. Thank you. Thank you. Thank you.

To Alyssa: You were there before I even typed my first word. Everything from your encouragement, to your tough love, the incredible illustrations you designed, and your honest words have been crucial in the creation of this book. I appreciate you more than you know.

To authors L.M. Whiteley and Rebecca Gulley: Thank you for answering all my questions throughout this process. I would have freaked out so much more without you.

To my daughter: I am so blessed to have such an understanding child. From the countless hours you sat next to me as I wrote, to the encouragement you gave me when I was stressed, you're as much

a part of this book as I am. But you better not read it until you're
18.

To Mary Beth: If you were still here, you wouldn't read this
book because it would make you blush. But you would be so damn
proud of me anyway. I love you. Until I see you again...

About the Author

Meribeth Richards resides in Kentucky with her husband, her daughter, their two dogs and their two cats. Oh, and now there's a fish...

From an early age, Meribeth always enjoyed writing and considered it a hobby. In college, her English professor asked her to switch her major to English, creative writing, or literature. Meribeth declined. Then she was given a scholarship from the department of journalism. Meribeth accepted. But she quickly found that writing what people demanded of her was not the type of writing she preferred. She's a dreamer and wants to write whatever the hell makes her happy.

So Meribeth is a teacher. When she isn't in the classroom teaching children how to read and write, you will find her reading or writing on her own. Romance novels were never part of her library until her best friend, Jaime, introduced her to the spicy world. Now she can't get enough and writes in hope others will add her books to their endless TBRs.

You can connect with Meribeth on her website www.meribethrichards.com or follow her on social media:

Instagram: @authormeribethrichards

Tiktok: @authormeribethrichards

Facebook: @authormeribethrichards

www.ingramcontent.com/pod-product-compliance
Lightning Source LLC
Chambersburg PA
CBHW050009120726
47903CB00006B/1695